TOUGHEST
Catch

a love me tender novel

ISBN: 9798349210099 (Paperback)

Library of Congress Control Number: 1-14347924991

Any references to historical events, real people, or real places are used fictitiously. Names, characters, and places are products of the author's imagination.

Front cover image by author.

Book design by author.

First printing edition 2024.

Untapped Publications, LLC

CONTENTS

TOUGHEST Catch

Prologue

I STOOD AT THE back of the old chapel, waiting with bated breath.

This wedding had been nine months in the making. There had been countless consultations. Many revisions. A few tears, mostly happy but some frustrated. We'd made compromises. Gone on tours, tastings, and fittings, all of it in an attempt to create the makings of one perfect day.

The chapel was full. The décor was dreamy. The ring bearer hadn't thrown a fit before his trip down the aisle, and the flower girl had everyone in the palm of her hand as she twirled, danced, and sprinkled rose pedals on her way toward the altar.

But none of that mattered now.

Now the only thing that mattered was the very next moment.

Their entire future hung in the balance, and I could hardly breathe as I waited.

I could always tell.

In a single moment, I could see the future in a groom's eyes.

I'd been planning weddings for more than a decade. Since I'd started my own company, I'd carefully curated precisely two-hundred and two of them. Of those, I'd seen one-hundred ninety-eight brides make it down the aisle.

Luckily, the four who didn't tie the knot figured out forever wasn't for them *before* the ceremony began. Sucked they didn't get any of their deposits back, but it was better than marrying the wrong person. Or worse—getting humiliated in front of more than two hundred people. I'm sure it might not have felt like it at the time, but I knew from experience.

In any case, I made it a point to refund seventy-five percent of my fee to the broken couples. It was the least I could do.

I'd seen just about every version of a groom there was.

The crier.

The proud chested.

The smirker and the grinner.

The nervous and the calm.

I'd seen the groom who couldn't take his eyes off his bride, as well as the groom who could barely take his eyes off his shoes.

I just knew—in one glance—I knew whether or not they were going to make it.

So far, I hadn't gotten a single one wrong.

Now it was time to see what *this* couple's fate would be.

The bridal march began to play.

The ushers swung open the doors.

All heads turned to catch a glimpse of the gorgeous bride.

But *my* eyes stayed unwaveringly fixed on the groom.

Instantly, he pulled his upper lip between his teeth as his eyes grew glassy with tears.

He blinked rapidly, in an attempt to clear his vision, but he didn't lift a hand to his face.

He didn't want to miss it.

He didn't want to obscure the view of his bride for even a second.

He'd won, and she was his prize.

One glance, and I was finally able to free my breath.

Relaxing, I leaned my shoulders against the wall at my back and smiled.

It was going to be a good day. The perfect day.

Ethan and Maggie were going to make it for the long haul.

This was the beginning of the rest of their lives, and I got to help make their big day a dream come true.

I had the best job.

CHAPTER
One

Channing

O N TUESDAY MORNING, I was the first to arrive at the office. This was usually the case, given my condo was only five minutes up the road. I could have walked most days but for two very good reasons I didn't.

First, I lived in Austin and didn't relish the idea of showing up sweaty every morning. Texas had two and a half seasons—primarily summer and not-summer.

Summer was why pool culture was an actual thing. Summer felt like being shoved in an oven and forgotten half the year.

Occasionally we got winter. And by winter I mean ice rain. If it happened, it lasted about a week. Anything more than that, and our whole infrastructure would go to shit.

If it snowed, it was basically the apocalypse, and everyone stayed home.

We'd managed to get through January unscathed.

Not-summer lasted approximately four-to-five non-consecutive months. Not-summer could be relatively warm or slightly cool. If we were lucky, not-summer almost felt like autumn or spring.

The second reason I didn't make it a habit of walking to work, even in the not-summer months, was because it was rare I spent all day behind my desk. My appointments had me all over the place, which meant having my vehicle close by was a must.

Our offices were just a couple blocks from the heart of downtown Austin. It was a corporate building filled with a variety of businesses. From the outside, it certainly didn't fit my aesthetic—seeing as I was not a corporate gal—but on the inside, my team and I managed to make our corner of the ninth-floor home.

We also had an incredible view of the Colorado River, which only added to the charm.

I'd opened Rusty Barn Wedding Co. five years ago. When I first got into event planning, I never imagined I'd start my own business one day. I was twenty-four when I got into wedding planning, and twenty-seven when I found my niche. It was my own disaster of a wedding that helped me hone my personal brand.

I was twenty-six when I thought I was getting married to the love of my life. Dylan was the youngest of three and his mother's baby. She had her own ideas of what our wedding should be. I was naïve and blinded by love, so I made a ton of compromises throughout the entire planning process. If there was one word I could have used to describe the overall theme, it would have been *glam*.

I was not glam.

Whimsical? Yes.

Bohemian? Definitely.

Country? Without a doubt.

But while not glam, I *was* young, excited, and anxious to start the rest of my life, so I went with *glam* in an attempt to start my relationship with my soon-to-be mother-in-law on the right foot.

In the end, all my compromises had been for nothing.

In a beautiful gown, in a Methodist church filled with five thousand dollars' worth of flowers and two hundred and forty-three guests, I was left standing by myself at the altar. I had never been more humiliated or heartbroken in my entire life.

I couldn't say how I managed to go back to work after that, but it was all I knew. It was what I was good at. I couldn't simply redirect my passion and start down a new career path, not on top of everything else. While it might have been true that getting jilted at the altar eradicated any desire I ever had of getting married, I still loved helping other people curate their dream weddings.

Except, after the awful glam debacle that ended in heartbreaking fashion, it got harder and harder to find happiness at work when I was forced to put my ideas in a box and stow them away because the client had a totally different vision. Every time it happened it reminded me of the biggest failure of my life. Obviously, I was in the business of making couples happy, so I sacrificed my creative genius for the good of the company—but one day I woke up and decided to be brave and take control.

Not long after my thirtieth birthday, I took a risk, and Rusty Barn Wedding Co. was born.

It paid off. Majorly.

We could afford our office lease after just a single year, something of which I was very proud. We were a small outfit, with just four of us, but we kept up with the best of them. More than that, we kicked ass—and that wasn't me being arrogant, it was true. I poured my whole self into my business, and our success was clearly documented in my calendar, which was booked solid for the next ten months. When couples walked into our office, if they weren't instantly sure they'd come to the right place, then they weren't in the right place. It was that simple.

Every day, I got to design beautiful, modern, country-chic Texas weddings, and I loved every minute of it.

"Hello, hello. *Buenos días*. Good morning, good morning!" belted Libby as she rushed into my office.

I looked up from where I sat behind my desk, unable to contain my smile. Libby—formally known as Olivia Chavez—was a firecracker in human form. At five-foot four, she was petite in almost every way—the exceptions being her personality and her hips; hips that made the pencil skirt she wore that morning look *awesome*. Every pair of shoes she owned, outside of the tennis shoes she begrudgingly donned for exercise, had at least three inches of heel.

She was my first employee and had been part of the team for four and a half years. Libby was my right hand, and I didn't know what I would do without her. She was also my best friend, which could have been by chance or just an occupational obligation.

It was a toss-up on any given day.

My life *was* my job, so my circle of friends was pretty small.

Fortunately, she was as loyal as she was feisty. Outside of my sister, Libby was the most trustworthy person I knew. We'd been through some crazy times together, and every moment of it meant a whole lot.

"Guess what, guess what, guess what!" she continued to repeat herself as she plopped into one of the chairs across from me.

I lifted my eyebrows, my smile stretching into a grin as I tried not to laugh. It wasn't exactly a character trait of hers to be grumpy so early in the day, but her excitement that morning was abnormally high. Her dark brown eyes, usually big and bold with the perfect application of makeup, were *bigger* and *brighter* than usual. Not to mention her dimples, which gave her the unique ability to be beautiful and adorable at the same time, were deep as her cheeks strained to keep up with her cheesy grin.

Giggling softly, I replied, "I have no idea, but I'm dying to know."

Crossing her ankles, she made a dramatic show of coolly brushing her long, straight, black hair over her shoulder before she let all her excitement burst as she squealed, "I'm getting *married!*"

My eyebrows shot up even higher, and my mouth opened with a gasp. As I processed her announcement, I hoped my face conveyed *happy* surprised not *is-she-crazy* surprised.

When she read my expression and threw her head back in laughter, I had my answer.

There was no bullshitting Libby.

She was definitely my best friend.

She was also wild, fun, and didn't understand the concept of half-assed.

Libby and Patrick met at his pub three months ago.

They'd hooked up and had been almost inseparable since that first night.

I knew she was falling fast and hard, but three months was like the blink of an eye. I'd barely met the guy. Between the craziness of the holidays, plus three Christmas weddings and one *huge* New Year's Eve wedding, every attempt to get me to join Libby at the pub had been foiled.

I'd seen Patrick only a handful of times. Twice when he came to pick her up from the office. Once when he saved our butts and delivered three kegs out to a farmhouse reception in the middle of nowhere after one of our vendors fell through last minute. Granted, given that experience, he was in my good graces. Not to mention how happy he made Libby.

But *three months?*

"I know. I know what you're thinking. We haven't been together that long. Trust me, I'm with you—he totally took me by surprise.

But when he woke me up this morning and asked me to marry him, I couldn't say no. When I'm with him it just...it feels *so* right. We even picked a date already."

"Wow. Really?" I asked, still trying to shake off *is-she-crazy* vibes.

"Yeah. Well, I guess, we're a little bit flexible depending on the availability of the church, but we're aiming for some time in early May. We want to do it before it gets too hot. Plus, June is when we really start to pick up around here. And, listen, I know it's a lot to ask, because it's super short notice, we're booked solid, and it feels like the Jackson-Ford wedding is breathing down our necks, but I'd really love it if I could hire you and Rusty Barn to help me plan it."

She was talking a mile a minute, but I caught every word.

She was right. We had a lot on our plates, including one of the biggest weddings of my career. It wasn't every day a congressmen's daughter walked through the door interested in hiring the Rusty Barn crew to plan the wedding of the season. It was even more rare that the same socialite came with the promise of a full spread article in *Southern Bride Magazine*.

All this, of course, Libby knew.

Suddenly, *is-she-crazy* morphed in my mind to *is-she-pregnant?*

I didn't ask.

But—was she?

Did people still have shotgun weddings?

Then again, she was Mexican American and Roman Catholic.

Tradition ran deep in those roots.

I closed my eyes, and my mouth, and shook away all my thoughts. I took a breath, then looked at my friend and knew my answer. We were more than halfway through February already, which left us with just about no lead time, but it didn't matter. This was Libby we were talking about.

"Sweetie, of course we'll help you. And you don't have to *hire* me. You're family."

Libby's dimples reappeared as she replied, "Thank you!" She barely took a breath before she continued, "Okay, so, I've thought about it, and we'll try to keep it pretty small. Just family and close friends. Then again, we're both Catholic—I'm Mexican, he's Irish, so *small* is relative—but all that aside, I thought it could be perfect if we hosted our reception at The Four Horseman. We wouldn't have to worry about trying to book it last minute because it's his place and not at all an in-demand wedding venue but still special to us. Perfect, right?"

I tried not to laugh again, even though I found it incredibly amusing how it was classic Libby to be able to think through all of this sometime between when she woke up to Patrick's proposal and now—before our nine o'clock staff meeting.

Nodding, I admitted, "That's actually a wonderful idea."

"I'm so glad you agree. Also, now I can finally get you to come check out the pub. In fact—we should go tonight. He'll be there. You can scope it out, we'll sit at the bar, and we can have our first consultation meeting. They serve *awesome* fish-n-chips. Their burgers are good, too. Anyway, the point is, we should go. Tonight. My treat."

I opened my mouth to respond, but before I could get a word out, Jorge peeked his head in the room.

"Morning," he greeted, curiosity lacing his tone.

Jorge Esteban was the last to join the Rusty Barn crew a little more than two years ago, but he'd fit in from day one. He was a total sap when it came to weddings, and he had a gift when it came to floral design and décor.

Like me, he was thirty-five and unattached. Though, unlike me, he was a serial dater. He liked the idea of a happily-ever-after, but he had commitment issues—an old lover saddling him with that baggage. He was handsome and flirty, if not often lonely, and I worried about him sometimes.

But who was I to give relationship advice?

"I heard fish-n-chips. Are we planning an outing to The Four Horsemen?" he asked, quirking a single eyebrow.

Coincidentally, Jorge hadn't been too busy to join Libby at Patrick's establishment.

And apparently, the fish-n-chips really were notable.

Twisting in her chair, Libby didn't hesitate to announce, "I have news."

At this, Jorge stepped fully into my office. As usual, he looked e-ffortlessly cool in printed slacks and a striped, short-sleeved button-up. The colors clashed but somehow worked at the same time. I didn't know how he did it, but he knew how to mix patterns like nobody else. Not to mention, his shoe game made *me* jealous.

When Libby shared that she and Patrick were getting married, his jaw dropped so fast, it was a wonder it was still attached.

Libby and I both laughed. Amusement still coating her tone, she told him, "We're aiming for May. And, so you know, I want peonies and succulents *everywhere*, which means you better start sourcing, like, yesterday."

Jorge waved his hands in front of him, leaning back as he did so, like he was literally reeling with this information. He didn't drop his hands, as if to brace for her answer when he asked, "Girl, are you pregnant?"

I pulled my upper lip between my teeth to prevent my face from expressing I'd wondered the exact same thing.

"What? No!" she insisted with an eye roll. "We just don't want to wait. I'm thirty-one. He's thirty-seven. It took us this long to find each other, and it kind of feels like we're late to forever." She lifted one of her shoulders in a shrug and let it fall as she continued, "I don't want to be any later."

Hearing that was all I needed. Libby could be impulsive, but she wasn't stupid. She was in love. Moreover, she deserved to have the wedding of her dreams—even if we had less than three months to plan it.

"Don't you worry. We're going to make this happen, even if I have to call in every favor I'm owed. Promise," I assured her. "We'll start tonight. I can meet you at the pub at six."

"Okay!"

We heard Phoebe humming as she came down the hall. She stopped when she noticed all of us in my office.

"Am I late for something?"

Phoebe Daniels had joined Rusty Barn not long after Libby, and she was a *godsend*. She came with experience that couldn't be taught and connections that mattered a great deal. I, of course, had my own reputation with plenty of contacts around the major metropolitan hubs of Texas; but Phoebe had a rolodex—an *actual* rolodex—of every catering vendor we knew and trusted. Whether we had a bride who wanted smoked brisket or vegan lasagna at her reception dinner, Phoebe could help curate the perfect menu with the best local chefs.

As a bonus, Phoebe didn't just come with previous work experience, she came with plenty of life experience, too. At forty-five, she was the only one of us who had started a family of her own. She had a husband of twenty years, and a teenaged daughter who was always happy to lend a helping hand during the summer months.

Even though her wavy, shoulder length locks were streaked with gray, she was all about keeping cool in stressful situations—a character trait that came in handy often.

"We were just chatting," I assured her as she entered.

Like the news would never get old, Libby announced once more, "I'm getting married!"

Not for the last time, I was incredibly grateful for Phoebe. She was the first one of us who responded not with shock or worry but pure, unadulterated delight.

"What? No way! Libby, that's so exciting." No sooner had she gushed than she grew serious and asked, "Let's see the ring. How'd he do?"

Libby stood, as did I. I made my way to the front of my desk, joining the others as we gathered around her outstretched hand. She wiggled her fingers, showing off her two-carat princess cut diamond.

"Classic," murmured Phoebe.

"Perfect," Jorge agreed.

"Beautiful," I added. Wrapping my arm around her shoulders, I gave her a squeeze and whispered, "Congratulations, sweetie."

Ange

H E LOCKED THE FRONT door of his house, his goldendoodle abandoning him on the porch as she headed for the truck he left parked in the driveway. He didn't mind. She knew the drill. Trailing after her, he unlocked the door of his Toyota and opened the driver's side.

"Ladies first," he told her. A smirk tugged at the corner of his mouth as she leapt up into the cab and climbed her way over to the passenger seat. "Good girl."

He stowed his tumbler full of black coffee in the cup holder, started his vehicle, and rolled her window down halfway. It was the middle of February, which meant the air outside was just brisk enough to remind him of the real winters he'd endured most of his life—until he found his way to Texas. It'd been nearly four years, and it still made him laugh a little to hear people moan about how cold they were when it was fifty degrees outside.

If anyone would have told him five years ago that he'd be living on a quiet street near downtown Austin, working behind the bar as a co-owner of a pub with his best friend, enjoying a simple life as a bachelor with his dog—he would have laughed. Back then, such a reality didn't seem even remotely possible.

His life had taken a drastic turn, one he never saw coming.

Now, he'd never been more content.

He was thirty-seven years old, and he felt it, which was a relief. When he was thirty-two, sprinting at full-speed in the rat race that was his career on Wall Street, he felt closer to fifty than thirty. Every day was a grind, but chasing money always was. He was good at his job, managing a hedge fund, but it was all-consuming. Days were often long, taxing, and stressful—and home wasn't exactly a respite.

He'd fallen in love what felt like a lifetime ago. They'd met through friends in the city, and their relationship progressed at the same speed as the rest of life. Fast. They had some version of happy for a while, but it didn't last. None of it did. It wasn't until he was forced to slow down that he took a good look at himself and realized he was exhausted and not the least bit fulfilled.

Then again, a global pandemic had that effect on a lot of people.

Now the only time he got out of bed before the sun came up was when he was getting ready to go out on the lake to catch some bass. Most days, he left for work just before nine—and he lived so close, he was parked out back ten minutes later. That day, the most stressful part of his morning would be making sure he got the liquor order in before the pub opened at eleven.

Moving to Austin had been one of the best decisions of his life.

He thought this, not for the last time, as he stepped out of his truck, Penny leaping out behind him. On his way toward the back door, he sifted through his keys for the right one, knowing he'd be the first to arrive. He usually was. Though, that didn't mean Patrick was a slouch. They were equal partners, even if his old friend avoided the opening shift more times than not.

It was no secret Pat loved The Four Horseman. It was his pride and joy. He'd opened it seven years ago and busted his ass doing it. Even though the two of them had ended up worlds apart, they'd kept tabs on each other since they'd graduated from Notre Dame. Ange knew it was always a dream of Patrick's to open up his own Irish Pub. He'd been proud of him, even if he never got a chance to make it down for a visit before the whole world shut down.

That year had been tough on a lot of bars and restaurants. Pat was one of the lucky ones. Not because he had enough business to survive, but because he was a smart guy with the right investments. He had enough capital to keep himself afloat for a little while. When people started going out again, he was optimistic—as always—but it was still a struggle. He took out a loan from his dad. When that wasn't enough, he asked Ange if he'd be interested in becoming a partner.

The timing couldn't have been more perfect.

Ange didn't know a thing about running a bar, but he wanted it.

And when Ange wanted something, he wasn't afraid to go after it.

He needed the change. He had the capital. They made it happen.

It took a couple years to bounce back, but they'd done it.

Together.

Now, business was good.

Life was good.

Simple.

Right.

Penny led the way down the hall toward the small office he shared with Pat. As soon as she stepped inside, she headed straight for her dog bed in the corner and made herself comfortable.

Ange got to work.

It was ten o'clock when he heard the backdoor slam shut. He was behind the bar; but without the music playing, the hum of conversation between patrons, and the commotion in the kitchen, noise traveled far. He listened absentmindedly to the sound of the approaching footsteps. The closer they got, the more certain he was who had arrived.

Ange could have looked at the schedule to see who was slated to arrive when, but he rarely spared a glance at the thing. Pat was in charge of that. Moreover, they had a solid crew. The people who worked at The Four Horsemen wanted to be there. Pat had a way of making everyone feel like family, so they didn't have to worry about flakes or drama with the staff. They all had Pat and Ange's number, and they were good about communicating if there was ever an issue.

That's not to say they were perfect. Every family had their unique measure of dysfunction, but they were loyal. Especially Jack. Pat had made sure to take care of his head chef during the pandemic, which earned him a degree of loyalty that would never be broken.

It was Jack who was headed his way just then. Ange would recognize the heavy, lumbering cadence of those feet anywhere.

"Hey, there, beautiful," he cooed.

Ange smiled at his tablet, appreciating the tone Jack always took with his Penny.

The man was six-foot-four, weighed nearly three hundred pounds, and could throw back shots of rye whiskey like it was sweet tea. At fifty-three, he'd lived long enough to be surly without apologizing, and he was never shy about speaking his mind. He'd yet to become a grandpa, on account of his only son was too busy *dickin' around*—as he often put it—and his wife would not allow a dog in their house. This meant Penny got a whole lot of affection from the old man.

She was a sweetheart and made sure to always gave it right back.

Jack appeared in the open doorway between the side of the bar and the hallway, Penny scrapping by his legs on her way to stand by Ange.

With a chin lift, Jack muttered, "Mornin'."

Ange mimicked the gesture. "Morning, Jack."

It was all he said before he turned back toward the kitchen.

A half-smile pulled at Ange's lips.

Classic Jack.

"Come on, Penny. You're not supposed to be back here, girl."

He returned her to the office, gave her a treat, then went to the stock room to finish up his liquor order. He was almost finished when he heard Hector arrive.

Hector couldn't sneak up on someone if he tried. He was always humming, dancing, or laughing. He wasn't just the life of the party—he *was* the party. He was twenty years younger than Jack, and they couldn't have been more different; but in the kitchen, they were the dream team. Ange knew Jack put up with Hector's antics because he worked harder than anyone, which earned him Jack's respect.

And Jack's respect was worth a whole lot.

Hector popped his head into the office long enough to say hello, then disappeared into the kitchen. Ange knew this for certain because, not thirty seconds later, Latin tunes could be heard drifting down the hallway.

Yeah. Life was good.

Simple.

Right.

At eleven, Ange gave Penny a loving rub down, closed her in the office, then headed for the front to unlock the doors. Willow, the youngest on their roster at twenty-six, was just outside, her gaze locked in on her phone as her thumbs moved swiftly across the screen. When Ange opened the door to let her in, she looked up and grinned.

She had purple hair. That day, she'd styled it in two, messy, pigtail buns. She was quirky, to say the least, but she was hard not to like. She also had a knack for remembering a table's worth of orders without writing a single thing down.

"Hey, boss."

"Hey, Willow."

With her gaze redirected back onto her phone, she continued texting as she entered the pub and told him, "Just gonna drop my stuff. Be back in a sec."

He left her to it, then went to turn on the overhead sound system and the televisions that flanked the liquor shelves. Twenty minutes later, the bar was set up the way he liked, and Willow was at the end of it, rolling a bin full of silverware. When the front door opened, they both looked up, anticipating their first customer. Instead, they saw Patrick.

He was grinning from ear to ear.

He stopped in the middle of the pub, spread his arms open wide and announced, "She said yes!"

Ange frowned, confused. "What?"

"Libby," he chuckled as he dropped his arms. "I asked her to marry me, and she said yes."

"Oh, my god! Congratulations," cried Willow.

Ange coughed out a laugh, though his eyebrows were still knitted together in confusion as he replied, "I thought you were going to ask her this weekend. Didn't you have a whole thing planned?"

"Yeah. I did," he said, finally approaching the bar. Pat bellied up to it and confessed, "But then I woke up this morning, and she was laying in the bed next to me. She was on her stomach, hugging the pillow under her cheek—her hair was everywhere, and I thought—*shit*, man. I want to wake up to my woman, naked and gorgeous, right next to me for the rest of my life." He shrugged. "I couldn't wait."

"Aww. That's so romantic," Willow murmured dreamily.

Ange shook his head, his smile clearing the tension at his brow. "Fuck, man. Congrats."

He'd meant it. He was happy for his friend.

Patrick had never been married. Truth be told, before Libby, he got around. A lot. Seeing as he was an owner of a bar, he didn't have to go far to find willing company. In spite of his own failed attempt at marriage, Ange thought Pat would be better off if he could find someone and settle down. Granted, he'd only known Libby for a hot second, but Ange liked to believe that when you knew, you knew.

It hadn't been like that with him and Stephanie. Not in the beginning. Their relationship had progressed as one would expect. They'd followed the timeline set by society and their peers. He knew he loved her. He knew he wanted to get married. It seemed one plus one equaled two, and so they went for it. But marriage had been complicated. They got caught up in the life they thought they were supposed to live. They became a power couple, keeping up with the Jones' on the Upper East Side.

Once Ange realized he desired more than that, it became very clear he and Stephanie didn't want the same things. That's when he knew. She was more in love with money and his ability to make more of it than she was in love with him. It was so obvious at the time, he wondered how he hadn't seen it before. Then again, he'd been so focused on making money it wasn't until he reconsidered his priorities that he saw it.

They fought about it for months, and their divorce had been ugly—but he had no regrets.

When you knew, you knew.

And Pat knew.

"It's about time someone tamed your wild ass," teased Ange.

"I'd tell you to go fuck yourself if you weren't absolutely right," said Pat, still grinning.

"I'm happy for you. Really."

Ange reached out a hand across the bar, and Pat was quick to clasp it with his own. Rather than let him go after a simple shake, he adjusted his grip until they were holding on to the meaty part of each other's hands, beneath their thumbs. Ange watched as Pat's expression sobered a bit before he spoke again.

"You know you're my best man, right?"

This time it was Ange who grinned.

If Ange was honest, he hadn't always been the greatest friend; but Pat never let time or distance sever their connection. In retrospect, it was as if Pat had been the tether keeping Ange connected to the realist part of him. He got lost for a while, but Pat had been there to bring him back to himself. He owed it to his friend to stand by his side for this.

"I'd be offended if it were anyone else."

"Good. Now, buckle up—I told Libby she had free rein over the wedding, and we're getting married in May."

"May?" gasped Willow. Both men looked her way as she added, "I've met Libby. She is extra in all the best ways, and weddings are how she makes a living. There's no way y'all are gonna have a wedding that's anything less than totally fab, and you're getting married in May? That's, like, tomorrow."

Pat merely waggled his eyebrows before drumming his palms against the bar top.

"Like I said, buckle up. She'll be here tonight with her best friend, who happens to be her boss and our new wedding planner." He pointed at Ange and continued, "Your first order of business is to help me survive my woman wanting to talk flowers and shit all night."

Great, thought Ange.

CHAPTER Three

Channing

I HELD THE DOOR open for Susan and Jennifer as we stepped out of the print shop. They were my last appointment of the day. Libby and I referred to the mother-daughter pair as the Dynamic Duo.

I hadn't seen Jennifer make a single decision without getting her mother's vote of approval first. It wasn't so much that Susan seemed to be the kind of mom who was essentially planning her second wedding via her offspring; more like Jennifer was self-aware enough to know she was incredibly indecisive and could use the guiding hand of a woman who had both good taste and sound judgement.

That afternoon we'd arranged to meet in order to approve the final proof of her custom designed wedding invitation. At first glance, it was fairly simple. It had a muted color palate with minimalistic design. The card stock was a burlap brown. The calligraphy etched on the inside was black.

Elegant.

Understated.

But it was the envelope which housed the invite that brought the whole thing together.

Wrapped around the paper was a thick cut of delicate, cream-colored lace. It was held together by a thin strand of twine tied in a little bow. Finally, on each strand, was a dime-sized, wooden medallion, "J+L" stamped in the middle, like initials on a tree.

We all agreed the final product was beautiful. Now we just had to wait for three hundred of them to be printed and carefully pieced together.

I'd planned weddings of all different sizes. This one, for sure, was going to be a grand affair. Half the guests were going to be family and family friends, the majority of which were people I understood to be friends of Jennifer and Logan's parents rather than their own. Neither of them seemed to mind this, especially as Jennifer's father was footing the better part of the bill. Mostly, the two were merely young, head-over-heels in love, and looking forward to their fairytale wedding.

The ceremony was scheduled for late August, which felt both a manageable distance in the future and right around the corner. There was still plenty of work ahead of us, but we'd crossed off a major item on our checklist that day.

After a round of goodbyes, I pulled out my phone to see the time. It was nearly six, which meant it was time for me to meet Libby at The Four Horsemen. Since the pub was only about a block away, and the heels on my boots were chunky enough to make them comfortable for almost any duration of time on my feet, I decided I'd walk rather than try to find another parking spot downtown. Certain this would make me a couple minutes late, I shot Libby a text to let her know, then I opened my email app.

While Jennifer and Logan's wedding was still a few months out, Tiffany Jackson and Henrick Ford's big day felt like it was the week after next. I tried not to put too much pressure on it or show the Jackson's preferential treatment, but it was nearly impossible. The guest list consisted of five hundred people, many of whom were well-to-do and traveling from out of town. I was also dealing with a bride who wanted it all.

The party favors alone were worth three months of my mortgage payment.

All that to say, I made it a point to stay on top of my emails. If I didn't have some sort of correspondence in regard to the Jackson-Ford wedding at least once a day, it was a valid concern that something had gone wrong; and I didn't want anything to go wrong.

Or, more accurately—anything *else*.

When I scrolled through my inbox and saw an email from Jorge, I braced.

We'd been having issues with our florist. This was not unusual when working with Blossoms & Balloons Floral Design, which was why we avoided hiring them as a vendor as a general rule. Unfortunately, when a bride put all her stock in a florist she thought she could trust, it was hard to argue with her—especially since flowers were such a huge part of a wedding. I'd never recommend B&B Floral Design, but that didn't mean they didn't come recommended, which was why Tiffany *insisted* she wanted no one else.

But we were three months out from her wedding, and we had yet to finalize her arrangement designs.

I opened Jorge's email, read the single sentence in his message, and breathed a sigh of relief. The consultation had gone well, and he was moving forward with a design. I made a mental note to sync with him the next day in order to find out how I could help with next steps.

I was about to close my screen when I got a reply from Libby, letting me know she was a few minutes behind herself. This was all the excuse I needed to take my time and enjoy my cool, not-summer evening stroll.

As I drew near the pub, I had to admit I felt a little guilty I'd never been before. Earlier that morning, it hadn't been a big deal. Now that the woman I claimed as my best friend was going to *marry* the owner, it felt pretty lame that I'd never so much as stepped foot inside. Close friends were hard to come by—especially ones as tried and true as Libby.

I'd learned that the hard way.

I wanted to be the kind of friend who showed up. And not just when it was convenient for me. For too long, I'd let work be my excuse for just about everything. It was why I barely knew Patrick.

Well—that, and he'd only been around for three months.

Regardless, I needed to do better.

Right then and there, I vowed I *would* do better.

It was almost a quarter after six when the pub came into view. The first thing I noticed were the tall, double, red doors against the black painted facing of the building. *The Four Horsemen* was in big, Celtic font above the entrance, the letters painted gold and lit by the lamps that hung along the top edge of the roof. To the right of the door was a wooden pub sign, protruding from the building, *The Four Horsemen* printed in the same font. Below it was a golden horse up on its hind legs, kicking its front hooves.

I made another mental note that Libby and Patrick would *definitely* be taking photos in front of those red doors, with a kissing shot under that pub sign.

As soon as I stepped inside, I was greeted by the sound of AC/DC and the buzz of conversation from a number of occupied tables. At a quick glance, I guessed maximum occupancy was anywhere from a hundred and twenty to a hundred and fifty people. That night, it wasn't packed, but it was far from empty.

"Have a seat anywhere. We'll be right with you!" called a red-head as she passed by me with a tray full of food.

"Thanks," I murmured distractedly.

I wasn't ready to sit. I was taking it all in.

I walked a few steps away from the door, so as not to be in the way, and continued to survey the place.

As one would expect, the pub was very masculine, earthy, and warm. There were a combination of high top and regular tables, all of which were surrounded by heavy, wooden chairs. Along the front windows, on either side of the doors, and the entire left side wall were booths covered in dark, espresso colored, pin-cushioned leather. To the right was a hallway I assumed led to the restrooms and maybe the kitchen further back.

Finally, there was the bar. It was a decent size with wooden barstools complete with seat backs, the leather cushions a shade of forest green. The liquor wall was brick-faced with shelves that spanned from the countertop to the ceiling. There was a thick, wooden, sliding ladder, which clued me into the fact that the bottles on the top were not just for show—merely big spenders.

I was on the verge of picturing just how we could utilize the bar for a wedding reception when my eyes caught his, and I froze.

He was standing behind the counter.

There was something in his hands, but I couldn't see what.

It didn't matter what.

In that moment, I wasn't sure anything mattered except for *him*.

I was aware of his dark hair—so dark it looked almost black but wasn't.

It was trimmed short on the sides but longer and thick on the top.

Long enough to be messy if he wanted it to be, but it was obvious he didn't.

I liked that for reasons I knew were pointless.

His face was also covered in a beard the same dark hue.

It wasn't too long or short, but trimmed and clean.

I liked that, too.

Too much.

He was incredibly handsome.

Rugged, but not overly so.

Except, it wasn't merely his good looks that had me transfixed.

It was his eyes.

No.

It was the way his eyes were *looking* at me.

Directly at me.

I could tell, even from a distance, they were green.

I wasn't sure if I'd ever seen a man with green eyes in person.

Plenty of blue. Tons of brown. Hazel, too.

But not green.

They were beautiful.

More than that, they were looking at me.

And I mean—*at* me.

I didn't know if it had been one second or a thousand. All I knew was that those eyes were staring at me like it might have killed him to look away.

My skin began to tingle, my whole body aware that somehow, in one glance, he could see all of me.

Not just my body, but my soul.

And the weirdest part was...

I swear I saw his, too.

"Hey, *chica*."

Libby's voice pulled me from my trance, and I looked to see her standing beside me. I could barely offer her my attention. For reasons I couldn't understand, I needed to see those green eyes again.

Immediately.

I shifted my focus back behind the bar, but his eyes were focused down at the glass he was busy drying in his hands. I dropped my gaze to my feet and slowly freed a breath from my lungs, wondering if I'd seen into those eyes at all, or if I'd made the whole thing up.

"Uh, hey," I muttered, forcing the words out.

I drew in a cleansing breath as I tried again to give Libby my attention.

She nudged me with a playful jab of her elbow, smiling at me as she asked, "Scoping the place out, aren't you?"

This made me laugh. For a moment, I'd forgotten I was standing in the middle of the room. I wasn't even sure how long I'd been there.

"Maybe," I admitted jokingly.

"It's in your nature. I get it. You're always *on*—but tonight, first things first." She looped her arm around one of mine and said, "Patrick saved us a couple spots at the bar. Let's get a drink."

As we made our way to the bar, I saw two upside-down wine glasses in front of two vacant chairs. All the other spots weren't taken, but those two were right in the center. Casually observing the other occupants, I noticed most of them had their attention on one of the two televisions mounted on either side of the liquor display. The TV on the left was showing a hockey game. The one on the right was basketball.

I wasn't interested in either.

When I settled onto a chair, I couldn't help but to look at the man working behind the bar. Up close, there was more of him to notice.

He was wearing a blue flannel button-up, the sleeves of which he'd rolled up his forearms. It was pretty apparent, by the way the fabric of his shirt clung to his biceps and broad shoulders, he took very good care of himself.

He was busy uncorking a bottle of white wine. As if he'd felt my gaze trained on him, his focus shifted, and his eyes found mine. Warmth spread across my chest, and that's when I knew.

I hadn't imagined it before.

And his eyes up close?

Gorgeous.

They stayed trained on me only until Libby said, "Hey, Ange!"

Then the unfathomable happened.

He looked at Libby, smiled, and got a whole lot better.

I immediately dropped my attention to the glossy, mahogany surface in front of me.

It was too much.

God, that smile was too much.

How it revealed his straight, white teeth against the contrast of his dark beard.

The way it made the skin at the corners of his eyes crinkle.

Those eyes—green and gorgeous—had grown more vibrant with the expression.

So, yeah, it was safe to say I found this man to be incredibly attractive.

I needed to get over it. Promptly.

For one, I didn't make a habit of staring at attractive men, and I wasn't going to start that night, either. Secondly, it didn't matter how handsome he was. I wasn't interested.

I'd long since given up on the idea of marriage for myself, which meant there was no point in dating. Every once in a while, I'd let a guy buy me a drink. If I was really aching for it, I'd let him take me to bed—but that was rare. I was busy. I didn't have time for games. Most of the men I interacted with were engaged to other women, and that was how I preferred it.

I was pulled from my thoughts when I heard the man say, "I'd congratulate you, but you've said yes to putting up with Pat for the rest of your life. I think that calls for *best of luck,* dimples."

Libby laughed, and I was relieved to give her my attention. As I looked at her, I was reminded why I was there. My best friend was getting married, and I was there for *her.* This grounded me, and I began to relax a little.

"He *is* Irish, so I guess luck is on my side."

No sooner had she finished speaking than Patrick appeared through the doorway behind the bar. His face lit up at the sight of Libby, and I relaxed a little more.

Patrick was handsome in his own right. He was leaner than the stranger with the green eyes, but no less impressive. His hair was cut shorter on the sides and longer on the top, too—only he styled his loose curls messily. It worked for him; his brunette locks tinged with a natural auburn undertone. His face was narrow and masculine, his strong jawline visible underneath the hair I didn't consider long enough to be called a beard. And when he smiled at his bride-to-be, the brown of his eyes shimmered like pools of melted chocolate.

"Hey, baby," he greeted before leaning across the bar for a kiss.

Libby met him halfway and murmured, "Hi, *mi amor.*"

Patrick looked my way as soon as he'd doled out his *hello* to his fiancée. His smile was still intact when he said, "Hey, Channing. Good to see you. Thanks for comin'."

"It's good to see you too, Patrick. Congratulations on winning my girl, here."

His smile stretched into a grin, and that made my heart happy. "Libby?"

We all looked to the man with the green eyes as he raised the chilled bottle of wine in silent inquiry. Libby nodded with a "yes, please," and he reached for the overturned wine glass in front of her, righting it before he filled it.

"Can I get you something to drink?" he asked me, mid-pour.

"Wait! You two haven't met, yet," cried Libby. We both looked at her, then at each other as she continued, "Ange, this is Channing. Channing, this is Ange. He co-owns the pub with Patrick. Oh—and he's also Paddy's best man."

"Hi," he murmured, extending his hand toward me.

I slid my palm into his, ignoring the way his big, warm, calloused hand felt wrapped around mine. I also tried, and failed, to ignore the way his thick, dark lashes framed those eyes.

My god, I needed to stop obsessing over those things.

"Hi. Nice to meet you," I managed.

He nodded as he let go of me and repeated, "Can I get you something to drink?"

I pulled myself together enough to say, "I'd love an old fashioned—with bourbon, not rye, please."

"You got it."

He took away the glass in front of me and got to work, Libby earning my focus once more as she said, "*Speaking* of wedding parties—Patrick and I agreed to keep it super low-key."

I shook my head, interrupting her as I chuckled, "Are you sure you've only been engaged since this morning?"

A sheepish grin brought about her dimples, and she peered out of the corner of her eye at Patrick, who's expression said it all. Even still, he told me, "She's been blowin' up my phone with text messages all day."

Reaching for my arm, Libby held on with both hands as she assured me, "I swear, I will not let my responsibilities at work slip. I wasn't thinking of myself all day, it's just—"

"Relax, sweetie, I was only joking. If your mind isn't working a million miles an hour, it's an off day." I patted her hand reassuringly. "Now, what were you saying about your bridal party?"

"Right," she breathed as she let me go. "Well, Patrick has two sisters, and you know I have four brothers. Honestly, we don't know each other's families very well yet, so I'd rather none of them be *in* the wedding. All that to say, our wedding party will be super low-key, and by that I mean we're just going to have a best man and a maid of honor."

"Great. That simplifies things nicely."

"Right..." Libby repeated the word, this time a little apprehensively. "The thing is, I couldn't imagine asking anyone else but you to be my maid of honor. And I know it's so much to ask, given you've already agreed to help me plan the whole freaking wedding, but it would really mean the world to me and—"

"Olivia!" I reached for her hand and gave it a squeeze. She sealed her lips closed, and I paused a moment, looking at her until I knew she was calm enough to see what I was trying to convey before I drove it home. "I would be honored. My answer is yes. Of course."

Libby's grip around my hand tightened, and I watched as her eyes began to fill with tears. She drew in a shaky breath, and I smiled. I knew then, I wasn't merely sitting next to my best friend—I was sitting next to a nervous bride-to-be.

"I just want to get it right," she murmured, blinking away her tears. "I want a perfect, intimate wedding that doesn't look like it was thrown together in two and a half months even though we're going to throw it together in two and a half months."

With my free hand, I reached up and touched my palm to her cheek, wiping away a rogue tear. "Sweetie, trust me. I do this for a living, and I'm very good at it. We've got this."

A strained giggle forced its way out of her mouth as she threw her arms around me. I hugged her back as she said, "Damn. You really are the bride whisperer."

We shared a laugh. When she was ready to let me go, she did—reaching for her glass of wine. When I looked, my old fashioned was waiting right in front of me.

I didn't leave The Four Horsemen until nearly ten o'clock, Libby and Patrick walking me safely to my car before we bid each other goodnight. I knew nearly all there was to know about Libby, so when we weren't discussing wedding details, I took the opportunity to get to know Patrick. He'd shared plenty, but what I'd remembered most was that he was warm and inviting, much like his pub.

The pub he co-owned with Ange.

But I tried not to think about him.

Patrick was great with his customers, and it was nice watching him interact with a few of the regulars who sat at the bar. His personality was magnetic, and he was as funny as he was smart. I understood how Libby could be taken by him.

Oh, and the fish-n-chips—worth the hype.

Extra crispy batter around thick pieces of cod.

Double fried French fries.

Delicious.

Except, after I readied myself for bed and slipped between my sheets, it wasn't Patrick and Libby, their wedding, or the great meal I had at the pub that invaded my thoughts as I tried to find sleep.

It was Ange.

I closed my eyes, and all I saw were his.

Green and gorgeous.

CHAPTER *Four*

Ange

HE WAS IN BED, laying on his back, covers down at his waist. Penny was curled up next to him, her head resting atop the left side of his hip. The faint light of the rising sun was peeking through his blinds. He was staring up at the ceiling, but that wasn't what he was looking at.

He was replaying memories from the night before.

In his mind's eye, he couldn't take his eyes off of her.

Channing.

She had thick, blonde hair that fell in big, soft curls down her chest and back.

She'd stood in the middle of the pub in a long-sleeved, navy dress covered in some sort of floral print. It clung to her in such a way he could make out the delicate shape of her breasts and the narrow length of her waist—the subtle curve of her hips hidden in the folds of the ankle-length skirt.

He thought she had a cute mouth.

He couldn't explain why, just knew he thought it.

But it was her eyes he couldn't seem to forget.

They were blue, like the clearest sky.

With his fingers submerged in Penny's copper curls, he stroked her absentmindedly as he replayed the sound of Channing's laugh. Somehow, it had been *poised*. He didn't understand how a laugh could be *poised* without also sounding *pompous*, but she was far from pompous. What she was, was confident.

Ange heard Channing when she reminded Libby she planned weddings for a living.

"...and I'm very good at it."

After nothing more than the way she seemed to guide Pat and Libby through early-stage wedding decisions, Ange believed her. She wasn't arrogant, she just knew what the hell she was talking about.

He liked that.

He liked the way she looked at him even more.

She'd sat at the bar for hours, and she'd glanced his way more than a few times. But she wasn't begging for his attention with her eyes. She wasn't even *asking*. Channing didn't flirt, didn't play coy, didn't get drunk and throw a line at him—nothing.

He'd been working behind the bar for only a few years, but he'd seen it all.

Until Channing.

Until he stared into those blue eyes, and they'd stared back.

"...with bourbon, not rye, please."

Even her decisive choice of whiskey was appealing.

When was the last time he found a woman appealing?

Not just pretty. Not merely desirable for a night.

He couldn't remember. But he knew one thing...

He wanted to see Channing again. Soon.

He thought about how Libby had suggested she and Pat might have a joint bachelor/bachelorette party. With everything getting thrown together so quickly, she thought it would be easier—especially for Channing—and fun. Pat, who seemed intent on letting his bride have whatever she wanted, had no objections.

Channing, on the other hand, did.

She made one attempt to change Libby's mind, but it didn't take.

A ghost of a smirk played at Ange's lips as he remembered watching Channing mentally stow away that topic of conversation for another day.

Yeah, she was very good at her job.

Maybe that could be his *in*.

He could stop by her office under the guise of wanting to discuss how he could help with any pre-wedding stuff. It might have been lame, but it was an excuse he could work with.

He couldn't remember the last time he found a woman appealing—until now.

He needed to get her out of his system, one way or another.

His mind made up, he moved to get out of bed, Penny perking up instantly.

"Time to get a move on, girl. Got places to be."

CHAPTER *Five*

Channing

I WAS STANDING BEHIND my desk, gathering what I thought I needed for the next few hours into my oversized purse. With any luck, I wouldn't be late.

I really didn't want to be late.

Blake had called demanding an hour.

When Blake called demanding an hour it meant I'd let work consume me to the point where I hadn't seen my sister in four weeks. In this case, regrettably, it had been longer than that. I hadn't seen her since right after the new year, which was pretty deplorable, given we only lived twenty-five minutes apart.

Blake was older than me by two years. We were born and raised in a suburb of Dallas, which was where our parents still lived. We were convinced we could get them to retire in Austin, but dad still had a few years left before he'd be ready to slow down.

As far as work ethic was concerned, Blake and I both came by it honest.

We had always been close growing up. We got on each other's nerves constantly, but it was mostly because we were two sides of the same coin. My sister and I ended up in Austin for almost the exact same reason. Both of us went to UT, fell in love with the city and then with a man.

Even though things didn't work out for me in the romance department, I was happy I stuck around—in part because it worked out beautifully for my sister.

Blake and Derek had been married for nearly twelve years. They had two unbelievably pretty little girls and a successful cookie business they ran together, with not just one but *three* store fronts. It was good for me to live nearby, so I could be a part of their lives in a real way. With no family of my own, I didn't have to slow down if I didn't want to; but for Sylvie, Camille, and my big sister, I was reminded to take a breather every once in a while.

That afternoon, I had an appointment scheduled away from the office. Not sure if I'd make it back before the end of the day, I scanned my desk once more to make sure I had everything. I stopped dead in my tracks when a soft knock against my open door beckoned me to look up, and I saw him.

Ange.

Right there.

In my office.

For a moment, I didn't know what to do with this reality.

He looked good out from behind the bar—better in the light of day.

He was wearing leather work boots with dark khakis, which fit him really well, and a gray tee underneath a denim button-up he hadn't bothered to button up. Like the previous evening, he'd rolled up his sleeves over his forearms.

Damn, but he was handsome.

I wasn't interested, but facts were facts.

Having reminded myself he was hot, and that I would get over it and move on, I came unstuck, strapping my purse over my shoulder.

"Hi. I'm—I'm on my way out. I wasn't expecting you. Are you here for Libby or...?"

"Hey. Sorry, I should have called. I didn't have your number," he said casually, tucking his left fingertips into his front pocket. "I actually came to see you."

"Oh? Why's that?" I asked, trying my best to look him in the eyes without staring.

Green. Gorgeous.

"I wanted to see how I could help with any pre-wedding things." He lifted his other hand, twirled a finger around—indicating my office—then added, "I'm sure you have the wedding part down, but if I can help in any way, I'd like to. I know Libby mentioned a joint bachelor/bachelorette party. Noticed you weren't too keen on that idea."

Half a laugh spilled from my lips, amazed he'd taken note of that. "You are correct in your assessment of my thoughts. I think—well, to be honest, it's a bad idea.

"It's completely acceptable to combine a bridal shower with a bachelorette party, but not a bachelor party. Men and women want very different things at these sorts of events. Not to mention, the whole point is to celebrate the end of a significant chapter in your life—namely, all the years you lived before this other person came into your world and changed everything—and I think it's silly to spend that night with the one person who will—hopefully—be with you henceforth for every other chapter of your life for the rest of forever. And...uhm..."

I lost my words for a moment when I noticed him smirking at me.

Like everything else, he wore a smirk well.

Then I realized I had been rambling.

I also remembered, I had someplace else to be.

"Anyway," I said with a shrug. "I'll talk Libby out of it, don't worry."

"Okay," he replied with a dip of his chin, his smirk stretching into a smile. "My offer still stands. I'm happy to help wherever I can."

"Great. I appreciate it."

I meant that. It was sweet how he was stepping up as a best man. It spoke of both his character and of Patrick's. Nevertheless, I was going to be late if I didn't get out of there.

"I'm so sorry, but I really do have to go."

"Right. Sorry for dropping by unannounced. Maybe we could find time to talk things over after work. How about dinner one night this week?"

Dinner.

Dinner.

Was he asking me out as a woman or as Libby's maid of honor?

I wasn't sure how I felt about an invitation to dinner in either of those scenarios. Moreover, I didn't have the wherewithal or the time to figure it out. So, I did the next best thing.

I reached for one of my business cards on my desk and made my way toward him. Offering it, I quickly responded, "Here's my card. My mobile number is at the bottom. We'll sort it out soon. Now, I hate to be rude, but—"

"Go," he chuckled, pocketing my card. "I'll see myself out."

"Okay," I murmured, waving goodbye as I hurried toward the stairs.

As I went, I tried not to think of how good he smelt. Like citrus and sandalwood.

I knew we were on the ninth floor, but there was no way I wanted to be caught with all that was him in an elevator. Certainly not with that pleasant, woodsy scent or a pending dinner offer between us.

I was definitely going to be late.

Approximately eighteen minutes later, I was ten minutes late. Partly due to my run-in with Ange, but partly due to the fact that it took me longer than usual to find parking. Fortunately, after I walked quickly into Hotel Zaza, headed straight for the restaurant, I spotted Blake and Camille already seated at a table near the front window. Neither of them looked bothered by my tardiness as they chatted.

"Hey. Sorry I'm late," I greeted with a wave as Blake looked over at me upon my approach.

"Hey, you. It's okay. You look cute," she said as she stood to wrap me in a hug.

"Oh, thanks."

"Hi Aunt Channing," came Camille's little voice from the seat behind me.

I turned to look at my favorite four-year-old niece. In a few years, I knew my sister and Derek were going to be in serious trouble because their daughters were going to be total knockouts.

Both of them inherited curly hair from Derek's side, while they got Blake's blonde hue. Even though my sister had hazel eyes, Camille and Sylvie each had different shades of blue, which stood out beautifully against their skin tone. Blake's pale skin combined with Derek's dark melanin made for the silkiest pale brown complexion on both of them. Add to that Sylvie's sweet heart and Cami's feisty personality—they were definitely going to have guys lining up around the block in another decade.

I crouched down to wrap Cami in a hug as I replied, "Hi, beautiful. I'm excited to have lunch with you!"

"Me, too."

I freed a contented sigh as we all settled, already relieved my sister had called demanding an hour.

"I ordered the baked goat cheese. I didn't know how hungry you'd be, so I stopped there. We can order a few more appetizers and share or get our own plates. I'm fine either way."

"I'm down to share, so long as we get the Brussel sprouts as one of the apps this time."

"Deal."

Blake and I had been to Group Therapy enough times to memorize the menu. The first time we dined at the swanky upscale restaurant, it had been as a bit of a joke, given the name. We ended up loving it. It was at the top of our list of "go-to" places to meet when we wanted to go out downtown.

"Sylvie will be disappointed she missed you while she was at school. You'll have to come to dinner soon."

Dinner.

Suddenly, I had Ange's voice in my head, inviting me to dinner one night this week.

I ignored it, smiled at my sister and promised, "I will."

"Okay—tell me what's new with you. I know work is good, 'cause you're buried in it."

I was happy to have news to share that wasn't tied to work. At least, not directly. I told Blake about Libby's engagement, which took the focus off of me for a few minutes. I didn't mention Ange, but that didn't mean he didn't keep popping up in my thoughts.

Honestly, it was more annoying than anything else.

When I was ready to change the subject, I shifted the conversation in Blake's direction. It was easy to get her talking about Derek and the girls. Our food arrived and as we ate, she told me about a few new recipes she was experimenting with for the cookie shop.

Before the girls were born, she was pretty involved in both the business and the baking side of The Cookie Ranch. She'd been baking for as long as any of us could remember. All through college, she would stress-bake during finals week, then sell her treats to various study groups whenever she went to the library. Years later, it wasn't until Derek encouraged her to open up shop that she seriously considered it. They did it together and found success, which hadn't been astonishing to anyone except Blake.

When Sylvie was born, she took a step back and let Derek handle all of the business side. Three years after that, when she had Cami, she took an additional step back. Now, she oversaw new recipe creation and all custom sugar cookie orders.

I loved it when I had a couple who wanted cookies at their wedding reception. It gave me an excuse to work with Blake, Derek, and their team. It was seriously cool when our worlds collided like that.

Most of our shared plates were empty and I was feeling full and happy when I unconsciously glanced out the window. I gasped when I saw her, turning in my chair and tilting my head so my hair formed a curtain that hid my face.

"Channing, what are you—?"

"Don't look," I told her.

"Don't look at *what*?" asked Blake.

"*Ava!*" I whisper-shouted, as if she might be able to hear me through the glass. "Is she gone?"

"What?"

I saw my sister direct her gaze out the window, and I hissed, "I told you not to *look*."

She quirked an eyebrow at me, her annoyance on full display as she replied, "First of all, I can't tell you if she's gone if I don't look. But more importantly, you know I hate it when you do this. She does not deserve for you to hide from her."

I stared at Blake for a moment, enduring her attitude because she was right.

I *did* know how much she hated when I hid from Ava.

I also didn't care.

"Is she gone?" I asked softly.

"Yes. She's gone. She didn't see you. You're fine."

I straightened and gingerly swept a bit of hair behind my ear.

I'd only seen her for as long as it took for me to register it was her—but in that fraction of a second, I saw she was pregnant. Jorge hadn't mentioned this to me. Then again, Jorge knew I wanted as little to do with Ava as humanly possible. She might have been the owner of B&B Floral Design, and I might have had to endure putting up with her shoddy work on the rarest of occasions, but that didn't mean I gossiped about her.

Though, this new discovery was one I'd just seen with my own eyes.

That meant they were expecting baby number three.

It shouldn't have hurt.

In fact, it didn't.

Not exactly.

It was more like a dull pinch somewhere deep in my chest that came about once every eight or nine months when I accidently saw her around town. Luckily, I'd only had the misfortune of dealing with her for three weddings over the last five years, so any other spotting of the woman was, indeed, an accident.

Greater still, I had a staff who dealt with her, so I didn't have to. This they did graciously, and I loved and appreciated them all the more for it.

"Channing Davenport…"

I gave my sister my attention but didn't speak a word.

I had an idea of what was coming.

"You are beautiful and talented and successful. You have a generous heart and great legs. If I've said it once I've said it a million times, you need to put yourself out there again. You need to stop hiding. Stop hiding from Ava, stop hiding from men, stop hiding from what I know, deep down, you want. You used to dream of so much more than a life spent planning other people's weddings while you go to bed alone night after night."

"Mmhmm," I hummed with a nod. Then, for the nine-hundredth time, I patiently reminded her, "The operative words being *used to*—I *used to* dream of more. I *used to* dream of marrying the love of my life. And then, after dad walked me down the aisle and gave me away—I watched the love of my life literally run away with my best friend, leaving me alone at the altar. You were there. I know you remember."

Blake leaned against the table, shortening the distance between us as she countered, "And you and I both know, as much as he had us all fooled, Dylan was *not* the love of your life, because the love of your life would *never* do that."

This was true, but I had no intention of conceding my point.

"Blake, I'm happy. I have my family, whom I love, and work and my friends—"

"You work so much your friends and your work are the same thing. You can't list them separately."

Smiling, I reached across the table for her hand. She gave it to me, her worried expression softening a little. "I promise I'm good."

She gave my fingers a squeeze and replied, "I'm never going to stop wanting more for you."

"I know."

"I love you. Like, a lot."

My smile grew. "I love you a lot, too, sis."

"And I love you three!" chimed in Camille, not to be left out.

We both turned and giggled with my niece.

She wasn't old enough to understand, but I was grateful for her perfect timing and the lightness she'd gifted our table. The tension broken, we moved on to another subject. Not long after, we settled our bill, gave each other another round of hugs, and then I left for my afternoon appointment, willing my brain to put the memory of a pregnant Ava Butler out of my mind.

It had been a weird day.

By the time I'd finished my appointment and gone to run an errand, it was late enough in the afternoon that I decided to head home rather than return to the office. I had a few things left to do, but I felt like doing them from my couch in a pair of leggings and thick socks.

After all my attempts to put up mental blockers to keep my thoughts from wandering where I didn't want them to go for the last several hours, I was exhausted.

I'd just stepped off the elevator onto the eleventh floor of my building and was on my way to my unit when my phone sounded with a text alert. I dug it out of my purse, saw the unsaved number, then stopped in my tracks right in the middle of the hallway.

I knew, before I even opened the message, it was from Ange.

Knowing that knocked down all the make-shift blockers I'd thrown up, and that familiar pinch in my chest came back.

Ava was pregnant. Again.

It had been nearly a decade. I wanted to be over it. I wanted to be happy for them. Clearly, they were meant to be. Except, I couldn't help but think—she was living *my* life, or the life I thought I wanted with the man I used to love. Together, they'd ripped that future right out from underneath me.

I hadn't lied to my sister. My life was good. Maybe not always *great*, but definitely good. I didn't want Dylan anymore. That ship had sailed a long time ago. Neither did I miss Ava and the friendship I thought we had. Would it have been nice if we could be two business owners in the wedding industry who partnered together on the regular to deliver an *amazing* product? Sure. But that was never going to happen.

It just bugged me knowing they'd simply started a life together and never looked back.

And it bugged me that it bugged me. Still—after all this time.

Why couldn't they have moved to Vermont or somewhere far, far away where I'd never see them again?

I sighed and continued down the hall.

It was fine.

I would be fine.

No, I *was* fine.

I opened Ange's text.

Hi. This is Ange. About that dinner. When are you free?

I still didn't know what he was after, and I hadn't allowed myself the chance to think about it. Considering the afternoon I'd had, and the lecture I'd gotten from my sister, I felt like telling him yes.

It was just dinner.

It didn't have to mean anything.

In two and a half months, he'd walk me down the aisle at Libby and Patrick's wedding. It wouldn't hurt if we got to know each other a little. Maybe we could be friends.

As I approached my door, I stopped long enough to type and send my reply.

How about tomorrow night? You name the time and place.

I didn't second guess myself. Neither did I wait for a response. Instead, I dropped my phone into my purse, dug out my keys, and let myself inside.

CHAPTER *Six*

AT TX COCINA. SIX-THIRTY.

We were going to a modern Mexican restaurant. It was conveniently located just down the street. As I suggested, Ange had picked the place and the time. Currently, it was a quarter after six, and I was closing up shop for the day. Or at least, I was trying.

I heard Jorge on the phone. He sounded like he was barely hanging on to any modicum of patience. I got up from my desk and headed for the door. I hardly had a chance to stick my head out into the hallway, and he was coming my way.

His face said it all.

I reached out a hand, signaling my offer to take the phone. He was one step ahead of me.

"Mrs. Stafford, I've got Channing right here. I under—"

She cut him off, and he rolled his eyes so hard it was a wonder they didn't get stuck.

"Okay. One moment, please." He put us on mute and handed me the phone. "She's certifiable."

I took the phone as I reminded him, "Her daughter is having an outdoor wedding in two days, and there's rain in the forecast. They're at the top of their budget as is and adding a tent—while practical—is not exactly how they dreamed it up."

Jorge folded his arms across his chest. "Well, I'm not *God*, and I didn't order the rain."

"Yes, I know," I said on a soft laugh. "Let me try."

I tapped the screen to unmute the call, then pressed the phone to my ear. It took me nearly ten minutes, but I managed to talk the woman off the ledge. I was getting ready to hand the phone back to Jorge when I saw Ange hit the hallway, headed toward us. My eyes locked with his green ones, he smiled, and I forgot what I was saying for a second.

ATX Cocina. Six-thirty.

We were meeting there, weren't we?

Why was he here?

Mrs. Stafford's voice in my ear reminded me I was in the middle of something.

"Sorry, could you repeat that?" I asked, shifting my focus onto Jorge.

His raised eyebrows spoke of his curiosity, while his smile was a clear indication of his approval. This time it was my turn to roll my eyes. I hadn't told Libby about my dinner plans. I hadn't told anyone. Now I wondered how long I had before Jorge inquired about an explanation as to why Ange showed up at our office clearly looking for me.

I finished with Mrs. Stafford, pressed the mute button, then handed Jorge his phone.

"When you boil it down, she wants firepits not heat lamps. In the event of rain, tents can't handle firepits, so we're going to have to get creative." I snapped my fingers, an absentminded tick, as I tried to recall a wedding we'd done last year with an aesthetic I thought could work if we needed to pull an audible. "The Carter wedding! Send her pictures."

Jorge's eyes widened in enlightenment. "Yes. Genius. I'm on it." He unmuted the phone, put it to his ear and picked up where I left off, headed back toward his office as he spoke. He waved his fingers at me in a silent *thank you*, and I watched him until he disappeared through his doorway.

That situation handled, I then turned to look up at Ange.

"Hi. I thought we were meeting at the restaurant."

He shrugged nonchalantly as he replied, "I assumed you'd walk from here, and I figured we could go together."

"Oh. Okay. I just need to grab my purse," I said, hooking a thumb over my shoulder.

He dipped his chin in a nod of acknowledgment, and I went to collect my things.

We were headed for the elevator when he asked, "Do you deal with difficult clients often?"

"Uhm, occasionally. Less often than you might think."

We boarded the elevator.

The lift car filled with the scent of citrus and sandalwood.

I forced myself to keep talking. To think of anything else.

"Most of the time, it's not so much that the client is difficult as it is they are dealing with a lot of emotions during what can be a stressful time. I've learned it's my job to step back, examine the bigger picture, and then help them see past whatever obstacle we're up against."

"In this instance, the obstacle being rain?"

The way he said it made me laugh, and I nodded. "Yup. And rather than say—*I told you so*—we just have to be ready with a backup plan. But I do always warn couples who want an outdoor wedding between February and May that the chance of rain is a coin flip. More so than in the summer months."

"It's supposed to be lucky, isn't it? Rain on a wedding day."

I smiled up at him as we stepped out of the elevator and into the lobby, headed for the exit.

"Yeah, that's how the saying goes."

"How long have you been in business?"

"I've been in the industry for more than a decade now, but I started Rusty Barn about five years ago."

"And you love it?"

We stepped outside, and a cool breeze swept by, causing the flowy fabric of my jumpsuit to dance around my legs. I'd styled my hair half up and half down that day, but a single strand blew across my face. I swept it away then tucked my hands into the pockets of my blazar as I replied, "I do."

"Why?"

"Uh…because it's fun?" I shrugged.

"Oh, come on," he stated challengingly. "The real answer."

"Okay," I conceded. I peeked up at him out of the corner of my eye, then directed my attention in front of me as I gave him the real answer. "It is fun, most of the time. But I think what I love the most is being able to take someone's idea and make it a reality—a reality better than they imagined. I find that I get a lot of clients who come into my office thinking they know what they want, but what they want is limited to what they know.

"I'm fortunate enough that I can be somewhat selective when it comes to accepting business from couples. My brand is very specific. Because my team and I are specialists, when a bride and I truly connect on her vision, and then we can go execute it, on the most important day of her life—I mean, how could I not love that?"

It was a rhetorical question.

He'd opened Pandora's box, so I kept going.

It was easy talking to Ange about my work, given how passionate I was about it. Without even noticing it, I talked for the entire walk to the restaurant. It wasn't until he opened the door, and we approached the hostess stand, that I realized I hadn't given him a chance to get in a single word edgewise.

I wasn't sure if I felt bad or relieved by this. He'd unwittingly chosen a topic of conversation that allowed me to ease into the reality that I was about to sit down to dinner with a man I found *very* attractive. Something I hadn't done in I couldn't remember how long.

It wasn't going to go anywhere, and I knew that, but still.

"Hope you don't mind waiting a few minutes for a table. I spend all day behind a bar."

"I don't mind at all," I told him, offering him a reassuring smile.

Those green eyes took in my expression, then settled as he looked at me in that way that made my chest feel all warm and tingly. So as not to get lost in his stare, I decided it was time to get him talking.

"So—*Ange*, is that short for something?"

"Yeah. Michelangelo."

My eyebrows shot up my forehead, and I had to make a conscious effort not to let my mouth fall open. I was so unprepared for that answer. Unfortunately, I wasn't quick enough to stop myself from asking, "After the Ninja Turtle or the sculptor?"

My breath caught when he threw his head back and laughed.

Oh, dear god.

I knew, in that exact moment, I couldn't be friends with this man.

A woman could not be friends with a man whose laugh made everything around her cease to exist.

The sound was deep and rich and beautiful.

Coupled with his smile, it was downright devastating.

Before I could get my wits about me, he was speaking again.

"That was good. But no—my mom just had some very grand, romantic ideas about what my name should be when I was born. Michelangelo Castellanos was a name my father could stand. I've gone by Ange since I could speak. *Mike* never really took."

Still recovering from the effects of his laughter, I didn't hesitate to reply, "I like Ange. Mike doesn't seem to suit you."

I could tell he liked what I said by the way his eyes seemed to grow warmer as he looked at me. I felt powerless under his gaze, which is why I was incredibly grateful when the hostess let us know our table was ready, drawing Ange's attention away from me.

I took a deep breath and let it out slowly, working on getting myself together as we were escorted to our table. We were seated in a spot that had a booth on one side with a chair on the other. He offered me the booth. I slid in as gracefully as I could manage.

In an effort to keep him talking, I was ready with my next question the moment we were left alone. "I talked your ear off about the joys of wedding planning, so now it's your turn. When did you and Patrick open up The Four Horsemen?"

He grinned, and I immediately wondered how I was going to survive this dinner. There was only so much goodness I could endure before it started to feel masochistic.

I braced, then he started talking.

"Pat opened the pub seven years ago. I hopped on board at the end of twenty-twenty."

"Oh. What did you do before?"

"I was a hedge fund manager on Wall Street."

I sat back, now incredibly intrigued.

The man across from me was more than a handsome, rugged, bartender. I hadn't let myself think about that before. I wasn't convinced it was a good idea for me to think about it then—but he was just as much of a person as I was. He came with his own unique story, and it would have been a lie to say I didn't want to hear it. At least a little of it.

I'd agreed to this dinner impulsively. I couldn't explain why because I hadn't allowed myself to think about it. Nevertheless, it was happening. We were two adults, mostly strangers, whose worlds had collided. The night was young, the conversation was easy and enjoyable, so I did what anyone in my situation would do.

"Okay," I started, speaking around a smile. "I think I'm going to need more backstory."

He chuckled—which was pleasant, but not as assaulting as his full laugh—and I braced again, wanting every word he was about to say.

"Pat and I met at Norte Dame. We were roommates, freshman year. We've been best friends since. He always talked about wanting to open a pub, but his parents wanted him to go the university route to explore his options. After we finished our undergrad, we both headed to grad school. It's how he ended up in Texas and I landed in New York. Got my MBA from Columbia and then got a job on Wall Street."

Our server arrived with chips, salsa, and two waters. She asked for our drink orders and was gracious enough to wait while we took a second to peruse the menu. Ange ordered a beer. I ordered the house margarita. When we were alone, to my delight, he jumped right back into his backstory.

"Anyway, Pat took a job in software sales for a few years, made some good money, made some smart investments, saved up what he needed and then opened the pub. I got a job, got married, put my head down, got lost in the grind, then got stuck in a rut."

A frown of confusion tugged at my brow for a fraction of a second when he mentioned he was married, but I controlled my features and kept listening.

He didn't miss a beat and kept talking.

"Twenty-twenty hit and it gave me the opportunity to reevaluate my life. It became glaringly obvious I needed a change. Pat approached me about investing in the pub, and the timing couldn't have been more right."

He stopped, leaving me on the edge of my seat. Granted, he'd given me what I wanted—a snapshot of how he and Pat ended up co-owners of The Four Horsemen—but he'd also piqued my interest and left me with more questions.

Namely—*was he married?*

I hadn't noticed a ring. Then again, I'd never looked. I just assumed...

I glanced down to sneak a peek, but his left hand was underneath the table.

Damn.

Though, lack of evidence aside, he didn't *act* married.

Maybe dinner really was just about helping out in his role as best man.

But that didn't make sense. Not entirely.

Though, admitting *that* would have meant what *did* make sense was that we were out on a date.

Damn.

I'd avoided reading into his true intentions because I had other things on my mind. Now I wish I hadn't done that. I wasn't interested in dating him. Handsome as he was, I wasn't interested in dating *anyone*. Dating could be messy and complicated. I neither needed nor wanted those things added to my plate.

However, that didn't mean Ange wasn't interest*ing*.

I realized I had two options.

Let my curiosity slide or dig deeper.

Who was I kidding?

There was only one option.

"So, that's it?" I blurted, tilting my head to showcase my confusion. "You just packed up your life and moved across the country?"

The corner of his mouth curled in a half-smile that could have been sad. Or retrospective. Or self-deprecating. I couldn't tell which, and I didn't have a chance to read into it before it was gone.

"It was a little messier than that, but yes. Essentially. Marriage didn't work out. I took what was left after the divorce and headed straight for Austin. The rest, as they say, is history."

Okay. Not married. Got it.

Only—I really didn't.

How could someone quit this man?

He'd said more words but left me with more questions.

Was it him? Was it her? Why didn't it work out?

I shoved my questions aside, deciding I'd heard enough.

Why his marriage didn't work out was none of my business.

I wasn't interested.

"What about you?" he asked, extracting me from my thoughts. "Have you ever been married?"

My mouth fell open, having not expected the question. I then watched as his eyes focused in on my lips, and I was quick to snap them closed. It took a second, but his eyes traveled back up my face until they found mine, and then he was smirking at me again.

I reminded myself, for the dozenth time, I wasn't interested in getting involved with Ange, which meant I could be honest without fear of his judgment.

No, I should *be honest.*

I drew in a deep breath, my shoulders rising with the inhalation—then I blew it out in a huff, my chest collapsing and my shoulders dropping before I let it all hang out.

"No. I've never been married. There was a time in my life when I thought that's what I wanted, but I changed my mind. I'm not some wild feminist or anything, I've just decided marriage isn't for me. And, trust me, the irony of my profession juxtaposed with my life choices is not lost on me."

Before Ange had a chance to respond, our server came back to the table with our drinks. Neither of us had even so much as glanced at the dinner entrees. When we were asked if we were ready to order, I didn't read into it when Ange told her we needed a few more minutes to decide. She told us to take our time, that she was around should we have any questions, and then she was gone again.

I took a sip of my margarita, then looked down at my menu, entirely missing the way Ange was staring at me. This was why I was caught off guard, again, when he asked, "What changed your mind?"

"Hmm?" I hummed, lifting my gaze.

He wasn't smiling, his expression clearly one of curiosity as he semi-repeated, "What changed your mind about marriage?"

I didn't hesitate.

"Well, I got really close. Made it all the way down the aisle before my groom took one last look at me, then looked *behind* me, stepped over the train of my wedding gown, grabbed my best friend by the hand, and then made a run for it."

My explanation came out as fast as I could get my mouth around the words. When I was finished, I lifted my drink to my lips and took a healthy swig.

Ange stared at me, wide-eyed, and muttered, "*Fuck.*"

This made me smile.

"I know." I shrugged. "At the time, it felt like a nightmare. Looking back on it, it's more like a scene from a movie. Just not a movie about me."

He opened his mouth to say something, but I didn't want to hear whatever it was. I didn't want to talk about me anymore.

"I can say with absolute certainty this will *not* happen at Libby and Patrick's wedding. Anyway, what are you thinking of ordering? I'm considering the salmon."

I dropped my chin and pretended to look at the menu, hoping he would take the hint we weren't going to keep talking about that time I was jilted at the altar. I kept my head down for a good thirty seconds before I peeked over at him from beneath my lashes.

He was *not* looking at his menu.

My chest got warm and tingly.

This lasted a good thirty seconds.

Then he said, "Short rib."

My chest got warmer, and I smiled.

A few minutes later, we ordered our dinner. While we waited for it to arrive, we talked about Libby and Patrick. As we ate, we talked more about work. He asked why I'd named my business Rusty Barn Wedding Co. He told me how Patrick landed on The Four Horsemen.

Apparently, it was an old Notre Dame football thing. It referenced four players in the offensive backfield from the nineteen-twenties. There was a framed article about them that hung in the bar.

I made a mental note to look for it the next time I was there.

After we finished our meal, Ange ordered us another round of drinks.

I didn't object.

We talked about the city of Austin. What we loved about it. How much it had changed since I'd moved there, since he'd move there.

When the bill came, he frowned at me when I reached for my purse, then pulled out his wallet and covered the whole thing.

Now, it was nearly nine o'clock, and he was walking me through the parking garage, under the office, to my car.

I'd told him it wasn't necessary.

He disagreed.

I didn't argue.

"Nice wheels," he said, jerking his chin in the direction of my red Toyota 4Runner.

Even though it was late, there were still two other cars parked in the same row as mine. Amused, I looked up at him and asked, "How do you know which one is mine?"

He closed one eye and pointed right at my Toyota. "Rusty Barn."

"Ahh," I murmured with a nod. "He's observant."

My vanity plate—RSTY-BN—really was a dead giveaway.

"I have my moments," he replied with a shrug.

"So, you'll let me know what you find out from Patrick?"

We were definitely at the end of...whatever this night was. I still wasn't sure how to categorize it. Nevertheless, we did discuss our friends' upcoming nuptials and the *pre-wedding things* he and I wanted to take on in our respective roles as maid of honor and best man. Seemed like a safe enough way to wrap up the conversation.

"Yeah. I'll be in touch, for sure."

That felt ambiguous.

I ignored said ambiguity.

"Great. Well, thank you again for dinner."

He dipped his chin in a nod. "Anytime."

I lifted one hand in a lame wave, reaching for my door handle with the other. "Have a good night."

"Night, Channing."

He waited until I closed myself inside my vehicle. I then watched from my sideview mirror as he turned, tucked his fingertips into the front pockets of his jeans, and took his leave.

ANGE

He headed for the exit of the garage. He got as far as ten paces and then he couldn't help himself. He turned to catch another glimpse of her.

His timing was perfect.

She'd pulled out of her parking spot and was stopped long enough to shift into drive. He caught her profile and smiled.

As he made the journey back to the pub, where he'd left his truck earlier that evening, he did so contemplating how he could convince her to go out with him again.

One dinner hadn't been nearly enough to get her out of his system.

She wasn't appealing. She was fucking captivating.

He needed more.

A lot more.

CHAPTER *Seven*

Channing

I STOOD OFF TO the side, out of the photographer's shot, watching the revelers with their dying sparklers bid farewell to the newly-weds.

It hadn't rained.

Everything went as planned.

My job was done.

And yet—this one didn't feel like a win.

"Ugh, my feet," Libby moaned. She circled an arm around my waist, leaning into me as she gave me a little of her weight. I rested my arm around her shoulders as she said, "I cannot wait to get home, take off this dress, and crawl into bed with my man. It's been a long ass day."

"Yeah. I hear ya," I muttered, looking once more at the nineteen-fifty, Ford pickup as it drove off—tin cans dragging along the gravel road as it went.

The truck had been a nice touch. The photos they'd taken with it and the wedding party at sunset, right after the ceremony, were going to be amazing.

I wished it would have rained.

Then again, I doubted luck would have changed the look in Craig's eyes when he saw Jodie walking down that aisle.

"Hey, are you alright?"

I gave Libby a squeeze then let her go, sighing as I replied, "Just ready to get out of here."

"You go. The crew has already started clean-up. I'll make sure they don't need anything else, and I'll be right behind you."

Any other night, and I would have insisted she go home first; but I knew she was right. Whoever stayed behind wouldn't be there for long. I relished the chance to be on the road headed back to Austin. I'd forced so many smiles that day, my cheeks ached. I couldn't take it anymore.

Nevertheless, I asked, "Are you sure?"

"Yes. Please, go," she said, waving her hands in a shooing motion. "I'll text you later, and I'll see you Tuesday morning."

"Thanks, Libby. Get home safe."

"Right back at'cha, chica."

The drive from New Braunfels to Austin was about forty-five minutes. After twenty of those minutes, I knew I didn't want to go home. I didn't feel like being alone. I didn't want to lay awake in bed thinking about the look that told me all I needed to know.

They weren't going to make it.

I wished I didn't believe it down to my core, but I did.

What I wanted to do instead of going home was have a drink.

No sooner had the thought crossed my mind than I pictured Ange standing behind the bar at his pub.

It had been two days since we'd gone out to dinner. In that time, I hadn't heard from him at all. He hadn't called, texted, or randomly dropped by the office. Rather than read into what it might mean, I was relieved. I decided his silence meant that dinner had simply been a meal.

It wasn't complicated.

It wasn't messy.

It was good food and great conversation.

That was it.

Having come to this conclusion, it seemed like a harmless idea to stop by the pub for a drink. Moreover, if Ange was working, I'd have someone to talk to. No doubt, he would distract me from the disappointment I felt that night.

I was fifteen minutes out when my mind was made up.

It was nearly midnight when I parked half a block away from my destination.

It wasn't until I was standing outside of the pub, my hand on the handle of the door, that I looked down at myself and realized I was definitely overdressed.

My dress was wine-red. The underlayer was a solid, spaghetti strapped, form-fitting slip that stopped mid-thigh. The outer layer was matching red lace. The sleeves stopped at my elbow, the skirt extended to the floor, and there was a generous slit up the side. The thin, gold belt wrapped around my waist matched the platform, chunky-heeled, strappy sandals on my feet. My makeup was heavy enough to befit an evening wedding, and my hair still held a little curl as it draped down my back.

I hesitated only as long as it took for me to decide I didn't care if I was dressed to be at a different sort of bar. I wanted to be at this one. Then I yanked at the door and stepped inside.

As soon as I crossed the threshold, I noticed the layout had been rearranged. To my right, where there used to be a few tables and chairs, there was a live band. I'd arrived just as the guitar player started strumming the iconic opening riff of "Dead or Alive" by Bon Jovi. The song reminded me of summers when I was a kid, my dad out in the garage tinkering with the lawn mower, or some other thing that needed fixing, classic rock turned up on the radio.

Thinking of dad reminded me of the way he still looked at mom, and the disappointment I'd been holding onto all night was assuaged a little.

Yeah. I was at the right bar.

It appeared the cover band provided a decent draw. I took in the rest of the pub, noticing it was still decently full. When I looked toward the bar, I didn't pretend I'd done so for any other reason than to see if Ange was still there. I spotted him a fraction of a second before he spotted me. This meant I got a front row seat to his reaction of me, in his pub, wearing a wine-red dress, platform, chunky-heeled, strappy sandals, and makeup heavy enough to befit an evening wedding.

It happened so fast, if I'd have blinked I would have missed it.

Those green eyes of his widened as his head jerked back—like someone had gone over and flicked him hard right in the middle of his forehead.

Then, slowly, his mouth spread into a smile, activating the creases at the corner of his eyes.

This time, it wasn't just my chest that grew warm and tingly.

My belly turned to mush, and I couldn't help it...

I smiled right back at him.

Then I reminded myself I wasn't interested.

It didn't matter.

I knew, without a doubt, I was *definitely* in the right place.

I lost his eyes as I watched him scan the length of the bar. He then waved me over, pointing to an empty spot to my left. I clocked it and headed that way. He met me there.

"I like the dress," he said instead of hello, speaking loud enough for me to hear him over the music.

My disappointment was assuaged a little more.

"Thanks."

He wasn't the only one behind the bar, but it was busy enough he didn't waste any time before he asked, "Bourbon old fashioned?"

I nodded, pleased he'd remembered. "With an extra cherry, please."

"You got it," he said with a wink.

He turned to go make my drink right as the sound of an electric guitar solo filled the pub. I glanced over my shoulder at the band, more than a little impressed. The hoots and hollers from a few of the patrons let me know I wasn't alone.

"Bastards sure can play," drawled the man next to me. He'd leaned a little in my direction to ensure I heard him. He was facing away from the bar, one of his elbows propped on the back of his chair, a glass of beer in his opposite hand.

"Yeah. They're good," I agreed.

He then shifted his attention away from the band and onto me as he said, "And you're awfully pretty to be walkin' into a pub and sittin' at a bar all by yourself."

I assessed his steady, brown gaze and allowed myself a moment to decide whether or not I wanted to engage.

He looked to be about sixty, but it was hard to tell. His weathered skin indicated he spent a lot of his time outdoors, and his deep, gravelly voice made him sound like cigarettes had been a vice of his for as long as I'd been alive. He had a head full of gray hair and a thick mustache to match. He was tall and lanky, but something about him made me sure it would have been a mistake for anyone to underestimate him.

"If you're here to find yourself some company, it won't take long," he continued. "You want to be left alone, it's your lucky night. I make a great wingman. Don't talk much, but I've got a knack for pest control."

I liked him instantly.

"Not looking for company," I confessed with a slight shake of my head.

He offered me his empty hand. "Name's Russ."

I accepted his gesture. "Channing."

"Nice to meet you, darlin'."

He freed my hand and returned his attention to the band.

Their next song was Def Leppard's "Pour Some Sugar on Me."

Russ was right. The bastards sure could play.

About halfway through the song, Ange returned with my old fashioned. He didn't rush to another customer, but asked, "Did it rain?"

He knew I'd come from a wedding.

He remembered we'd all feared rain.

I wrapped both hands around my glass as I shook my head.

Ange frowned. "The look on your face indicates that's not a good thing—but isn't it a good thing?"

"They could have used the luck. They're not going to make it." I brought my drink to my lips and took a sip. The bourbon felt warm on its way down. When I returned the glass to the counter, Ange was still frowning at me.

"What does that mean?"

"As a couple. They're not going to make it. I give them three years. Five, if she's not strong enough to let him go."

I thought back, this time not picturing the groom but his bride. Jodie was so sweet and naïve. I didn't realize it until a few hours ago, but her ignorance—shrouded by love—was all too familiar.

"I'm going to need you to hold that thought." Ange held up a finger, wordlessly conveying he'd be back, and then he went to check on another customer.

I sipped at my drink, enjoying the burn of the whiskey and the vibe of the band.

By the time Ange came back, I was chewing on my extra cherry.

"You want another one?"

I looked into my empty glass. I was already feeling the effects of the alcohol. I hadn't eaten since before the ceremony. It was getting pretty late, but I wasn't ready to go home, and I *did* want another one.

"Yes, please," I answered.

Speaking over his shoulder, Russ muttered, "Put this one on my tab."

I jerked my head in his direction. "Russ, that's sweet of you, but—"

"Don't waste your breath," Ange interrupted. He was smiling when he said, "There's no arguing with Russ."

"He's right. You should listen to him," said Russ.

I looked from one man to the other, then shrugged.

"Thanks, Russ."

"Pleasure's all mine."

Ange took my empty glass and returned two minutes later with a full one.

This time, he'd given me three cherries.

"You still holding onto that thought?"

"Yeah," I said on a half-hearted chuckle. "Kind of hard to forget."

He spread his arms wide, pressed his palms flat against the bar, and leaned toward me a little. "How do you know they're not gonna make it?"

I hesitated to respond. Not many people knew about my sixth sense.

Blake was a skeptic.

Derek found it amusing.

Libby bought it. Every time.

On the verge of tipsy, I decided to try my luck with Ange.

"I can always tell. It doesn't matter if they have a first look before the ceremony or not. There's a moment—one *precious* moment—when a groom sees his bride as she starts to walk down the aisle. I can tell, by the way he looks at her, if they're going to make it or not."

Ange smirked at me, and I could see it in his eyes he was a skeptic.

"No shit?" Russ grumbled.

I turned to Russ and stated adamantly, "No shit."

"Okay. What'd you see today?" Ange asked.

I detected amusement in his voice, but I chose to ignore it.

"He looked at her, then he looked out at their guests. He did this, like, three times as she made her way toward him. It was quick, but it happened."

What I didn't share was that I couldn't tell if Craig had been looking at a specific person or not. It was hard to see from my vantage point. I hoped, for Jodie's sake, that it wasn't a specific person.

"Hmm," Ange hummed.

I took this to mean he was coming around and cried, "Exactly!" before taking a swig of my drink.

He chuckled and my chest tingled.

I ignored it.

"So, how many weddings have you planned where the couple doesn't make it?"

"Not that many," I stated proudly. "We do anywhere from thirty-seven to forty-five weddings a year. Not counting the last three years—although, sadly, one couple barely made it a year and a half, and their wedding was two years ago—there have only been three divorces so far.

"I mean, obviously, I don't take any credit for the success of these marriages. I merely predict whether or not they'll last. And a lot of marriages end up working out. I know people always say the divorce rate in our country is fifty percent, but it's pretty nuanced, given men and women get remarried multiple times, but that's not the point."

"And what is the point, darlin'?" asked Russ, sounding genuinely curious.

Shifting slightly so I could address them both, I answered, "The point is, ninety-nine percent of the time, when I see a groom catch sight of his bride, I get a hit of dopamine knowing I got to play a part in what will be one of the best days of their lives. But every once in a blue moon, I don't get that feeling. And it sucks."

Russ dipped his chin slowly, his voice rumbly and low when he replied, "I get that."

I held up my hand, excitedly pointing at my new friend, and looked behind the bar at Ange.

"See? He gets it."

Ange didn't say anything. He just grinned at me.

My belly turned to mush. Again.

I ignored it as I took another sip from my glass.

Thirty minutes later, the band was packing up, and Russ was closing out his tab.

After his bill was settled, he reached into his wallet for a twenty-dollar bill and tossed it on the bar. He then looked to me and said, "Was nice talkin' to you, Channing."

In the hour we'd sat next to each other, we hadn't talked that much, but the feeling was mutual. I let him know this, then waved goodbye as he headed for the exit.

"Last call," said Ange, reaching for the empty glass in front of me. "Want one more?"

I was enjoying a lovely buzz, which meant part of me *did* want one more. It'd been a while since I'd let loose. Long enough I was sure I'd regret it later that morning whether I had another drink or not.

But I also knew my limits.

"If I have another one, I'll definitely need a ride home."

"Babe, you want another, it's on the house, and I'll get you home."

Suddenly I couldn't find my words.

All I could do was nod.

Ange made me another drink, then started closing down the bar.

At a quarter to two, Harper—the other bartender who I'd met at some point that night—locked the front doors behind the last customers to take their leave.

Well, besides me.

I was still at the bar. I'd just popped my last cherry in my mouth when Ange asked, "Harp, where'd you park?"

"Out back. On the corner."

He jerked his chin in acknowledgment then said, "Give me ten minutes?"

"You got it, boss. Want me to take Penny out real quick?"

"Sure. That'd be great."

"Cool," she said before disappearing down the side hallway.

It took me a minute to replay their exchange and make sense of it. When I got it, I accidently spoke my thought aloud and said, "You walk your female staff to their cars after closing. That's sweet."

Ange didn't look away from his task, but I still caught his quarter-smile as he replied, "Better safe than sorry."

I nodded, even though he couldn't see me do it. Then, realizing we were alone in a quiet, empty pub, I suddenly felt awkward and irritatingly useless.

"Can I—can I help with anything?"

I stood as soon as I was finished speaking, as if to express he could put me to work. Except, the moment my feet hit the ground, I lost my equilibrium and was forced to grab hold of the back of my chair to keep from stumbling.

"You okay?" he asked, no longer smirking.

"Mmhmm."

I'd had three old fashioneds, seven whisky soaked cherries, and I was pretty sure at least one glass of water without standing up. I just needed to get used to my sea legs.

I also needed to pee.

"I'm going to run to the bathroom really quick."

His eyes pinned on me, as if he was afraid I'd fall over any second, Ange replied, "Take your time."

Embarrassing as it was, after I slid my purse over my shoulder, I made my way slowly across the room without stumbling once, and I was pretty proud of myself.

I took my time in the bathroom. Mostly to ensure I didn't stumble in there, either. It would have been a lot easier had I not been wearing platform, chunky-heeled, strappy sandals—but there was no way I was walking barefoot around The Four Horsemen.

It wasn't dingy, but it was still a pub.

After I'd handled my business, I felt a lot better, if not still a bit tipsy. I walked out of the bathroom, intent on finding some way to help out rather than sit uselessly at the bar.

I hardly got two steps before an adorable, fluffy dog came trotting toward me.

I gasped as she sniffed at my feet before she looked up at me with her cute, little, beady eyes. She seemed like she would be outrageously soft to the touch, and I didn't hesitate to reach down to find out. Her tail wagged excitedly as I submerged my fingers into her curls, and I giggled as she tried to lick at my wrists.

"Hi, there. You are such a sweetheart," I cooed.

"Her name's Penny."

Both Penny and I looked down the hallway as Ange spoke. When Penny abandoned me to go love on him, I straightened, trying my damnedest to ignore how much I liked that a rugged, handsome man owned a goldendoodle—of all dogs.

"You ready to go?"

It was then I spotted Harper, waiting just beyond Ange, her jacket on with her purse lopped around her forearm. Apparently, it was time to go.

"Yup."

After Ange locked up, he took Penny and me to his truck first. Fortunately, he was parked pretty close. Also fortunately, I managed to climb up into his massive Toyota Tundra without any assistance. Once Penny and I were settled, I watched as he walked Harper to her car on the corner.

It really was very sweet of him.

He folded himself into the seat next to me not two minutes later.

I got a whiff of his scent.

I closed my eyes, willing myself to ignore it.

He started up the truck, I opened my eyes, and he peered at me through the darkness—barely broken by a nearby streetlamp—and asked, "Where to?"

"Uh, right. I live off of Third and Bowie. My building is right next door to Lifetime Fitness."

"Got it," he said with a nod, shifting into reverse.

"Thanks," I murmured when we were on our way. "For the ride."

"No problem."

Silence settled in the cab of his truck.

My condo was only a five-minute drive away, but thirty seconds with no words exchanged between us made me hyper aware of my surroundings.

I was in Ange's truck.

He was taking me home.

Even though I kept telling myself I wasn't interested, it felt like all the nerve endings on my skin were buzzing with some sort of electric current that could only be explained by the fact that I was in Ange's truck, and he was taking me home.

I needed to break the silence.

I blurted out the first thing I could think of.

"Okay, I'm dying to know—how does a cool, bearded, hedge-fund turned pub-owner bachelor wind up with a designer dog?"

I shouldn't have asked.

I should have endured the silence.

His reaction was so much worse.

He threw his head back and laughed.

I melted into the passenger seat, my thoughts coming out in a whisper before I could stop them.

"I really wish you wouldn't do that."

Still chuckling, he took his eyes off the road long enough to glance at me and ask, "Do what?"

"Laugh," I replied, still at a whisper.

He sobered. "Channing, I'm not laughing *at* you."

"No, I know. I know. Actually, that might be preferred."

"What?" he asked, his confusion quite evident.

"Back to Penny. How'd you end up with a goldendoodle instead of a lab or a rottweiler or something?"

"Stephanie picked her."

Stephanie.

His ex's name was Stephanie.

He kept going.

"We got her when she was a puppy. She wasn't supposed to be my dog, but I fell in love with her all the same. She chose me, too. I didn't even have to fight for her in the divorce."

"Oh."

I was so distracted by the details of what he'd shared, I didn't realize we'd arrived at my place until he put his truck in park and asked, "This you?"

I looked out the window. "Yup."

"Hey…" he called softly before I could so much as reach for the door handle. He waited until he had my attention then asked, "Why don't you like it when I laugh?"

Truth serum still working its way through my bloodstream, I answered simply, "Because I love it."

I didn't wait for him to respond. Immediately, I turned to let myself out of his truck. I needed to get inside. My filter was malfunctioning, and I could feel my guard slipping, which meant it was time to call it a night.

Once my feet were on the ground, I turned to thank him one last time. But when I looked back into the cab of his truck, he wasn't there. I turned again, and saw he was headed toward me—Penny at his heels.

"What are you—?"

"It's late and you didn't trust yourself behind the wheel, so we're walking you to your door."

I thought about arguing with him, but I wasn't that drunk. I knew he'd win in the end. He was that guy who walked his female employees to their cars after closing time. So, I nodded, turned, and headed for the front entrance of my building. I did this carefully, still feeling a little unsteady on my feet.

We made it to the elevator, then all three of us piled inside. Neither Ange, nor I, said a word as I pressed the button for the eleventh floor. Just like in his truck, the silence made me keenly aware of the man beside me, where we were, and where we were going.

The higher we climbed, the harder it was for me to remember why I wasn't interested in him.

After a long night of work, he still smelled like citrus and sandalwood.

I liked that. Too much.

Part of me wanted to say something.

To break the silence.

To bring me back to my right mind.

But it hadn't been ten minutes since the last time I'd done that.

And it had backfired.

Royally.

The elevator chimed as we reached the eleventh floor.

I stayed silent, stepped out, and headed for my unit.

Ange and Penny followed.

It felt like forever before I saw my door.

When we were close, I reached into my purse for my keys. Having found them, I looped the main ring around my index finger, palmed the rest, then stopped and turned toward Ange.

"This is me."

"Good."

"Thank you for getting me home."

"You're welcome."

I stared into his eyes, my chest warm and tingly, waiting for him to leave.

He didn't leave.

He stared back at me.

Then he smiled.

"Babe, you gonna unlock the door?"

I couldn't explain how it was possible one word could make my brain short circuit—but it wasn't the first time it had happened that night. Only this time, my words didn't get lost in my mind, they fell right out of my mouth.

"I want to kiss you. But I know it's a *bad* idea because I'm drunk. And I don't make a habit of kissing men when I'm drunk. So—I think I'm not going to kiss you."

His smile turned into a grin, and it was a miracle I didn't whimper.

Damn, but he was handsome.

"I respect that. Maybe some other time, then."

"Mmhmm."

He chuckled, then reached for my keys.

My breath caught at the feel of his fingers grazing mine.

He unlocked my door, twisted the handle, pushed it open, then handed me back my keys.

"Thanks," I breathed.

Ange was being nice.

He hadn't plied me with liquor and convinced me to let him drive me home.

He didn't walk me to my door, suggesting a nightcap.

He was seeing me home safe.

He wasn't going to leave until I was inside—just like the other night, when he didn't leave until I closed myself into my car.

He was being a gentleman.

So, when he leaned down to kiss me on my cheek, I knew it wasn't some calculated move.

Neither was mine. I just couldn't stop myself.

Before I lost the feel of his lips and the tickle of his beard, I reached out in front of me to grab either side of the button-up he hadn't bothered to button up, and then I turned my head until my lips met his.

I'd made my move, and now it was his turn.

He didn't disappoint.

I felt his hand in my hair as he reached for the back of my neck. He held me steady, tilted his head, opened his mouth, and slid his tongue along the closed seam of my lips.

My turn.

I opened up for him immediately, tightening my fists around his shirt, pulling him closer as I got a taste of his mouth.

He then hooked his other arm around my waist, dragging me so close I was up on my tiptoes and my grip wasn't about me bringing him closer, but about me holding on for dear life.

He tasted so good, the feel of his beard scraping at the sensitive skin around my lips was so nice, his body was so warm and hard and unrelenting, I was out of moves. All I could do was whimper into his mouth.

The second I did, he was gone.

At least, part of him was.

He still had one hand in my hair, one arm around my waist, and he was so close I could feel his breath against my face as we both panted.

His eyes were smoldering. As they stared into mine, my core temperature rose, and I felt myself melt against him.

He felt it, too.

"You sure?"

I wasn't.

But after that kiss? I didn't care.

I shrugged, then moved to wrap my arms around his shoulders.

When I reached for another kiss, he beat me to it.

With our lips still locked, we were on the move.

He lifted me a couple inches off the ground and carried me into my condo. I assume Penny followed, having heard the sound of dog tags before I heard my front door slam shut. I dropped my keys and purse at our feet, causing a clatter we both ignored.

I had giant, floor to ceiling windows in my living room, which meant we weren't completely shrouded in darkness, downtown Austin serving as our nightlight. Ange got us past my kitchen and to the mouth of my short hallway before he muttered against my lips, "Bedroom?"

"Last door on the left," I breathed, anxious to be there already.

He got us there, put me down—one hand splayed open between my shoulders, the other reaching down to palm my backside as he leaned into me and *owned* my mouth.

God, but he could kiss.

I held on tight with one arm still around his shoulders, my free hand finding its way into his hair.

It was thick. It was soft. It was awesome.

There was nothing to do except grip it greedily with my fist.

He liked this. I knew because both of his arms constricted around me when I did it.

I liked that.

He abandoned my mouth, dipped his head, and kissed his way along my neck.

I liked that, too.

But I wanted more.

I knew by his next words, he did too.

"How do I get this off?" he asked, skimming a hand up my side, stopping at my breast.

His thumb grazed over my hardened nipple, and I couldn't find my words.

I turned around instead, gathering my hair over my shoulder and down my chest.

Fortunately, he didn't need further instruction. I loosened the belt. He found the zipper, and I was suddenly in nothing but a strapless bra, a thong, and my platform, chunky-heeled, strappy sandals.

We needed to level the playing field.

Facing him once more, I stepped out of my dress, then pushed his outer shirt off his shoulders. He worked his arms out of the sleeves as I began to tug his tee up his chest. With his button-up on the floor, he reached behind his head, grabbed a fistful of his shirt, and then it was gone.

I was about to reach for the button at his jeans, but before I could, his hand was back at my nape. He wanted my mouth—indicated clearly when he sweetly demanded, "Come here," before his lips were on mine.

He got no objections from me.

Not even when he unfastened my bra with his free hand, tossed it aside, and pulled me flush against him—all while exploring my mouth with his tongue.

My nipples pressed firmly against his bare chest was sensational.

Needless to say, my thong was *soaked*.

I didn't make a habit out of kissing men when drunk.

Occasionally, I'd let a man buy me a drink.

If I ached for it, I'd let him take me to bed.

This was rare.

This was rare because most of those infrequent sexual encounters were clumsy and awkward, neither of us really sure what the other person wanted. Sometimes a guy could get me there, sometimes he couldn't.

But this was not that.

Not at all.

Ange gripped me around the waist, leaned into me, grabbed the side of my thigh, then hoisted me up. I gasped, my legs instinctively circling around his hips. Then I moaned, my swollen clit having come into contact with the button of his jeans.

Suddenly I didn't mind he hadn't let me take them off earlier.

We were on the move again—and then I was flat on my back, my comfy, fluffy, duvet comforter like a cloud underneath me.

Ange put a single knee on the bed, like he was going to come toward me, then he looked down and changed his mind. I watched as he stood, made quick work of his boots and socks, and then he was back.

He lifted one of my legs, greedily feeling his way from my knee to my ankle before he fumbled with the clasp of my sandal. I was just getting ready to reach up to help him when he figured it out, freeing my foot, and discarding the platform heel. My other one was soon to follow.

Then he was hovering over me, his hand between my breasts. I couldn't see the green of his eyes, but I could feel his stare, and it made me squirm in excitement beneath him. My breaths came quicker as he lightly traced his fingertips across the plain of my stomach before slipping them beneath the fabric of my thong.

The second he made contact with my sex, my hips jerked, and he swore.

"Beautiful," he whispered against my lips.

His dipped his tongue into my mouth at the same time he inserted two fingers inside of me.

I moaned, reaching for either side of his face, needing to touch him.

He groaned, giving me the friction I craved.

I didn't know if it was the whiskey or if it was just him, but I was completely uninhibited, and it was bliss.

It wasn't long before I was panting, my legs trembling, my orgasm building into something I knew would be marvelous.

I tore my mouth from his, pressing my cheek against his bearded one, reaching for his crotch as I whimpered his name.

"Right here, baby."

He thrust his erection into my hand as he spoke, and I was a goner.

Pleasure washed over me, causing even my scalp to tingle, and it was awesome.

I was still coming when he extracted his hand, yanked my thong down my legs, over my ankles, and off my feet.

Then I watched, Ange backlit by the city lights peeking through my bedroom windows, as he reached into his wallet and pulled out a condom. He held the packet in his mouth, needing both hands to drop his jeans and boxer briefs in one go.

I pulled my bottom lip between my teeth, more turned on than I ever was watching a man sheath himself. If I didn't want him so badly, I would have been disappointed we hadn't turned the light on so I could see him in all of his naked glory—but I didn't have the capacity to dwell on that.

I wanted him.

I wanted him so badly I couldn't think straight.

I'd told myself—repeatedly—I wasn't interested.

It was a lie.

He came back to me, propping himself up on his forearms resting on either side of my head—his lower body between my legs. I slid my hands along his sides and down his back, boldly reaching further to feel his firm backside. He jerked his hips, reminding both of us of the erection that lay heavy against my lower abdomen.

Ange found my mouth, kissing me hard until I was breathless. I held on to him, wanting more. Wanting everything he had to give.

Finally, he shifted, reaching down between us. He grazed the tip of his length along my seam, coating it before he positioned himself at my entrance. I held my breath in anticipation.

I didn't have to hold it long.

Oh, god—but he felt incredible.

"Channing, you good?" he asked, breathless, once fully seated.

I wasn't good.

I was great.

Exceptional.

Over the freaking *moon*.

I lifted my head until I could feel his breath against my lips, then sank all my fingers into his hair before I murmured, "Better than."

I felt his lips curl into a smile.

Then he started to roll his hips.

It wasn't long before we'd found a steady rhythm.

I knew he didn't mind my active participation when she slid his hand underneath the small of my back during one of my upward thrusts, his lips pressed against my neck as he muttered, "Just like that, baby—move with me."

Oh, I moved.

And when I felt my second orgasm coming on, I held tightly to his shoulders and moaned.

"Ange!"

"Wait for me, Channing."

Oh, god.

No one had ever asked me to wait for him before.

I'd never had a simultaneous orgasm.

I didn't know if I could wait.

But I was willing to die trying.

"Hurry," I breathed.

He rode me harder. Faster.

This did *not* help.

"Ange, hurry!" I begged, squeezing my knees tight against his sides, no longer able to meet his thrusts with my own.

I sealed my eyes closed tight, concentrating on holding on even as what grew inside of me felt totally and completely uncontainable.

"Come for me, baby," he grunted at last.

I let go, my insides clamping down around him so tight, it was a wonder he could move at all. But he did—and he did it coming with me.

And it. Was. *Awesome.*

CHAPTER *Eight*

Ange

H E WOKE TO THE smell of her hair. It was floral. Nothing sweet or overpowering. Just feminine and delicate. He liked it.

They were underneath her massive—though, surprisingly light—beige duvet comforter. They were both naked, and she was still in his arms.

It had been years since he'd woken with a naked woman still in his arms.

He liked that more.

No—he liked that it was *Channing*.

He'd wanted more of her, but he hadn't seen last night coming.

After their dinner at ATX Cocina, where she'd dropped the bomb that some dumb fuck had left her at the altar, cleansing her of any desire to get married—a truth she'd shared before putting a lid on it so tight a crowbar couldn't break the seal—he'd gathered she wasn't going to be an easy pursuit. He'd planned on playing the long game. He wasn't in any hurry.

Then she showed up to the pub in that dress, with those heels, that hair and makeup—all class and beauty. She sat at the bar, rambling on about how she could tell if a marriage would last, based on a single look, and he knew she was serious, which made it even cuter, and he lost a bit of his patience.

Even when she'd had a little too much to drink, she still played her cards close to her chest. Up to the moment when she told him she wanted to kiss him, but she thought it was a bad idea, she'd been trying her damnedest to deny either of them what he already knew he wanted, and what he hoped she wanted too.

Then she'd kissed him.

That kiss had changed the whole damn game.

Ange didn't know what time it was, only that it was late enough in the day that the sun lit up Channing's bedroom. He felt something warm and heavy at his feet. He lifted his head enough to see Penny sprawled out at the foot of the bed.

Channing seemed to like Penny when they'd met earlier that morning. Nonetheless, he wasn't sure how she'd feel about his goldendoodle in her bed. If she was bothered by it, he'd apologize and have a chat with Penny later. For the time being, Penny was content, which meant he didn't have to take her out. He preferred this, seeing as he was pretty damn content himself.

Before he rested his head back on the pillow, Ange reached down to press a kiss against Channing's bare shoulder. He'd been inside of her sweet, wet heat. He'd taken her body, but there was so much more of her to explore. Her skin was soft against his lips—a promise his future explorations were something to look forward to.

The second his kiss made contact he felt her body stiffen. This gave him pause. He couldn't tell if she was uncomfortable, or if he'd merely taken her by surprise.

Knowing there was only one way to find out, he repeated the act before he murmured, "Good morning."

"Hi," she whispered in reply.

When she didn't relax against him, he had his answer.

She was no longer coasting on a buzz.

She was stone-cold sober, and her guard was back up and fully intact.

Ange nodded to himself, now cognizant he had to play it smart.

He rolled onto his back, letting her go, and she bolted from the bed a second later. Penny's head lifted in curiosity, and Ange propped himself up on his elbows as he watched Channing yank open a dresser drawer and pluck out a piece of clothing. She was covered in an oversized shirt before she turned around, allowing Ange his first real glimpse of her in the light of day.

Her makeup was faded. Her hair was wild.

She looked like the most beautiful mess Ange had ever seen.

She also looked totally freaked.

Fuck.

"You okay?" he asked cautiously.

"Mmhmm," she hummed with a nod.

Yeah. She was freaked.

Fuck.

"I, uh, I should probably hop in the shower," she told him.

Ange took the hint, sat up, and began searching the floor for his jeans. "Sure."

Having spotted his clothes, he got out of bed, reached for his boxer briefs, pulled them on, then sought out Channing's blue eyes.

He tried again.

"You hungry? Let me buy you breakfast before I take you back to your car."

"Oh, uh—that's very kind of you, but I'm not really all that hungry. Plus, I, um, I've got a little work I need to do. And then, uh—I actually have plans with my sister. So, thanks, but—I can't."

Ange stared into those sky-blue eyes.

They stared right back.

He wasn't sure if he believed her, but she'd certainly made her point. She wanted to be alone. He dipped his chin in acknowledgment, then grabbed his jeans. Penny came over to say good morning. He gave her a short, absentminded scratch behind the ears and continued getting dressed. Unsatisfied with his affection, she went to the other human in the room.

"You should at least let me take you to your car," said Ange, tugging on his tee.

"Oh." That one had been for Penny, who had greeted Channing by licking at her bare legs. "Hi, sweetheart," she murmured, bending to give her a generous rub. As she did so, Channing looked up at Ange and said, "You don't have to give me a ride to my car. It's okay. Really. It's not that far of a walk, and I could use the fresh air after—uh—after all that whiskey."

"Are you sure?" he asked, walking over to his boots.

"Positive."

Ange felt like he'd taken five steps forward before they'd gone to sleep only to take ten steps back upon waking.

Neither of them spoke as he laced up his boots. When he was finished, he closed the distance between them, intent on at least giving her a proper goodbye.

She looked up at him. He looked down at her.

He went for her lips. She gave him her cheek.

His ego took a hit, but he didn't back down.

He kissed her cheek, then told her, "Talk to you soon."

"Mmhmm," she hummed.

He forced a smile—the first time he'd ever done such a thing in her presence—then headed for the door. "Come on, Penny. Time to go."

Ange didn't take in the details of her condo as he made his way through it. He closed the front door behind him, then paused for a long moment.

Nothing that had transpired since he entered her building had gone the way he anticipated.

But now he'd had her.

He knew what she tasted like. What she smelled like. What she felt like.

He knew what she sounded like when she was desperate for a release.

What they'd shared had been incredible. He wouldn't be convinced otherwise. He knew she felt it, too. She'd come so hard for him it was a wonder his dick still had circulation.

That had been real. That had been *them*.

He'd seen it in her eyes.

She wanted him, too.

Now, Channing was running scared.

He was sure of it.

By the time Ange got home, walked Penny, showered, and had a bite to eat, it was after noon. He'd thought about reaching out to Channing repeatedly, then remembered the way she'd given him her cheek before he left. He needed to be patient. The last thing he wanted to do was scare her even further into her hidey hole.

He reminded himself it was *Channing* who came into the pub.

It was *Channing* who'd said she wanted to kiss him before she'd done it.

Then they'd gone at each other like they couldn't get enough.

The sound of his name on her lips in a soft whimper did him in.

Fuck.

He needed a distraction.

Ange headed out to his detached garage, opened up the rolling door, and went about tinkering with his bass fishing boat. He'd built this one himself, after he'd sold the one he'd owned in New York. It was something he'd wanted to take on for a while—construct his own boat. Fresh out of a divorce, it felt like the cathartic thing to do. Build something new. Something he loved.

He'd been fishing bass since he was a kid. Born and raised in Michigan, he and his dad had plenty of lakes to choose from to catch the largemouths. Growing up, he looked forward to spring not merely because he was sick of the snow, but because he was ready to get back out on the water.

During his time in New York, he'd bought himself a boat as soon as he could afford it. Until he got married, he'd spent a lot of weekends getting out of the city and onto the lake. When he and Stephanie were dating, she'd indulged him by joining him on occasion. That stopped shortly after they were married. She said it was his thing—like some men who golf—and she was happy for him to have a hobby he enjoyed. Except, she complained any time he wanted to take off to enjoy it.

Ange had been out on the water a couple times that February, but with March on the horizon he knew he'd be getting out more. It was his favorite time of year in Texas. Not yet hot. Water just warm enough for the bass to be active. He could catch and release for hours. The best part was, he didn't have to go far to find a lake to cast in.

He spent half the afternoon tinkering and cleaning before closing up shop and heading back inside. He went straight for the fridge, grabbed a bottle of beer, then made his way to the living room. TV on, seat on the couch, his patience lasted until the bottle in his hand was half empty. He set it aside and reached for his phone. He shot off a text, then waited.

He finished his beer.

He grabbed another.

He waited.

An hour later, she responded.

Ange, I'm not so sure last night was a good idea. I'm so sorry.

He tossed his phone aside, downing the rest of his beer.

He called bullshit.

Why don't you like it when I laugh?

"Because I love it."

She wanted him.

He'd felt it.

He'd seen it in her eyes.

She was right.

The night before hadn't been a good idea.

It was impulsive, unstoppable, and so fucking natural it was beautiful.

It was *better* than a good idea.

He had every intention of ignoring her text.

They weren't done.

They were just getting started.

She just didn't know it yet.

CHAPTER
Nine

Channing

MONDAYS WERE MY OFFICIAL days off. People didn't get married on Mondays.

At least, not if they wanted anyone there.

While I didn't have a wedding to attend *every* weekend, Fridays to Sundays were prime. On the weekends where I didn't have anything scheduled, I typically spent most of Saturday catching up on work from home, then most of Sunday running errands and handling chores. If I had a wedding on either of those days, my weekend tasks were shuffled around accordingly.

Monday was my buffer.

This Monday in particular, I needed a buffer.

Except, not for my typical reasons.

I needed to clear my head. I needed to exert some energy.

I needed to wear myself out so I could forget and then move on.

Forget the texture of his hair between my fingers and the feel of his beard on my skin.

Forget the way he smelled and how he called me *babe* when we were fully clothed, but then I was *baby* when he was inside of me.

I definitely, *definitely* needed to forget.

So, I went to the gym.

I went to the gym often. I mean, it was right across the street. I didn't have a good excuse not to. Usually, I stuck to the treadmill. Three miles, two degrees of incline at speed level five, four times a week.

That morning, I did five miles.

Then I tried my hand at the rowing machine.

I'd never done it before. It looked simple enough. It looked exhausting enough. Figured it would be worth a try.

It was perfect.

I was spent and sweaty as I trudged my way home.

I dragged my feet from my front door to the primary bath, trying not to look at the bed as I passed. I'd already washed the sheets *and* my duvet cover.

Nobody liked to wash their duvet cover. It was a pain in the butt getting the comforter just right when you put it all back together; but in my case, it had been necessary.

I'd thrown my bedding in the wash the previous morning without delay. Like maybe if I washed the smell of him from my sheets, I'd be able to rinse away the memories of him naked—in my bed—from my mind.

My sheets were clean.

I was still actively working on the last part.

I stripped down and hopped in the shower. I took my time under the water, filling my thoughts with anything that had *nothing* to do with being naked. I thought about what I might eat that day. I mentally started constructing a grocery list. I reminded myself it was time for a new air filter.

When I was finished washing and conditioning my hair, I shut off the water and stepped out of the shower. I wrapped myself in a towel, wrapped another around my hair, then went about getting dressed. I picked the plainest pair of underwear I could find—gray, cotton, no-show panties. I had a comfy bra to match. Perfect. Not sexy.

I was not thinking about sex.

I was certainly not thinking of simultaneous orgasms.

I was getting dressed.

Next, I tugged on a pair of navy leggings, then slipped into a heather-gray, half-zip pullover. Gray was apparently the color of the day. It suited my mood, so I didn't think twice about it.

I let my damp hair down and thought about drying it, then decided that chore required coffee first. I padded barefoot to the kitchen. I was reaching for a Nespresso pod when a knock sounded at my door.

I blinked and stared straight ahead, not at all sure who that could be. I was not expecting any visitors. In fact, I hardly ever had anyone over. My condo wasn't that big. It had two bedrooms, but the living room was small, and I barely had the space for a kitchen table. I didn't mind the close quarters. I lived alone. I was two minutes from my office. I wasn't some master chef, so I wasn't hosting dinner parties. It was easier to meet people out, so I rarely had any guests.

Except, the night before last, I'd had a guest.

He hadn't come for my cooking.

There was another knock. It wasn't any louder than the first, but this one made me wince.

I palmed my Nespresso pod and made my way to the door. I peeked through the peephole and tensed when my suspicions were confirmed.

Just that quick, every effort I had taken to forget what it was like to be touched by Ange was demolished.

I remembered the way he kissed my neck. How his big, warm, calloused hand felt as he grazed the skin up my side before palming my breast. The sound of his voice, demanding yet gentle as he slid in and out of me, telling me to wait.

I hadn't planned on sleeping with him. Worse, if I was being honest, I didn't regret it. I couldn't. He'd been too good to me. It hadn't been a smart move on my part, but I was sure it was a night I'd never forget. No matter how hard I tried.

But there was a reason I ignored the way he made me feel; why I told myself over and over I wasn't interested in him. I'd spent enough time with him to know, he wasn't the kind of guy I could hook-up with and then move on from. I knew this, I *knew this*, and then I went and kissed him anyway.

Stupid. Stupid. *Stupid!*

And my text. *God*, that text.

So cold. Frigid, even.

Ange deserved better.

He knocked again.

I closed my eyes and tried not to panic. I'd already done the panic routine yesterday morning. I woke up in his arms, and I'd never felt so horrible about something that felt so good in all my life. I'd laid there, waiting for him to wake up, for at least twenty minutes. As soon as he let me go, I couldn't move fast enough. Then I'd *lied* to convince him he should leave.

I felt so bad about it, I ended up calling my sister so my lie that I'd had plans with her didn't remain as such.

I'd gone to her house for dinner.

My nieces had been thrilled to see me.

Derek made smoked salmon.

It was delicious.

Ange knocked a fourth time.

I couldn't ignore him. Not forever. Any attempt at trying would only make matters worse. Like a mature, well-adjusted adult, I had to get this over with.

I drew in a deep breath, blew it out in a huff, then unlocked my deadbolt and swung open the door.

Damn, damn, *damn*, but he was handsome.

He was in black jeans and an olive green, crew-neck sweatshirt.

He made simple look *so* good.

His eyes trailed down and then up the length of me.

My body felt his perusal as if it were his hands and lips reacquainting themselves with every inch of me rather than his eyes. It made my nerve endings buzz all over. Then his gaze settled on mine—green and gorgeous—and my chest grew warm and tingly.

Warmer and tinglier than usual.

Before Ange, it had been at least a year since anyone had touched me.

In my avoidance, I hadn't taken the time to do a true evaluation, but I was pretty sure no one—and I mean *no one*—had ever touched me as well as Ange.

That still didn't make what we'd done a good idea.

"Hi," I murmured.

I was still so tangled up in my own head, I hadn't heard him say hello.

Had he said hello?

His lips twitched in a smirk, and I watched as his face relaxed, as if he'd just made up his mind about something.

It was then I knew he hadn't said hello. He skipped straight to the point.

"If I'm bad company and a horrible lay, and you want to keep this—" he waved a hand between us "—strictly professional, I will turn around and leave right now. But..."

I waited for him to finish.

Then I waited some more.

I squeezed the Nespresso pod in my hand, feeling fidgety under his gaze.

When I couldn't stand it any longer, I asked, "But...*what*?"

He took a step toward me, my breath caught, and he finished.

"If I'm a risk, a big one—seeing as my best friend is marrying your best friend in a couple of months and there's no way either of us are getting out of being around each other for that, at the very least—well, then we're both in the same boat. And if we're in the same boat, we might as well see where it's going before we jump out and swim for shore. Water's still cold this time of year."

I didn't know what to say.

I didn't want to lie. Not again.

Not to Ange, and not to myself.

I'd decided so long ago that I wasn't someone who got mixed up in romantic relationships, I wasn't even sure how it was done anymore. I avoided messy and complicated.

Except—the way he'd framed it didn't seem so complicated.

He wasn't bad company. He was actually pretty great company. So much so, I'd sought him out when I was feeling low and didn't want to be alone.

Neither was he a horrible lay. Quite the opposite.

Then there was the alternative. And he *was* a risk.

Though—he thought I was one, too.

I wasn't sure how I felt about him thinking I was a risk, but a part of me thought it was actually kind of a nice thing to say. We were on level playing field.

And, in spite of the terrible way I treated the man who gave me two of the best orgasms I could remember after driving me home and making sure I made it safely to my door, he was at my door again—kindly offering me a choice.

I felt my shoulders slump.

I didn't want to lie.

Before I could figure out what to say, he smiled, and my belly turned to mush.

"Right," he said, nodding back toward the hallway. "Come on. Let me buy you breakfast. Penny's waiting downstairs."

Damn.

I didn't want to lie. Not again.

Not to Ange, and not to myself.

"...we're both in the same boat. And if we're in the same boat, we might as well see where it's going before we jump out and swim for shore."

I wasn't ready to jump out. No matter how many miles I jogged, or meters I rowed, I knew I'd still want to see where the boat wound up—especially if it meant I got to kiss him some more.

I sighed, then reached up to run my fingers through my still-damp hair. "I'm not fully ready for the day, yet. I just got out of the shower, and—"

"Channing, greasy spoons don't require makeup. Put some shoes on and let's get out of here."

Ange wanted to take me on a date. A breakfast date.

He'd seen me all dolled up, and yet he wanted to take me out now—in leggings with no makeup.

Keeping with the theme of not lying, I had to admit, that felt nice, too.

"Give me two minutes?" I asked, stepping aside to indicate he could come in.

His agreement was conveyed when he crossed the threshold and proceeded to wait.

I hurried back to my room, discarding my Nespresso pod on the dresser where I snagged socks from the top drawer before I went to my closet. I grabbed a pair of sneakers and made quick work of tucking my feet inside and doing up the laces. I then scanned my hangers until I found my white down vest—which went with my outfit, even if my mood wasn't so gray anymore. I shrugged it on, then began gathering my hair as I went from my closet to my bathroom mirror. I knew it would take forever for my hair to dry if I twisted it and clipped it up—but Ange was giving me two minutes, not forty.

Once I was satisfied with my hair situation, I paused for a second and looked at my reflection. Not at what I was wearing, but at *me*. I hadn't really looked at myself after what happened with Ange the other night. Now I knew why. I could see it all over my face.

I didn't want my first time with Ange to be my last.

I turned on my heel as I fought my smile and went to get my purse.

We were on our way to the elevator, silence tagging along as our third wheel, when it struck me.

My text hadn't been the only cold thing I'd done the day before.

He'd been so good. So gentle. And I'd panicked.

"Ange?" I murmured, reaching for the sleeve of his sweatshirt.

He stopped to look at me, a cautious curiosity in his expression.

That was my fault.

He considered me a risk, too.

Damn. I needed to clear the air.

"I just wanted to say—I'm sorry. For the way I acted yesterday. You didn't deserve it."

His face relaxed, and I felt my body do the same.

"Appreciate that. Seeing as you're letting me take you to breakfast, I think we can consider it water under the bridge now, yeah?"

I nodded, and we continued toward the elevator.

After we stopped at his truck to get Penny, Ange and I walked a block to 24Diner. We got a table outside. He ordered steak and eggs. I wanted biscuits and gravy with a vat of coffee. I got the former and settled for a single cup of the latter.

When Ange asked after my sister, I was relieved I didn't have to tell him I didn't actually go see her. Instead, I told him about our dinner. I admitted I didn't spend as much time with my nieces as I would like, and I was glad I got to put in a couple hours that weekend. We talked casually about family for a while.

I learned Ange had a younger brother. His name was Nicodemus—because, of course it was. Nico, as he preferred to be called, was a couple years younger than me. He still lived in Michigan, but his job as a welder in the oilfield meant he traveled for work quite a bit. Ange told me they'd been pretty close growing up, but when he left for college, they started to grow apart, their lives headed in different directions. Then, not long after he'd married his ex, Ange and Nico had a falling out.

"Do you miss him?" I asked, unable to imagine falling out with my own sister.

"Yeah."

He didn't say more, and I didn't press.

We finished our breakfast, then Ange got the check.

"What now?" he asked as we took our leave.

I looked up at him. "Do you have to be at the pub today?"

"Nope. We're closed Mondays."

"Oh." I didn't dwell on how convenient that might be for me. For future us. If there would be a future us. Instead, I suggested, "Do you want to walk around a bit?"

"Sure."

He didn't ask me where to. He didn't even hesitate. It took me a minute to figure it out, but he pointed us toward Shoal Creek Trail, and I was happy to follow. The trail was more like a path that meandered along the creek in the middle of town. It was a beautiful day out, the temperature still hovering in the mid-sixties, and there was a gentle breeze as we walked. Penny trotted along in front of us, her tail wagging like her favorite thing in the world was going exploring with her dad.

We'd been walking for nearly twenty minutes and were coming up on the public library when I saw her. This time, she wasn't alone. Ava was pushing a stroller carrying a toddler with one hand, holding the hand of a little boy with her other. The little boy was clutching a library book to his chest.

I stopped, sucked in a sharp breath, then did what I always did when I saw Ava. I turned, accidentally colliding with Ange, forcing him to stop. Seeing as he was blocking my path, I merely stood staring at his chest, praying she hadn't seen me.

"Whoa, you okay?"

I frowned as I looked up at him. Though, it wasn't his question that had me confused. What I didn't understand was how I'd managed to spot Ava *twice* in a week.

Nine years. Nine years, and I'd seen her maybe a dozen times. Even when we were working the same wedding, I evaded her like a pro with the help of Libby and Jorge. There was one time when we almost bumped into each other while she was entering the bridal suite to make a delivery and I was trying to make a mad-dash out, but that happened once and once only.

I'd never seen her twice in the same month, let alone a week.

Was the universe punishing me for something?

"Channing?"

Still staring up at Ange, I realized I needed to explain my seemingly odd behavior. With a grimace I admitted, "Do you see that pregnant woman with the stroller and the little kid?"

I watched as his eyes went over my head before they came back and settled on my face.

"Yeah..." He smiled, as if he found me amusing, and asked, "Are you hiding? From a pregnant woman?"

It sounded ridiculous when he said it like that. So ridiculous I felt a little embarrassed. Embarrassed enough that his smile didn't make my chest feel warm and tingly. This annoyed me—mostly because he was probably right, just like Blake was probably right when she insisted I needed to stop hiding. Except, at present, my embarrassment didn't change the fact that I didn't care what anyone thought. Not about t his.

"Yes," I stated before I walked around him, headed in the opposite direction.

I heard Penny's dog tags jingle as the both of them followed after me.

"Channing," Ange called.

I kept walking.

"Channing, babe, slow down."

He reached for my hand with his, effectively bringing me back to his side, and I slowed down. When he didn't let go of my hand, I looked up at him.

He gave my fingers a squeeze. "You want to talk about it?"

I didn't. The feel of my hand in his felt nice. So nice, it was helping to assuage my embarrassment. Since talking about hiding from a pregnant woman, whom I hadn't spoken to in nearly a decade, might have the reverse effect, I murmured, "No. I really don't."

"Okay. Then we won't."

He gave my hand another squeeze.

That felt nice. The squeeze and the acceptance.

He didn't let me go, so I didn't let him go either.

Before I could get lost in my thoughts, he asked, "So, do you like sports?"

I couldn't help but smile up at him in response to his completely random question. He caught it, returned it with one of his own, and the warm and tingly in my chest came back.

I told him I was a faithful Longhorns football fan and had been since before UT Austin became my alma mater—thanks to dad—but how I didn't really watch anything else. Given the backstory behind The Four Horsemen, I already knew he was a college football fan. He shared how he'd grown up watching Michigan, would always be a lifelong fan, but that he was loyal to Notre Dame, too.

As far as professional sports went, he was a Detroit Lions fan and, in a strange turn of events, a Toronto Maple Leafs fan. I knew nothing of hockey, but I did know Toronto was in Canada.

"It makes more sense than you think," he insisted. "We don't have a pro team in Michigan. Our choices were the Chicago Blackhawks, the Pittsburg Penguins, or the Toronto Maple Leafs. They're all about equidistant from where I grew up. And nobody does hockey like a Canadian."

I couldn't fault his logic.

By the time we'd exhausted the topic of sports, we were back at my building. When we got to my door, I unlocked it then asked, "Do you want to come in?"

"Yeah," he answered simply.

I nodded, opened the door, and we all went inside. My kitchen was the first room in my place. I set my purse and my keys on the island, then asked over my shoulder, "Do you want something to drink or—"

I didn't get a chance to finish my sentence before Ange's hands were at my waist, turning me to face him. My head jerked up just in time to see his mouth descending to meet mine. My eyelids fell closed, and the hum that crawled up my throat would not be silenced. When he sought entrance into my mouth with his tongue, I opened up immediately. I then pressed up on my tiptoes, wrapped my arms around his shoulders and held on for the kiss of a man I was stubborn enough to think I could forget.

God, but he could kiss.

No. I didn't want my first time with Ange to be my last.

His grip tightened around my waist, and then I was up—my butt on my kitchen island and my knees spread open to make room for Ange between my legs.

I knew he liked this because he kissed me harder.

I told him I felt the same with a moan.

We did this for a while, and it was marvelous.

It was marvelous until it got better.

It got better when he reached down and pressed one of his hands between my legs. He wasn't even in my clothing; as if he was curious, he rubbed the meaty part of his palm against my center, eliciting a whimper. I knew that whimper was an answer to an unspoken question when I lost his mouth and he reached for the waistband of my leggings.

My hands went flying to the counter propping me up as my body acted faster than my brain, lifting my hips so Ange could pull off my leggings and my not-sexy cotton underwear. When both were at my ankles, he deftly slid off my shoes, which dropped carelessly to the floor, then completely rid my lower half of any garments.

I was half naked, on my kitchen island.

I'd *never* been half naked on my kitchen island.

Then again, I'd never had a hot guy strip me half naked on my kitchen island before.

The next second, I was on my back, and I was seeing stars.

This was because while I was busy thinking about how I was half naked, on my kitchen island, I missed it when Ange bent down so he could get a taste of me.

He licked, then groaned, and suddenly my arms weren't strong enough to hold me upright anymore.

Ange was not shy. He took what he wanted, and what he wanted was me in his mouth. I didn't know it until he was doing it, but I wanted that, too. So much so, I could barely breathe.

His tongue hit the perfect spot, and my back arched so sharply it was like I was a woman possessed. Consumed by the pleasure he was giving me I mindlessly reached down and buried my fingers in his hair. Somehow, this made what he was doing even better.

He was going to make me come, and it was all I could think about.

I was on the brink, my entire body so hot I was starting to sweat under the pullover and vest I still wore.

Then he was gone, my grip in his hair lost.

"No," I breathed, the word falling from my lips before I could process all that was happening.

I looked up at Ange, who now stood at full height, and he was grinning at me.

"I'll get you where you want to go, babe. Get you there faster if you help me out of these jeans."

No sooner had he said the words than I saw he was reaching for a condom out of his wallet. I didn't think twice about it. I sat up and went for the button at his jeans. My thumbs hooked on the inside of his boxer briefs, I pushed his clothing down as far as I could reach, and his erection sprang free.

I almost came seeing it in the light of day.

When he took over, rolling on the condom, I took the opportunity to shed another layer. My vest was gone, then his arm was around my waist, pulling me to the edge of the counter before he slid his way inside of me.

For a moment, he didn't move.

We were chest to chest. He propped his forehead against mine, and we were nose to nose. My hands were at his shoulders, gripping tightly to his sweatshirt, my whole being wishing he would move.

"Beautiful," he whispered.

At that, I melted a little, remembering how he'd said the same thing the first time he'd touched me. The way he filled me so completely now, I couldn't agree more.

Then he began to move.

My god, he felt sensational.

A whimper escaped my lips as I hitched one of my knees up against his hip. He immediately reached beneath my thigh to help me keep it there. This made his strokes feel even better.

My orgasm was building again.

No, not building. It was there.

"Ange," I gasped. "Ange, I'm gonna come."

"Do it, baby."

I threw my head back, relieved he hadn't asked me to wait. I wouldn't have been able to. I cried out in pleasure, my center constricting as I surrendered to my release.

I was just starting to recover when Ange stopped. I righted my head, and my eyes found his. The look he was giving me made my sex clench. I knew he felt it when I got a smile that turned my belly to mush.

He then instructed, "Brace yourself, baby."

When his free hand lifted my opposite leg, I nodded, then leaned back until I was propped up on my forearms. I braced—and he rode me hard and fast.

It. Was. Amazing.

My eyes held his until the unthinkable happened. I then moaned in ecstatic disbelief when I felt another orgasm coming on. I tilted my head back as my eyes closed and I concentrated on the feel of him pounding into me over and over—filling me full over and over.

Yeah—I was *definitely* going to come again.

"Channing," Ange all but growled.

It was hot. It fed the burn inside of me.

I didn't respond. I was on the verge.

"Channing—eyes on me."

He wanted my eyes. Seeing as I had a thing for his, too, I obeyed.

His green gaze was molten.

"Touch yourself, baby, and come for me."

Oh, yes. I wanted that.

I reached for my clit, and I barely had to touch it before I was coming undone.

And that wasn't even the best part.

The best part was, I wasn't coming alone.

I got to watch Ange find his release.

He kept his eyes on me. He bit his bottom lip—*hard*. He groaned, and the muscles in his neck bulged. His fingertips dug deeper into my thighs, and he jerked erratically inside of me until he was spent.

Now, that? *That* was beautiful.

I barely had a chance to lock all I'd seen into my memory banks before he dropped one of my thighs, caught me behind the neck, hauled me up, and kissed me hard.

Good lord, the man could kiss.

We clung to each other until we needed air. When he pulled away, my hands were holding his bearded cheeks, and his fingers were buried in my still-damp hair.

Like my clothing, he'd discarded my hairclip when he decided I shouldn't have it on anymore.

We panted, desperately trying to catch our breath.

When I could manage to speak, I stated unnecessarily, "We just had sex on my kitchen counter."

I *felt* his cheeks lift with his smile as he chuckled and replied, "We'll rest for a bit, then we'll go again, but in the bed."

There were so many things I liked about that statement I couldn't put it into words. Not to mention, I'd recently experienced another simultaneous orgasm followed by a searing hot kiss, so there weren't that many words in my head at the moment.

Instead, I merely nodded and whispered, "Okay."

After Ange left me to discard his used condom, I had just enough time to slip back into my not-sexy cotton panties and give the counter a quick wipe down. That was all I had time to do before he came back and I learned *we'll rest a bit* consisted of him carrying me to my bedroom, stripping me naked—then stripping himself naked—before kissing me until he was ready to *go again—but in the bed*.

He took me slower the second time.

We did not share a simultaneous orgasm, but that didn't make it any less incredible.

Drunken sex with Ange had been unforgettable.

It did not take me long to discover sober sex with Ange was even better.

It was late afternoon. I was wrapped around his side with my cheek resting on his chest. He had one hand underneath the covers, his fingers tickling the small of my back. I was sated and content, happy I'd decided not to get out of the boat.

I didn't know where it was headed, but neither did Ange.

He wasn't bad company, and he was far from a horrible lay.

It was as simple as that.

We were enjoying the ride, and that was enough.

"What's her name?"

Ange asked out of nowhere.

I frowned at his chest.

"Who?"

"The pregnant lady."

My body was so worn out, I didn't have it in me to tense—but my mind braced.

"Come on," he encouraged gently. "Is she a rival wedding planner or something?"

Seeing as I was naked in Ange's arms, after he'd delivered *four* orgasms using various parts of *his* naked body, I figured I couldn't get more vulnerable. So, I answered him.

"Her name is Ava. Not exactly a rival, but she is a florist that tends to make my life harder whenever I'm forced to work with her. And, in another life, we'd been best friends."

Ange's fingers stopped moving against my back.

"That was *her?*"

"Mmhmm."

"*Shit,*" he breathed.

Something about his reaction made me feel comfortable giving him more. I shifted, until I was propped up on his chest and I could see into his eyes.

"We'd been best friends since junior year of high school. We applied to all the same colleges. When we both got into UT, we were ecstatic. We lived together all four years," I began, giving him the reader's digest version.

"Ava dated a little bit here and there, but she was kind of a free spirit. She liked to have fun and she wanted to find herself and start a career before settling down, so she wasn't into anything serious. She was actually how I met Dylan.

"It was our senior year. They'd met at a house party. They hadn't messed around or anything, but he'd been interested. He invited her to tailgate with him and a bunch of his buddies before a game, and she brought me with her. Ava was Ava and she flirted with everyone. Dylan lost interest and struck up conversation with me." I dropped my gaze, looking down at my cheeks as I whispered, "At least, I thought he'd lost interest. I'd learn, four years later, I was wrong."

"That's all sorts of fucked up," muttered Ange.

I met his eyes once more and shrugged. "It was a long time ago."

"Still fucked up."

He wasn't wrong, so I didn't argue.

"You run into her often?"

"Do I *see* her sometimes? Rarely, but yes. I also do my very best to make sure she does *not* see me. One might say I've made an artform of it."

"Why?" he asked matter-of-factly.

"Because I don't want her to see who I am now. She's in the industry, so she's aware of Rusty Barn Wedding Co., but I mean *me*, outside of work."

This brought a scowl to his handsome face. "Babe, you're gorgeous. You've got a great body and fantastic hair. You're smart, and funny, and cute as fuck. You *own* your own business. And while I haven't been to one of your weddings, I've seen enough of you to get that you kick ass at what you do. What they did to you was fucked, but you turned out better than alright. Why not flaunt it?"

He'd said a lot. All of it nice. He thought I was cute and had fantastic hair. He'd said it like he thought I was crazy if I didn't believe it, and that was nice too. I didn't know what to say in response, which was why I mumbled, "You sound like my sister."

"Smart woman."

"I can't explain it, okay? She stole my life, or, the life I thought I wanted. She broke my heart. She doesn't get any more of me. Not even so much as a glimpse."

My eyes widened after I realized what I'd confessed.

It was true. It was exactly how I felt—I'd just never spoken it aloud before. I'd never been able to articulate it so clearly. If all it took was a couple rounds of sex with Ange to get that out of me, I was glad I hadn't spent the last nine years and thousands of dollars on therapy.

Nevertheless, Ange was not my therapist. I'd shared enough. It was time to talk about something else.

Feeling more vulnerable than I thought I could get whilst being naked with him in bed, I started to maneuver out of my current position.

He moved faster than me, circling his arms around my waist so I couldn't move.

"Channing—"

"I'm hungry. Are you hungry?"

"Chan—"

"Do you want to stay for dinner?" I continued, cutting him off. "I can cook something. I'm no Julia Child, but I don't suck at throwing something together."

He stared at me.

I stared back.

We did this for a solid thirty seconds.

Then I watched as his expression shifted, and his arms around me loosened.

"Yeah. I could eat," he conceded.

I didn't fight my smile. "Great."

I pressed a quick kiss against the corner of his mouth then rolled away from him and got out of bed.

A while later, after we'd eaten grilled cheese sandwiches and a heated-up carton of pre-made, organic tomato soup, Ange said it was time he got home so Penny could have some dinner, too.

It was hard to believe the day we'd had. Even harder to conceive it was ending.

I walked them to my door, not at all sure where to go from here.

I had no reason to worry. Ange was one step ahead of me.

"I'll call you tomorrow. We'll make plans."

"Okay," I agreed with a nod.

We were staying in the boat.

We were seeing where it would go.

That meant, when he leaned down to kiss me goodbye, I let him have my mouth.

CHAPTER *Ten*

T HE NEXT MORNING, I skipped the gym. I'd done enough cardio in one day to last me the whole week, and my body felt it. My arms and shoulders were sore after my attempt at the rowing machine, but I couldn't be bothered to complain about it.

This was because I was sore in other places.

Other places that conjured very satisfactory memories every time I was reminded of said soreness.

I was gathering what I needed for our weekly staff meeting when Libby breezed into my office, flashing me her dimples. For a fraction of a second, I tensed, wondering if she knew what I had done that weekend.

Or, rather, *whom*.

"Good news," she announced, not bothering to sit. "Mama Chavez to the rescue—we have a church, which means we have an official date! May fourth."

I relaxed, then returned her grin with a smile of my own.

Ange didn't strike me as someone who would kiss and tell, so I wasn't all that surprised by the fact that he hadn't told Patrick, who would undoubtedly tell Libby. What *did* surprise me was the realization that I didn't want to tell Libby, either. Not yet, at least.

I shoved all of that aside and focused on the matter at hand. Libby and Patrick now had an official wedding date. Moreover, it was the date we were hoping for, as we had no other weddings scheduled that weekend *and* it was a couple weeks before the Jackson-Ford hoopla.

"That *is* good news." I hugged my laptop and my everything-binder to my chest as I grabbed my travel tumbler full of coffee. I then made my way around the desk and started for the door as I asked, "Which church?"

Libby, who had fallen into step beside me, scrunched her face a little.

"Uh-oh. That is not a face I want any of my brides to make when they're telling me about where their ceremony is going to take place."

"Okay, it's not that bad," she admitted. "It's just not my first choice. Or my second. But we couldn't get the cathedral on such short notice, and Our Lady of Guadalupe—the church my family has been attending since I was baptized—was also booked through August. But, my mom called around, and there was an opening at Saint Austin. Again, not my first or second choice, but a solid third choice. And, at this point, I understand beggars can't be choosers. I won't compromise on getting married in a Catholic church, but I suppose I can bend a little on which one."

We entered our conference room, and I set my things down in my usual spot, in the middle of the six-seater table.

"Saint Austin," I mused, trying to picture it in my head. "If I'm remembering correctly, that's not too far from here, right?"

Libby, as always, took the seat to my right. "Not walkable to the pub, but a super short drive."

"It's not ringing a bell as someplace we've done a wedding before. Maybe in my pre-Rusty Barn days, but I can't remember. I'll look up pics later."

Rusty Barn Wedding Co. did plenty of weddings in churches of all kinds, but we did far more outdoor ceremonies, and even more ranch or farmhouse type venues. I didn't name my company *Rusty Barn* for nothing.

"I know I'm going a bit out of our wheelhouse, with the church and the pub—"

"Stop," I insisted, turning in my chair to face her dead on. "This is your wedding. *Yours*. And we're in the business of making dreams come true—this one in particular because it hits so close to home—so, you need to stop worrying. Just because we've never done a reception in an Irish pub before doesn't mean we aren't capable of turning it into a rustic paradise fit for you and your groom, okay?"

Sheepishly, she nodded. "I didn't think I'd be *that* bride," she murmured.

I laughed. "I still love you, though."

"Thank God," gushed Libby with a playful eyeroll.

Phoebe was the next to join us, and Jorge was soon to follow.

It took us a little over an hour to recap the wedding we'd done over the weekend and then go through our separate lists of priorities for the week ahead. We were juggling a few weddings, and we all had plenty to do, but if we managed to stay on top of our responsibilities, I was sure things wouldn't get out of hand. With our upcoming weekend free of any ceremonies, that meant a solid week of dividing and conquering.

By ten thirty I was back at my desk. An hour later, I was working on a pile of invoices when Jorge walked into my office. He didn't knock, and when I looked up to see him approach, I suspected his visit wasn't going to be a pleasant one.

"B&B is saying they're not sure if they'll be able to handle the number of hydrangeas we need for the Jackson-Ford wedding. Rather than share this information with me exclusively, Tiffany was looped into the email thread. This resulted in a phone call where she said if the arrangements we agreed upon can't be delivered, maybe we should reconsider centerpieces for the tables."

I frowned. "It took two months to agree on floral arrangements and design. Everything was finalized and signed off last week. I thought we were all good."

"We were good, until Ava went back on her commitment to deliver enough hydrangeas to cover fifty barrels."

I shook my head. This wasn't happening. This couldn't be happening *again*.

When Tiffany and her mother informed us they wanted to enlist B&B Floral Design, I had asked them why that florist in particular. They'd apparently been to more than one event where Ava had done an "incredible" job. Mrs. Jackson wanted a sure thing. Since she'd seen it with her own eyes, she was convinced Ava was a sure thing.

I didn't make it a habit of bad-mouthing vendors. Certainly, I had my own list of reliable people I liked to work with, and I was never shy about stating my preference; but I was also in the business of giving my clients what they wanted when it was possible. Ava had never completely screwed the pooch, but it was the little things—and in my world, the little things mattered.

They mattered a great deal.

The last job we did together was a small wedding nearly two years ago. There were only one-hundred guests. At the reception, we had agreed on these beautiful centerpieces—a spray of assorted flowers in adorable, old tin watering cans. All the blossoms were supposed to be white. *White*. When the centerpieces were delivered, all the flowers were white *except* the gerbera daisies. They were cream.

It didn't go unnoticed.

Not by Jorge. Not by me. Not by the mother of the groom, either.

In a mad scramble, Jorge and I reached out to every florist we knew until we had procured enough white gerbera daisies to rectify the issue. Fortunately, we had the lead time to replace all the cream ones, since the pieces were delivered well before the ceremony, but it was close.

Too close.

Not only that, I'd forked up the cash to cover the cost of Ava's mistake.

I had a reputation to protect.

Yes, I could have demanded *she* needed to reimburse me for her mistake and breach of contract, but I didn't want to deal with that headache. I ate the cost and vowed not to work with her again.

But Tiffany Jackson was a congressmen's daughter. She'd hired *me* to put on the wedding of the season. *Southern Bride Magazine* was doing a full spread on the whole affair.

I was living proof one should never say never.

All that to say, I did not consider Ava a "sure thing." Therefore, I'd learned to expect this kind of shit. But that didn't make the pill any easier to swallow.

"We don't want to do flowers on the tables," I said, reminding Jorge of something he already knew. "We already decided on the candle centerpieces. Tiffany loved them. She also loved the idea of lining the perimeter of the barn with barrels topped with mass arrangements—*fifty* barrels I've already sourced and put down a deposit for, I might add."

Jorge dipped his chin in a slow nod.

The simple act spoke volumes.

He was just as irritated as I was.

"You knew something like this was bound to happen. It always does with Ava."

I reached up to rub my forehead as I said, "She knows this wedding is being featured in *Southern Bride*, right? She knows that by playing these *stupid* games, she's shooting herself in the foot, too."

"One would think."

"Ugh," I growled.

I then took a breath and composed myself.

"We aren't doing this. We're three months out. Please call Tiffany back and convince her to stick with the previously approved design. Time is of the essence, and we need her to really grasp that reality. Then call Ava and tell her if she can't honor her commitment, we'll take a refund on the mass arrangements and work with another florist for all reception flowers. If you need my help getting someone to sign up for this massive project with such short notice, let me know—but hopefully the threat of bringing in competition will change Ava's tune. Also, please make sure you document this."

"Oh, don't worry," he assured me, arching a single eyebrow. "It has been added to the list of ways she's screwed with us."

"Thank you." I sighed, regretful he had to deal with this mess—a mess, I was pretty convinced, was a personal attack directed at me. "I'm really sorry about all this."

"You have nothing to apologize for. This is not your fault. You're the professional in this whole situation."

"True, but I'm asking you to—"

"To do my job," he stated, cutting me off. "I'm the director of floral décor and design at Rusty Barn Wedding Co, in case you forgot. You pay me to do this. I'm only here to keep you in the loop. Consider yourself read-in. I'm off to make a few phone calls."

I sighed again, this time in relief.

Jorge left to make his phone calls.

My weekend high was now gone. Thanks to Ava, it hadn't even lasted until noon. I went back to my invoices, hoping a bit of productivity would cheer me up a bit.

Then my phone rang.

I glanced at the screen, saw *Ange Castellanos* was calling, and suddenly Ava was the last thing on my mind.

"Hello?" I answered on the second ring.

"Hi, babe. Did I catch you at a good time?"

I sealed my eyes closed tight and smiled as the effect of his greeting rushed through me.

Why did it feel so good to hear him call me that?

"Mmmhmm, now is fine," I murmured in reply.

"Calling about those plans. Dinner. A proper date this time. When are you free?"

I blinked my eyes open and tried to sort through what I had on my plate the next few days.

What I didn't do was stop to think about how I wasn't a woman who went on dinner dates.

I had Ange in my ear, and I wanted to be a woman who went on dinner dates.

"Um—I think I could do tomorrow. Thursday might be better."

"Thursday, then. It's better for me, too. I'll pick you up at your place. Seven o'clock?"

He'd pick me up at my place.

Seven o'clock.

This meant I'd have time to go home and change into something date-worthy.

I nodded, even though he couldn't see me do it, then confirmed, "Yeah. Okay."

"Great. I'll see you then."

"Okay," I semi-repeated.

"I've got to go. Bye for now."

"Bye for now."

He disconnected, and I pulled my phone away from my ear to stare at it.

Ange was going to take me to dinner Thursday night.

A proper date this time. No room for ambiguity.

Then again, we were well past ambiguity.

I smiled to myself as I got back to work, Ava now totally forgotten.

CHAPTER *Eleven*

I HAD THREE LITTLE black dresses.

I might not have been a woman who went on dates, but I wasn't a recluse. Every now and again, when I was invited for a night out, I would say yes. Sometimes that meant drinks with Libby and Jorge when we had a Saturday night free. Or if Blake wanted something a little more adventurous than lunch at Group Therapy, we'd meet there after dark. On such occasions, I enjoyed the thrill of wearing a dress not suited for the office.

I wasn't sure where Ange was taking me for dinner. I knew only that he would be at my door in twenty minutes. I'd been home long enough to give new life to my hair and layer on the appropriate amount of makeup for a date after sunset. Now I just needed to decide on a dress.

One of my LBDs was a lacey number I'd ruled out on account of he'd already seen me in—and taken me out of—a pretty great lacey dress.

He'd called tonight *a proper* date.

I took this to imply we weren't going to another diner.

The question remained, did I want to give off *sexy-but-classy* or *flirty-and-sassy*?

I pictured Ange in my mind's eye.

His hair—trimmed short on the sides but longer and thick on the top.

Long enough to be messy if he wanted it to be, but it was obvious he didn't.

His beard—not too long or short, but trimmed and clean.

When my thoughts drifted to what it felt like to run my fingers through his hair, or to feel the sensation of his beard as it scraped against the sensitive skin on the inside of my thighs, I shook my head to clear it.

Then I reached for *sexy-but-classy*.

The shape of the dress was the *sexy*. It was sleeveless, with a wide, deep V-cut neckline, allowing me to show off what little bit of cleavage I had. It cinched naturally at my waist, the skirt sculpting my backside and hugging my legs until the hem, which landed just shy of mid-thigh.

It was the details that made it *classy*. There was a simple ruffle around the outside edge of the shoulder straps. The skirt was designed to culminate in a cascading ruffle that draped from my right hip. It was subtle, feminine, and me, which was why I always felt great when I wore it.

I opted for my nude, strappy, stiletto heels to finish the look.

Once dressed, I applied a spritz of perfume, then went about gathering what I needed from my big purse into a reasonable clutch.

I'd just snapped it closed when a knock sounded at my door.

My belly tensed with a sudden bout of nerves.

I wasn't a woman who went on dinner dates—but Ange was on the other side of my door.

Whatever it meant, we were in the boat, and I was reminded—for the first time in a very long while—I *wanted* to be a woman who went on dinner dates.

He knocked a second time, and I forced one foot in front of the other until I was standing in an open doorway, not even kidding myself into thinking I could do anything but stare.

That's because Ange was wearing a charcoal-gray button-up that fit him so well, it was impossible to think of anything but all the strength he possessed in that body of which I knew he took exceptional care. He hadn't rolled up the cuffs of the shirt, and it was tucked into a pair of dove-gray chinos, the straight leg of which bunched a little over the top of his classy, ankle-high boots.

Damn, but he was handsome.

Somehow I knew, this was not an outfit he wore often.

Tonight was a *proper* date.

He'd dressed accordingly.

I liked that. A lot.

I'm not sure how long I stood speechless at the sight of him before I realized neither of us had said so much as *hello*. I forced my eyes up and found his were staring, waiting.

I held his green gaze.

My chest grew warm and tingly.

When he continued to stare, I forgot I was nervous, and my belly turned to mush.

This lasted a solid forty seconds.

Then I couldn't take it anymore.

"Ange?" I whispered.

"We have reservations," he muttered.

"Okay," I said with a slight nod. "I'm ready."

"We have reservations," he repeated.

I tilted my head in confusion.

I didn't have a chance to voice said confusion before Ange reached for me.

One hand took hold of my waist. His other dove into my hair—his fingers weaving between my strands before he had me by the nape of my neck.

I sucked in a staggering breath, and then his mouth was closed around mine, his tongue taking advantage of the opening.

Instantly, I understood.

Except, with his lips on mine, I found I couldn't concern myself with such trivial things as reservations.

I draped an arm over his shoulder, snaking my other around his back as I pushed further into his hold.

He liked this. I knew because he opened his mouth wider and kissed me deeper.

I whimpered my appreciation, pressing up onto my tiptoes.

God, but he could kiss.

And kiss me he did—long and hard and deep and wet.

Before I was ready, he ripped his mouth away from mine—both of us breathless.

"We have reservations," he told me a third time.

His eyes—green, gorgeous, and absolutely molten after that kiss—devoured my face.

I bit my bottom lip in an attempt to hold back another whimper.

"Fuck, babe. Don't do that," he insisted, his grip around me tightening pleasantly.

Instead, I rolled both my lips into my mouth.

Ange gave me his quarter-smile as he shook his head at me.

"I'm hungry. Been looking forward to dinner all day, and we have reservations. Trust me when I say, if it weren't for two of the three reasons I just laid out, we'd be halfway to your bed right now and ordering pizza after I made you come."

A shiver raced down my spine.

Ange felt it, and his smirk stretched into a smile.

I swallowed then asked, "So, you like the dress?"

It was the exact right thing to say.

I knew this because, right after I said it, my whole world stopped.

Ange pulled me even closer, threw his head back, and laughed.

Seeing him laugh was one thing.

Feeling it while I watched it?

Exceptional.

When he recovered himself, his eyes—bright and shimmering with amusement—found mine as he replied, "Yeah, babe. I like the dress."

Now I was grinning.

"Noted."

"Lock up. Let's get out of here."

I locked up, and we got out of there.

Ten minutes later, my hand tucked into Ange's big, warm, calloused one, we were walking into Péché.

I wasn't sure what to expect—but I was more than a little flattered that a *proper date* was worthy of French cuisine. Moreover, I was pleasantly intrigued to learn rugged, bearded, pub-owners ate such a thing.

When we were seated at a table for two, I decided to say as much.

Ange smiled at me—eliciting that warm, tingly sensation—then said, "I have a more sophisticated palate than you might think."

"I suppose you did spend a number of years in a city known for having some of the best restaurants in the world. Are you a foodie?" I asked, half teasing, half curious.

"I don't like labels," he said with a wink.

I hummed a laugh and we both looked down at our menus, checking out our cocktail options. When our server came around, inquiring about our drink order, I got a New York Sour while Ange opted for a Sazerac.

"Do you miss it? The food scene in New York City?"

He shrugged nonchalantly. "Not particularly. It's a nice feature, but not worth the tradeoff."

"Is there *anything* you miss about the city?"

Ange frowned while he thought, as if no one had ever asked him that before. Finally, he said, "Christmas time."

"Really?" I asked, genuinely intrigued.

"Yeah. It's a crazy time of year anyway, and when you add in a bunch of tourists it turns into madness—but there's something about it that's magical, I guess." He paused. A hint of a smile appeared and disappeared just as fast before he went on to tell me, "My last Christmas in the city, I flew my parents out the week before. Steph's family always did Christmas in the Hamptons, which meant we did—"

He cut himself off, like he hadn't meant to mention his ex, then shook his head, and refocused. "Anyway, it was the first time my parents had ever been to New York during the Christmas season. My mom was obsessed. She wanted to go to the Christmas market every day. At the time, I didn't know it was going to be my last Christmas in the city. Looking back, it was a great way to go out."

Ange shifted his focus onto his menu, but I kept my eyes on him.

It was sweet how he considered Christmas magical.

The night was young, and already I was finding he was full of surprises.

"What do you do at Christmas now? Go to Michigan?"

"I've only made it back home once in the last few years," he admitted, offering me his attention. "Until I came around, it was pretty tough for Pat to get home for the holidays. I've stayed behind the past two years so he could try to make up for some lost time."

Our server returned with our drinks.

Like the last time Ange and I sat across from each other at dinner, neither of us were ready with our entrée order upon our server's first return visit. When he left to give us a few more minutes, we took the time to make our selections and were ready on his next trip back to our table.

"What about you?" asked Ange when we were alone again. "Are you team Christmas, or are you more of a Thanksgiving person?"

I grinned, knowing my answer was not typical. "Fourth of July."

His smile brought about his eye creases before he said, "Okay. I'll bite. Why?"

"It's just a quintessential, all-American summer holiday, with *fireworks*. How could you not love the Fourth of July? There's zero pressure. You get together with family or friends; you eat hot dogs and watermelon and corn on the cob...

"Growing up, my family lived in a cul-de-sac, and we would always have this neighborhood block party that was huge. We played yard games and shot off our own fireworks. It was the best. Now, my sister usually hosts at her house. Blake and Derek have a pool, so I'm typically in the water most of the day with my nieces, trying to stay cool. My parents will come down and stay for a few days, and it just feels lik e *home*."

I paused long enough to think about it, then continued, "Actually, since Cami was born, my parents make the trip down for most major holidays. It's easier all around. Between The Cookie Ranch and the girls, plus my job—it's not unusual for me to have a wedding I have to put on a day or two after a holiday. It's not ideal, but I charge a premium for certain dates of the year. Especially Christmas. Brides love a Christmas wedding. It can be convenient if people are already traveling for..."

I lost track of my sentence at the sight of Ange's amused grin.

That's when it hit me.

I was rambling.

Damn.

"Anyway…" I muttered lamely, reaching for my drink.

"Correct me if I'm wrong, but I can't help but notice a theme, here. I remember you telling me you have no interest in marriage, but it kind of sounds like you might be married to your job."

My spine straightened. I wasn't entirely sure how I felt about his comment.

My mouth moving faster than my brain, I retorted, "Says the man who hasn't been home for Christmas in the last two years."

He dipped his chin in a nod, as if conceding to my point. He then added, "Fair. But I'm not judging. I'm only curious to know what you do for you? How do you keep yourself from burnout?"

"Oh," I breathed, relaxing a little in my seat. "Well, having family close keeps me sane. If I go too long without a break, my sister's great about pulling my head above the water. And…" I hesitated, allowing the cliché to roll around my mouth before I spit it out. "You know how they say, if you do what you love you never work a day in your life? It's cheesy, but not too far from the truth."

"Okay," he said simply.

Something about his response made me ill at ease, like he didn't totally buy my answer. Or like he wasn't convinced my answer would hold up over time.

If I was honest, there were moments when I wondered if it would—if I could keep my head down and power through at the same rate forever, or if my life needed more than work and a few stolen moments with my sister to propel me.

I glanced down at my drink, spinning the glass slowly with my fingertips.

I remembered where I was. On a date. With Ange.

I couldn't say where we were going or what, exactly, we were doing—but I was enjoying it.

It was something for me.

I lifted my gaze and found his still trained in my direction.

Smiling softly, I added, "Plus, I'm here with you, aren't I?"

This earned me a smirk.

"Yeah, babe. That you are."

Dinner was delicious.

I was glad we made our reservation.

It was way better than take-out pizza would have been.

That said, when our server asked if we were interested in dessert, Ange took one look at me, I took one look at him, and we simultaneously declined.

Ange paid the check, then grabbed my hand, and we were out of there.

Neither of us spoke as we made our way through the lobby of my building toward the elevator. On our trip to the eleventh floor, Ange traced his thumb in slow circles across mine, and it felt like a whisper of a promise of things to come.

I'd never been so turned on holding a man's hand.

The pace of his stride down the hallway leading toward my unit had me practically sprinting on my tiptoes in my stilettos. Rather than exasperation, I had to fight the urge to giggle.

I had my keys out before we got to my door.

We crossed the threshold.

I discarded my things on the first surface I could reach.

Ange got the door—and then he had me.

His hands were on my waist, pulling me close. I gripped hold of his biceps and tilted my head back, ready for his mouth. He brought his lips to mine, but he didn't kiss me.

Instead, he said, "Penny's with the neighbor."

He got a dog sitter.

This was good news.

He confirmed this when he next spoke.

"Not in a hurry, babe," he continued, backing me toward my bedroom. "Plan on taking my time."

I nodded, incapable of words, too desperate for his kiss.

"But if I take this dress off and you aren't wearing any underwear—there might be a change of plans."

I planted my feet, my hands reflexively tightening around his arms as I thought about my earlier decision to go panty-less. It wasn't exactly a habit of mine, but it was Thursday, I hadn't done laundry, and I didn't have the right thong for this dress. Not to mention, a bra was simply not possible, laundry day aside.

As if he'd read my mind, Ange muttered, "Shit."

I lost my grip on him when he bent at the waist, shoved his shoulder into my belly, grabbed hold of the back of my thighs, and hefted me off my feet.

I squealed in surprise, trying to find purchase somewhere on his back as he carried me down the rest of the hallway. His shirt was too fitted for me to grab any of it, but I managed to latch onto his belt.

Ange stopped at the foot of the bed before I felt him slide a hand up the back of my thigh and underneath my dress. He palmed my naked backside then squeezed, and I couldn't help but squirm.

"Fuck," he whispered before trailing his fingers between my legs.

It wasn't long before I was dead weight over his shoulder, my hair hanging like a curtain reaching for the floor, my breaths coming quicker and shorter.

Was he going to make me come like this?

He slid two fingers inside of me, I moaned, and I knew.

He was going to make me come like that.

"Oh, my god—*Ange*," I gasped, on the brink of an orgasm.

I pulled at his belt, wishing I had access to him in other places.

Wishing he wasn't clothed.

Wishing I could *move*.

None of these things were going to happen.

But I was definitely going to come.

He circled my clit with his thumb, my breath caught, and then I moaned as my center constricted around his fingers.

I was still coming when he pulled out and put me on my feet.

Mercifully, he kept an arm around my waist, holding me against his chest while I recovered.

Though, recovery was no easy feat, since I wasn't on the ground two seconds before he gave me his mouth.

I whimpered in delight, then circled my arms around his neck and kissed him with all that I was.

"Pants, babe," he muttered against my lips. "Help me out of 'em."

I was happy to do this.

He went back to kissing me while I worked.

This was why I didn't notice he'd reached for his wallet and extracted a condom while I helped him out of his pants.

As soon as I had his zipper down, he lifted his mouth from mine and said, "On the bed. Hands and knees, babe. Shoes on."

I pressed my thighs together in excitement, then turned toward the bed and crawled on top.

I didn't have to wait long before Ange was there, working the skirt of my dress up to my waist.

Then I felt his weight on the edge of the bed.

I couldn't help it. I was panting.

The moment he slipped inside of me, I felt unbridled.

He didn't take his time.

He moved in and out of me with a purpose, and it felt *great*.

Ange had me by the hips, but that didn't stop me from rocking back and forth—meeting him thrust for thrust.

It was when he reached for a handful of my hair that I felt it.

I was going to come again.

I pushed back harder, whimpering as we came together.

Ange swore, then I lost the feel of his hand in my hair.

I felt his chest on my back, then his lips at my ear as he demanded, "Don't even think about it, baby."

He didn't need to explain, and that made me giggle.

The next thing I knew, I was up.

We were both on our knees. My back to his chest. One of his arms around my waist. His free hand inside my dress, cupping my breast.

My head fell back against his shoulder as he began to thrust at a new angle.

This was better.

I let him know this by clasping my hands around his wrists, silently insisting he not let go.

Just in case he needed further affirmation, I turned my head and grazed my tongue along his neck, just below his beard.

He squeezed my breast on a groan, then pounded into me harder. Faster.

"Yes," I whispered.

I arched my back, pressing into his arms, and that felt better still.

"Hurry—Ange, you feel too good."

"Almost there, baby," he promised.

I sighed, my grip around his wrists tightened, and I concentrated on what felt like the making of an atomic orgasm building in my core.

He didn't break his stride.

I closed my eyes and bit my lip. I was barely hanging on.

He buried his face in my neck and kissed me there—wet and frantic. *Oh, god.*

"Honey!" I cried.

His response came swiftly.

He let go of my waist, reached down to graze my clit, and I detonated.

It was so huge, I couldn't breathe, let alone make a sound.

As I trembled and shook—my mouth open, but my throat closed—Ange held me tight against him, groaning as he lost his rhythm whilst in the throes of his own pleasure.

When he was spent, my center was still contracting and releasing around him, so he kept thrusting. Slowly. Patiently. Blissfully.

"Wow," I finally managed on a pant when we both grew still.

His face remained buried in my neck, which meant I got the pleasure of feeling both his smile and his quiet chuckle.

"Change of plans," he muttered, just as breathless as I was. "Next round, I'll take my time."

Still floating on my post-orgasm high, I squeezed his wrists and merely nodded in reply.

CHAPTER
Twelve

Three Days Later

I FRETTED IN FRONT of the mirror. I had on my denim, puffy sleeve, baby doll dress with a ruffled hem that draped comfortably on my body and stopped a smidge past mid-thigh. I'd accessorized with a couple simple pieces of jewelry and put on a light layer of makeup and a spritz of my favorite perfume. My hair fell in soft, beachy waves down my chest and back. Admittedly, I'd spent a good amount of time perfecting it.

Ange liked my hair.

I liked that he liked my hair.

I wanted him to keep liking my hair.

Thus, I fretted in front of the mirror—because it was Sunday, we'd been doing whatever it was we'd been doing for only a week, and I could no longer deny it.

I wasn't just interested in Ange.

I liked him.

After our date Thursday, he stayed until morning.

After he left, I hadn't seen him since.

He'd texted. He'd called. We'd made more plans.

But it had been two days—and I missed him.

I wasn't sure how I felt about this.

So, I fretted.

I didn't know what the hell I was doing, but I knew I wasn't ready to stop doing it.

Once I admitted as much to myself, I stopped fretting and went to put on my shoes. We were staying in that night, so I went for my white, canvas slip-ons.

I was going to his place for the first time.

He was making steak.

On my way out the door, I made sure to grab the bottle of red I'd picked up from Whole Foods earlier that afternoon.

He didn't live far, and I was parked in front of his house in under fifteen minutes. At first glance, his home looked charming with great curb appeal. His house was dark blue with white trim around large windows. His front door was a maple shade of wood. The covered porch was large enough for seating, and he had a two-seater rocking chair situated to the right of the door.

I couldn't wait to see the inside.

I felt a little nervous as I walked toward his front entry. I refused to read into it and didn't tarry before knocking. Penny barked in excitement. I wasn't waiting long before Ange filled the doorway.

He was wearing a beige henley and jeans. His feet were bare, and I realized instantly that I liked this version of him.

Instead of hello, he stepped outside, caught me behind the neck, and drew me in for a kiss. It was deep and wet and delicious. It spoke of his longing, cluing me into the fact that he missed me, too.

I didn't like that.

I loved it.

I let him know this by melting against him and giving as good as I got.

My thong was damp when he pulled away, smirked at me, then said, "Hi."

"Hi," I replied on a giggle.

His smirk turned into a smile, then he took my hand and led me inside.

Penny was racing circles around me as soon as Ange had the door closed behind us. I handed Ange the bottle of wine I'd brought, then knelt to give his goldendoodle the hello she was owed.

"Hi, sweetheart. Oh, I know—I'm happy to see you, too," I cooed, giving her a generous rub.

"You're good with her. Why don't you have a dog of your own?" asked Ange.

I shrugged, scratching behind Penny's ears before I patted the top of her head and stood. "Just too busy, I guess. And I don't have a yard. I get that dog parks exist for a reason, but I've always thought a dog should have its own personal playground."

"Fair point." He nodded toward the kitchen. "You hungry? I'll throw the steaks on if you are."

I hesitated, my eyes doing a swift scan of what I could see of his place. I knew right away I couldn't wait. "Quick tour first?" I asked hopefully.

He chuckled then dipped his chin in a nod. "Sure."

Most of the house was constructed with an open floorplan. His living room was to the right of his front door, the small dining area to the left. On the other side was the kitchen. It was decently sized and had obviously been updated since the house had been built. He had three bedrooms and two bathrooms. Aside from the primary bedroom, he had a furnished guest room and an office that clearly doubled as Penny's playroom. He also had a screened-in back porch with a firepit and outdoor lounge furniture.

I didn't know what I expected, but I was impressed with how *cozy* it was.

We were back in the kitchen, he was preheating a skillet and un-corking the wine when I admitted, "Your place is, actually, really great."

"You sound surprised," he replied, amusement evident in his tone.

"I'm sorry," I said on a laugh. "I kind of am. It's so *homey*. And, no offense, but you don't strike me as someone who walks into a home and décor store and takes his time honing his aesthetic."

Grinning, he confirmed, "Definitely not."

"So, what? Is this what your place looked like in the city?"

"Oh, hell no." He poured me a glass of wine, then put our steaks on the stove. "The brownstone was—magazine worthy. And not in a good way. Every piece of furniture felt more like a status symbol than anything else."

"Okay, so how do you explain this?" I asked, sweeping my hand toward his open floorplan.

"Honestly?"

His green eyes were bright with humor.

I wasn't nervous anymore.

"Yes. The truth, sir," I demanded good naturedly.

"After I bought the house, I went to a few stores, found a sample of a room I liked, then ordered the whole thing."

"What?"

"Yup," he muttered on a laugh. "Rugs, pillows, lamps—someone had gone through the trouble of designing the look for the show room. It wasn't for nothing."

I looked over my shoulder at his living room, now seeing it in a whole new light. Teasingly, I said, "So what you're saying is, your house is not you at all. It's basically one big show room."

He flipped our steaks.

"Well, that's a little harsh. I did pick which collections I liked the best."

Conceding, I brought my wine to my lips and murmured, "Fair enough."

"If you're done judging me, maybe you could grab the salad out of the fridge. Steaks are just about done."

I chuckled, set aside my wine, and headed for the fridge.

The steaks were delicious.

The company even more so.

After we'd eaten and cleaned up in the kitchen, Ange poured each of us another glass of wine, then took me out to his back porch. He turned on the firepit, then sat sprawled in one corner of the couch. I sat on the other end, my feet now bare, my legs extended across the space between us. Penny sat next to me; her head propped on the cushion beside my thigh as I scratched absentmindedly at the curls on her neck.

My belly was full, and the wine had me feeling mellow. Ange reached over and grazed his fingers along the top of my foot, over my ankle, and back again. It felt nice. Then again, everything about that night felt nice. I watched him as he continued to touch me, totally at a loss as to how any woman in her right mind could have him and then let him go.

Feeling brazen, I broke our comfortable silence and inquired, "Could I ask you a personal question?"

His eyes found mine. "Shoot."

"You don't have to answer if you don't want to."

A half-smile played at his lips. "Can't know I don't want to if you don't ask, babe."

I hesitated for a second, then asked, "What happened with Stephanie? I mean, why didn't it work out for you two?"

He took a deep breath and blew out a slow sigh. His fingers stopped tracing my ankle. Instead, he rested his hand there before absentmindedly sweeping his thumb back and forth across my skin.

"We met when I was twenty-seven. I was starting to make some real money by then. I was young and dumb. Arrogant. I wined and dined her, thinking that was my best chance. She came from money. I didn't, but that didn't matter. I was finding success, and that counted for something.

"In the beginning, I think we really did love each other. After we got married, it wasn't like we changed—we just lost sight of what was important, I guess. Like I said, she grew up with money, so she was really great at spending hers and mine. I wanted her to be happy, so I did my part to make sure money was never an issue."

His thumb froze and his eyes lost focus.

I waited, not daring to interrupt.

"Twenty-twenty rolled around, the world shut down, and it was the first time I'd looked up from my work in years. I honestly don't know, if I hadn't been forced to slow down, how long it would have taken me to notice I wasn't happy. But I was. Unhappy, that is.

"I spent a lot of time out on my boat fishing that summer. It cleared my head. It brought me back to a peace I'd forgotten I'd once known." He paused and gave me his eyes. "Told you I had a falling out with my brother?"

I nodded in acknowledgment.

"We fought over Steph. He was convinced she'd married me for my money. I didn't see it. I was doing well, hoped to do even better, but she had a trust fund. I was adamant he didn't know what he was talking about. Like a total dick, I told him he was just jealous—jealous of the life I was making for myself. I'd gotten out of Michigan, and I wasn't going back. Anyway, come to find out, he was right.

"I told Stephanie I wasn't happy. I was tired of the grind. There was no fulfilment in it. Pat had approached me about the pub, I wanted to give it a go; I wanted to try something different; something simpler. She had absolutely no interest. She told me she didn't care whether or not I was happy—I had promised her a certain kind of life, and it was my responsibility as her husband to give it to her."

He paused once more, then shrugged and shook his head as if to clear it of the cobwebs of his past. "That's when I knew she didn't love me. I decided life's too short to spend it with someone who doesn't care about your happiness."

Ange was right. I'd told myself something similar after what happened with Dylan and Ava in an effort to get over the loss of two of the most significant relationships in my life. It worked. I eventually got over it. But the truth that neither of them cared about my happiness had stung, so I knew Ange had felt that hurt, too.

It made me a little sad. Much as there was nowhere else I wanted to be more than I wanted to be on his couch, by his fire, with the dog he didn't even have to fight for in the divorce—I was still sorry for the pain he'd had to endure for us to be in that moment.

I thought love should be simple. Easy. Pure. But it wasn't. It wasn't because humans were messy and complicated. Thus, *relationships* were often messy and complicated.

Ange was a risk.

He thought I was, too.

But there we were. Together. Doing whatever it was we were doing.

"Can I tell you something?" I murmured.

Ange lifted his brow, a smile curling the corners of his mouth, as if to express without words how ridiculous a question that was.

I smiled down at my wine glass, wondering if I'd had enough. Then I lifted my eyes and confessed, "I haven't told Libby. About...*this.*"

He held my gaze and shook his head as he said, "Haven't told Pat, either."

I'd figured as much. If Patrick knew, then Libby would know, and Libby would not be able to keep that in a bottle until I was ready to talk about it.

"I just..." I started and then I stopped.

I liked him, and it scared me.

I didn't say this aloud. Instead, I admitted, "To be honest, I haven't done this—" I waved a hand between us, "—with anyone in a long time. I haven't hidden it from her, or anyone, they all just know better than to ask at this point."

Ange didn't say anything in response. He looked at me, in that way he did, with those green eyes that saw beyond my exterior. I almost chickened out, but I liked him, so I had to know.

"I—I don't want to be one of those women who needs to define this, whatever we're doing. But, it's like I said, I don't do this very often. I've never really been part of the hook-up culture and I—"

"Channing?"

It wasn't until he said my name that I realized I'd dropped my gaze into my lap.

He didn't speak again until he had my eyes.

"You're not a hook-up, babe."

I hesitated then asked, "So—what would *you* say we're doing?"

"We're staying in the boat. You and me. For as long as it feels good."

I liked his answer. A lot. So much so, I set aside my wine and crawled over to him, until I was straddling his lap. He was quick to free his hands before sliding them up my thighs and underneath my dress.

That felt nice.

I leaned down to press a kiss against his lips, his hands went higher, pulling me closer, and that felt nicer. I said as much when I held on to the back of his neck, opened my mouth, and deepened the kiss. We took our time, the heat between us growing steadily as our hands roamed over one another. I sat on top of the bulge in his jeans for as long as I could stand it, then I ground down against it, longing for friction.

Ange groaned, then broke our kiss.

One of his hands was in my hair, and he gently pulled my head back as he sought out my eyes. "You on the pill?"

I nodded, and I swear his eyes got a shade darker.

"No more rubbers. Just you and me, yeah?"

My belly turned to mush, *and* my chest got warm and tingly.

"Okay," I managed on a breath.

He then reached into my thong and slid a single finger along my seam.

I shivered.

A lazy smile tugged at his lips.

"Right," he said, as if he'd just answered his own question. "Pull me out, Channing. Put me inside you."

I shivered again, bigger this time, and then I reached for the button at his jeans. As soon as I had his zipper down, he had his hips up. I pulled at his jeans and boxer briefs until they were out of my way, then I reached underneath my dress and shoved aside my thong before I took his length in my hand. I didn't mess around. I coated his tip, and then I took him inside of me.

His groan made my sex clench.

I knew he felt it when he muttered, "Fuck, yes."

That was all the encouragement I needed.

I rode him. In front of the fire. Out on his back porch.

It was heavenly.

Then he began to move with me, and I felt myself start to lose control.

"*Ange*," I moaned, dropping my forehead to rest against his. "Don't stop," I begged.

I bucked my hips hard, unable to help myself.

He thrusted his up harder, giving me what I needed.

"Honey—honey, I'm—"

"Wait, baby."

I whimpered in blissful agony, sealing my eyes closed tight.

"Please," I cried, throwing my head back.

He brought his lips to the base of my throat and semi-repeated, "Baby, *wait*."

Oh, god—he was killing me.

I didn't know if I was going to be able to make it.

I held tight to his shoulders.

Then he ran his tongue up my throat, nipped at my chin, and said, "Now."

I buried my face in his neck, let go, and my orgasm ripped through me so forcefully, I almost missed it as Ange came, too.

Then there we were, by the fire, out on his back porch, his softening length still inside of me and completely bare.

I worked to catch my breath, then lifted my head until I had his eyes.

"Fucking beautiful," he muttered unabashedly.

Yeah. I liked him. A lot.

"Doin' that again," he told me.

I smiled. "Okay."

"You head inside. Clean yourself up. I'll shut it down out here."

"Okay," I repeated, but I didn't move.

His arms were still around me, holding me close.

"No clothes next time."

This was my preference, too.

I said as much when I replied, "Okay, honey."

His arms constricted around me, he pressed a quick kiss to my lips, then he let me go.

"Up, baby. I'll meet you inside."

I nodded and obeyed.

A few minutes later, he met me inside.

We went to his bedroom.

We took off each other's clothes.

Then we did it again.

Twice.

CHAPTER *Thirteen*

Ange

"A NGE?" CHANNING CALLED, BARELY above a whisper.

He was in his bed. He felt certain Penny was, too, stretched out at his feet. He peeked open one eye and saw Channing was *not* in his bed. He closed his eye then forced himself to open both.

The sun was barely on its way up. Channing was covered in the dress she'd been wearing when she came over Sunday night, her hair contained in a loose braid that draped down one side of her chest. It was now Tuesday morning. It had come early. He frowned, wondering how Monday had come and gone so quickly.

He liked the dress—but he preferred her in his henley, hair everywhere, face bare, her walking around in no panties. He'd made his preference perfectly clear the day before. Repeatedly. In fact, as often as he could get it up. Halfway through the day, it had become a game. The only rooms in which they hadn't had sex were his office and the guest bath.

Next time, he thought.

Now, it was back to reality.

"What time is it?" he mumbled.

"Six. You don't have to get up, I just wanted to say goodbye."

"Shit. Okay." He ignored her comment and sat up, still stark naked, and threw the covers back. Penny didn't move as he stood and headed for his dresser.

"Ange, really—I know you don't have to be awake yet. I—"

"Babe," he started to say as he found a pair of jogger sweats and began to pull them on. "When have you ever known me to not walk you to your door?"

He looked back at her from over his shoulder. She'd rolled her lips between her teeth, silently indicating he had a point.

Cute as fuck.

A tired smile curled one corner of his mouth as he turned back to his dresser, opened another drawer, and plucked out a muscle shirt. He threw it on but didn't bother with shoes before he took Channing's hand and headed for the door.

By the time they'd made it to the driver's side of her 4Runner, he was fully awake.

"I had fun yesterday," she told him, delaying her departure as she stood beside her opened door. "I'm not going to make it through today without an obscene amount of coffee, but I'd say it was worth it."

"And then some," he agreed.

He slung his arm around her shoulders, pulling her toward him as he reached down for a kiss. She opened up for him right away, and he cradled the back of her neck with his free hand. Like always, she gave as good as she got. It made him want to pick her up, carry her back inside, and take her against the wall in his office. He got hard thinking about it, then slowed down their kiss in an act of self-preservation.

"You got to go. Before I don't let you."

She blinked up at him dreamily, then hummed, "Mmhmm."

He released her neck, then gently traced his fingertips down the side of her face, capturing a hair she'd missed and tucking it behind her ear.

"Cute as fuck," he whispered, staring into her sky-blue eyes.

She pressed up onto her tip toes in order to brush her lips against his.

"You'll call? We'll make plans?"

"Yeah, babe. I'll call. We'll make plans."

"'Kay. Bye for now."

Channing turned to climb into her SUV, and Ange let her go, closing the door behind her. She waved as she pulled away from the curb, and he watched her until he lost sight of her taillights. Hands in his pockets, he slowly made his way back toward the house, all the while mentally sorting through his schedule. As usual, he was working late for the next two nights.

There was no way he was waiting until Thursday to see her again.

Then he remembered her comment about needing coffee.

He was learning coffee was an essential part of Channing's mornings.

He was learning a lot of things about Channing.

Like how she wasn't shy about devouring a whole plate of food.

Or how she rambled when she discussed something she'd thought a lot about.

And how the best way to get her to open up about things that made her feel vulnerable was to give her an orgasm first. Maybe a couple, for good measure.

Yeah, he was learning a lot about Channing Davenport.

It would have been a lie to say he didn't like all of it a whole hell of a lot.

The truth of the matter was, he was already falling for her.

Ange stopped at his front door, his hand ready to twist the knob, his mind sorting through the possibilities.

He was up. He could hit the gym early. He didn't have to be to work until nine. He knew Channing would be in her office by eight. He'd spent the better part of the last day and a half with her, and already he was jonesing for more. He didn't think less of himself for it. There was no doubt in his mind she was worth the risk.

Now, going back to sleep seemed like a wasted opportunity.

Besides, he liked coffee, too.

It was a quarter after eight when Ange stepped off the elevator with a large black coffee in one hand, and a large vanilla latte in the other. He was hoping she'd go for the latte, but he was ready and willing to sacrifice the coffee if that was her preference.

He'd never stopped to pay attention to what other businesses occupied the remaining two-thirds of the ninth floor, but he noted how it was still pretty quiet as he approached the main entrance of Rusty Barn Wedding Co. He pushed the glass door open with his shoulder, then headed to the first office that branched off the hallway.

Channing was standing behind her desk, shuffling things around. By the looks of it, she hadn't been there long. Ange spotted the travel tumbler on the corner of her desk by her purse, no doubt filled with coffee. He wasn't deterred. Especially not after he got a good look at her.

Her thick, blonde hair hung straight down her back, half of it pulled up and away from her face. She wore a powder blue jumpsuit with short, ruffled sleeves and a cinched waist.

That was another thing he was learning about Channing. She was every bit as feminine as she could be, and he found that to be incredibly sexy.

Sensing his presence, she glanced up from her desk, said a quick hello, then dropped her gaze once more. He smirked at her when she did a double take, then froze, offering him a different greeting.

"Oh—wait. What—what are you doing here?"

He held up both coffees, making his way into the room. "Figured I was partly to blame for your need of an obscene amount of coffee, which meant I owed you one." He jerked his chin toward her tumbler and added, "I see you've already started."

"I bet whatever's in that cup is better than what I've got," she said, coming out from behind her desk to meet him halfway.

"Black coffee, vanilla latte," he said, lifting each cup respectively.

"Latte, please."

Channing reached for it without hesitation, then brought it straight to her lips. She held his eyes as she took a slow sip, then closed hers as she hummed her satisfaction. The sound went straight to his groin, reminding him of the way she whimpered softly during sex.

Ange had his hand in her hair and her body pressed to his a second later.

She gasped, her eyes flying open as she reached up and gripped his forearm. Then she giggled as he brought his lips to meet hers. Her giggle dissolved into another hum as her eyelids fell closed once more. When he sought entrance into her mouth with his tongue, she sighed and melted against him. Like always, she gave as good as she got. He didn't linger long, only needing a taste. When he broke their kiss, Channing blinked her eyes open slowly, then gave him a lazy smile.

Yeah. He was definitely falling.

"*Dios mio,* are you *kidding* me right now?!"

Ange felt it when Channing jolted against him, but she didn't pull away as they both looked toward her office door. Libby was standing there, mouth agape, her big brown eyes round in awe. She balled her hands into fists, lifted them toward her chest, then squealed, "This is *amazing!*"

That's when Ange felt Channing laugh. He gave the back of her neck a gentle squeeze as Libby continued.

"Does Patrick know? Wait, of course he doesn't know. If he knew, I'd know—and I definitely didn't know! *Dios mio*—I must know *everything.*"

Ange felt it when Channing moved to look up at him, and he shifted his gaze to meet hers. The cat was out of the bag, but he could tell she didn't mind.

"I'll let you handle this."

"Good idea," she murmured. "Thanks for the coffee."

"You're welcome." He pressed a kiss against her temple where he mumbled, "Later, babe," then let her go.

On his way out of her office, he jerked his chin at Libby in a silent farewell. The last thing he heard before he was out of earshot was, "Later, *babe?* You're *babe?* Channing Davenport, you have *seriously* been holding out on me. Spill it!"

Three hours later, Ange was behind the bar when Patrick waltzed into the pub, a shit-eating-grin spread wide across his face.

"Well, well, well—seems the hermit just needed a pretty blonde to finally coax him out of his shell."

Ange frowned playfully and retorted, "I'm not a hermit."

Patrick laughed as he continued toward the bar. "You do realize Libby is already planning your nuptials, right?"

Ange rolled his eyes. "Do I really need to remind you your woman does weddings for a living? Not to mention, she's knee deep in planning *your* wedding. Her head is in the clouds, my man. Channing and I are good with our feet on the ground."

"For real, though..." Patrick paused, leaning against the opposite side of the counter as he stared at Ange, eyebrows raised to denote his seriousness. "Really happy for you, man. It's about damn time."

"Yeah. It is," Ange agreed.

Pat knew better than anyone else how long it had been since he'd attempted anything resembling serious. What Pat didn't know—and what Ange wouldn't share—was that it had been two weeks since the first time he'd laid eyes on Channing; two weeks, and the thought of that woman wearing his henleys for the rest of their days?

It wasn't the worst idea he'd ever heard.

CHAPTER
Fourteen

Channing

Two Weeks Later

I T WAS FRIDAY MORNING. I was running around, getting ready for work, hoping I wouldn't be late. Ange was in my bed, still naked under the sheets. Even though he'd already taken me to great heights before I got in the shower, he was still a very tempting distraction—especially since I knew I wouldn't have him again for the next two days.

Though, naked and tempting as he was, I had places to be that day.

On that list of places was Group Therapy.

My sister had called demanding an hour.

I was pulling up the zipper at the side of my high-waisted, wide leg pants when I told Ange, "You don't know my sister yet, but I should warn you—the moment she finds out about us, she's going to want to meet you as soon as humanly possible."

He shrugged, like it didn't bother him in the slightest, then confirmed, "I think I can handle that."

We'd been in the boat for three weeks.

In that short span of time, we'd begun to establish a sort of routine.

If my Sundays were free, I'd catch up on what I needed to at home while Ange went fishing, and then we met up for dinner.

We spent our Mondays off together.

Thursday was our unofficial date night.

Depending on what I had going on, I'd spend Friday or Saturday night at the pub, listening to live music, sharing a drink with Russ, and eyeing the handsome man behind the bar.

Then we'd start the cycle all over again on Sunday.

I used to fall back on the excuse that I didn't have time to date. I'd convinced myself this was true—and in some ways, I made it a self-fulfilling prophecy.

But Ange was changing all that.

When he so easily accepted the idea of meeting my sister and her family, it made me want to kiss him. I hesitated for only as long as it took for me to get lost in those green eyes, and then I crawled across the bed and stole what I wanted.

He gave it right back, and then some.

His hand cupped my breast through my blouse, and I groaned pathetically, my lips still grazing his as I insisted, "Don't start."

"I didn't," he teased on a chuckle. "That was all you, babe."

I narrowed my eyes at him, annoyed he was right, then kissed him once more before crawling off the bed. I went to the jewelry tree on my dresser and was picking out my earrings when I heard him get up. Glancing over my shoulder, I got a peek at his backside before he pulled on his underwear.

"Remind me what day you have a wedding. Is it Saturday or Sunday?"

"Oh, honey," I began to say, turning to face him as I blindly inserted one of my studs into my ear. "I'll be MIA all weekend. I have an evening wedding on Saturday and an afternoon wedding on Sunday. I'm going to be a full-on zombie come Monday; but then I don't have a wedding for the next two weekends, so it's kind of a wash."

He nodded, buttoning his jeans before he asked, "Okay. Well, what are the chances you want to be a zombie on my boat Monday?"

I straightened, my arms falling to my sides as I gaped at him. This was the first time he was inviting me out on his bass fishing boat. He talked about it enough for me to know it was an important part of him. I knew he'd built it himself. He'd showed it to me once, but I'd yet to get on it.

I liked the idea of spending Monday on the lake with a handsome, rugged man and his pup. Honestly, I couldn't think of a better more relaxing way to end my crazy weekend ahead.

Before I could tell him as much, he grinned, and my belly turned to mush.

"Alright—zombies like to fish. Noted."

I smiled self-consciously, suddenly aware he'd read my mind via my face.

He did that a lot.

I didn't hate it.

He plucked his tee off the floor, pulling it over his head as he told me, "You can crash at my place Sunday night. We'll head out Monday morning."

I finally found my words and murmured, "Okay, honey."

We finished getting ready. Me for work, him for home—where he'd change, hit the gym, return home, shower, change again, and then head for the pub.

It had been three weeks.

We already had a routine.

And I didn't fight it.

Even though I was on time for my lunch date with Blake, she beat me to the restaurant. This time, it was just her and me. Sylvie was at school and Camille was spending the day with Derek's mom, which gave Blake the opportunity to get a bunch of errands done.

And to have lunch with me, of course.

Both of us were hungry enough to order our own entrees. While we waited, we went through our usual catch-up list. We talked about work, the girls, the last time either of us spoke to our parents and what they'd been up to. Derek's birthday was coming up. He was turning thirty-nine, and Blake wanted to make a big deal of it.

"He thinks it's silly, but I don't care. Everyone makes a big deal about forty. And I get it, you know? It's a new decade. But you gotta live it up the last year of your thirties. Besides, you know how the girls love birthdays."

"I do," I said, pushing around the last little bits of my lunch with my fork. "Let me know how I can help."

"I definitely will."

I'd been waiting for the right moment to tell her about Ange. We never talked about my dating life, for obvious reasons, and I was a little apprehensive. I really liked Ange, but I didn't want her to blow it out of proportion. Libby had practically gone insane, but she was a bride and easily excited. Plus, she only knew the post-Dylan version of me.

I couldn't blame her for freaking out over something she'd never seen before.

She loved me. She wanted me to be happy. And I loved her for that.

"Okay—something's on your mind. Spit it out," demanded Blake.

I coughed out a nervous laugh and immediately dropped my fork.

She impatiently raised her eyebrows at me. "Channing?"

"I started seeing someone."

Her eyebrows lifted higher in amazement. "Like...a *therapist?*"

"No!" I laughed, tossing my cloth napkin at her. "Like a *man.*"

I watched as her whole face fell, as if her jaw—which hung wide open—was in control of all the muscles in her face. "Shut. Up. Are you messing with me?"

I rolled my eyes. "Like I would kid about such a thing."

Blake clapped her hands over her cheeks. "Sweetie, are you serious?"

I could hear the tears in her voice, and I was quick to shake my head at her.

"Don't you dare cry."

"Okay. Okay, I won't. But, oh my god!" She dropped her hands and blew out a breath. After she cleared her throat, she somewhat-calmly asked, "What's his name? Where'd you meet him?"

"His name is Ange. He's Libby's fiancé's best friend. They co-own The Four Horsemen."

"Wow. That's great," she breathed. "Ange—that's an interesting name."

"It's short for Michelangelo."

"Michelangelo? Really?" she asked, not hiding the depth of her intrigue in the slightest.

I fought my amusement, certain my face looked almost exactly like hers when he'd told me the same thing.

"Yeah. His mom—she was pretty creative about naming her children."

"Okay," she laughed. "Well, how long have you two been—?"

"Just three weeks," I interrupted, hoping to get through all her questions in short order. "But I like him. A lot." I went on to confess, "If I think about it too much, it scares the shit out of me but there you have it."

"Well, first of all, don't overthink it. Enjoy it."

"I'm doing my best."

"So, tell me more. What does he look like? What does he do for fun? Is he from here?"

We discussed Ange for a few more minutes. I didn't give her *all* the details, but enough to convince her Ange was a good guy. Not surprisingly, he was pretty easy to talk about. There was still plenty about him I was looking forward to learning, but what I did know was good fodder for girl talk.

When I'd shared all I was going to over lunch, she reached for my hand, and I let her have it. "I'm so fucking proud of you."

I shook my head, embarrassed by her response.

She squeezed my fingers.

"I mean it, Chan."

"I know."

"Alright, so, when do I get to meet him?" She let go of my hand and reached for her phone. I didn't get a chance to respond before she said, "Pretty sure we don't have anything going on Sunday."

I couldn't help but laugh. "I have a wedding Sunday."

"Oh, okay. Let me see..." She quickly scrolled through her phone then countered, "How about Monday? Does he work nights or—"

"He works a lot of nights, but not Mondays. I'll check with him and get back to you."

Blake looked at me like I was being unreasonable. "Why don't you check with him now?"

"I—well—because I'm sitting here with you?" I stammered.

"Exactly. Perfect timing. If I know you're both coming to dinner Monday, when I stop at the grocery store this afternoon, I'll know to pick up what I need. Can't you call him?"

I scrunched my face at her. "You're not going to let this go, are you?"

She batted her eyelashes at me. "Absolutely not."

"Figured as much," I muttered, reaching for my own phone.

I pulled up Ange's contact info, initiated a call, and pressed the device to my ear.

He answered on the third ring.

"Hey, babe."

"Hi, sorry to bug you at work."

"Not a problem. What's up?"

I caught my sister's eyes across the table as I told him, "We have been invited to my sister's house for dinner on Monday night. Of course, you'd meet the whole gang. My brother-in-law and my nieces would be there, too. I just wanted to check with you before I confirmed."

"Hmmm," he hummed contemplatively. "I don't know—is it safe for a zombie to have dinner with two little girls?"

I burst out laughing.

My sister *beamed*.

Ange chuckled softly on the other end of the line.

When I'd recovered myself, I assured him, "As a matter of fact, they have these special regenerative powers that always seem to bring me back to life."

"Sounds like it's imperative we be there."

"Okay," I said, still smiling. "I'll let Blake know."

"Channing?" he called, his tone more serious than before.

"Yes?"

"I love your laugh, too."

My breath caught, having been totally unprepared for that comment.

He wasn't even in eyesight, and my chest grew warm and tingly.

Mercifully, he didn't wait for me to respond before he asked, "Did you need anything else?"

"No, honey. That's all," I managed to murmur.

"Alright. I got to go."

"'Kay. Bye for now."

"Bye for now, babe."

I pulled the phone away from my ear and stared at it for a second.

Blake recaptured my attention when she stated, "Well, I know what we're having for dinner Monday night. That man is getting spaghetti and meatballs with my homemade pasta."

I jerked at this announcement. "What? Blake, no. You don't have to do all that."

My sister's spaghetti and meatballs were no small task. She let the sauce simmer all day, cooking the meatballs in the sauce so they were tender and melt-in-your-mouth-delicious. While I loved her fresh pasta, such an effort for an introduction was too much.

She wholeheartedly disagreed.

"Channing—I get that you're not me, you're you, which means you didn't see what I just saw. But any man who can make my sister laugh like that and then say something I know must have been sweet, because your face went softer than I've seen it since the first time you held Camille in your arms—well—that man deserves my homemade spaghetti and meatballs."

I didn't have it in me to argue.

Monday night, Ange was going to meet my family.

I'd make sure he came hungry.

Blake never served fresh pasta without homemade bread, too.

CHAPTER
Fifteen

Ange

H E WAITED UNTIL THE last possible moment to wake her.

The boat was loaded and stocked.

The trailer was hitched.

Penny had been fed.

The coffee was made.

It was almost eight, and he was itching to get out on the water.

"Babe," he whispered, kissing the spot just beside her ear. "Babe, it's time to get up."

She frowned, then groaned before turning to bury her face in the pillow.

"Made coffee," he coaxed.

She sighed, blindly reaching out her hand in a wordless demand.

Ange chuckled. "I only share my coffee with zombies who are fully dressed."

Channing whined, then pushed herself upright.

She was still frowning.

Ange was still smiling.

He watched her take in his expression, then continued to watch as hers softened. She then kissed him, crawled out of bed, grabbed her weekend bag, and closed herself into his bathroom. Twenty minutes later, she came out in a pair of jeans that sculpted her great legs, a graphic tee that read *Raised on 90's Country*, and a plaid, fleece button-up she wore open. She had on a baseball cap, her hair pulled back into a ponytail, and her feet were covered in a pair of black Hunter boots.

Seeing her like that did something to him.

He didn't know what, but it hit deep.

"Now can I have coffee?" she asked on a yawn.

They took their coffees to go.

Lady Bird Lake was only ten minutes from Ange's house. Once they'd arrived at the familiar reservoir, it didn't take long for him to get them out onto the water. The cockpit in his boat had two seats, the ice chest between them doubling as a third. As he steered them further out onto the lake, Penny sat between them.

Channing, still waking up, hardly spoke. Ange didn't mind. Every time he glanced over at her, she had one hand buried in Penny's curls, coffee in her other, her face turned away as she took in the passing view. She seemed relaxed, and that did something to him, too.

The quickest way to Ange's heart was by his boat. Any doubts he harbored about whether or not he was falling in love with Channing were eradicated the moment she settled in next to him. He'd invited her along because he liked her company. When he was out on the water the previous weekend, he'd wondered what it would be like to have her come with him. But even the look on her face when he'd asked her to join him a couple days ago paled in comparison to what it felt like to look over and see his woman simply enjoying the ride.

And there it was.

She was his.

She'd carved herself a place in his heart only she could fit.

It should have scared him—how hard he was falling. How fast.

It didn't.

Knowing she'd made room for herself in his heart, he hoped he was doing the same in hers.

He wanted in there. All the way in.

He knew he'd wanted her since the night she'd told him she'd been left at the altar. It had been a month. He'd had her in a variety of ways, all of them noteworthy. He was still at a loss as to why anyone would forsake her for someone else. It damn near blew his mind.

When they'd arrived at a decent spot, Ange climbed out of the cockpit and started unloading his gear from its respective storage compartments. He felt Channing's eyes on him and looked her way. She smiled, took a sip of coffee, then sighed contentedly as she looked out over the view of downtown Austin's skyline.

She really was something else.

He was just getting ready to throw his first cast when she stood, put her hands on her hips, tilted her head to the side and asked, "So, are you going to teach me how to catch some bass, or what?"

Fuck.

He wanted in there. All the way in.

Channing

WE STAYED OUT ON the boat, catching and releasing, for hours.

It was everything I wanted it to be.

I even caught a *two-pound* largemouth bass.

Of course, *I caught* really meant I had the pole in my hand when it bit; then Ange had his body curled around my back, his hands covering mine until we reeled in my two-pounder. It was awesome. I even got a picture with the big guy before we let him go.

When we got hungry, we made our way back to shore, Ange hitched his boat to the back of his truck, and we headed to his place for lunch.

To my delight, when our bellies were full, we laid down for a nap.

To my greater delight, when I woke up, Ange made me come. Twice.

Now, we were getting ready to go to my sister's house.

I was having a great day.

While Ange was in the shower, I got dressed in his guest bathroom. Even though it was just dinner at Blake's, it was not an insignificant evening, and I put in what I deemed was the appropriate amount of effort. I'd styled my hair in a loose French braid, leaving a couple strands out to shape my face. I had on a light layer of makeup and a spritz of perfume. I swapped out the jeans I'd worn on the boat for my faded, high-waisted pair, and I coupled it with my black, crocheted, lace top with a generously cut V-neck and long sleeves. Since it was slightly see-through and wasn't lined, I had on a matching black bra underneath. To pull the whole outfit together, I planned on wearing a pair of cute, wedge sandals.

I was on my way to grab them when Ange walked out of his bedroom.

I froze at the sight of him.

Damn, but he was handsome.

Not only that, he'd also put in what he deemed was the appropriate amount of effort for an evening at my sister's.

And what he deemed appropriate made my belly turn to mush.

He was wearing a khaki button-up—which he'd seen fit to button up *and* tuck into his dark washed jeans. Like most of his shirts, this one accentuated his broad shoulders and impressive biceps. Tucked in, it also reminded me of his tapered waist and all the awesome that I knew existed underneath his clothes. He had on a great belt, and his whole outfit was pulled together with a pair of cowboy boots. He was in the middle of rolling the cuffs of his sleeves up over his forearms when he saw me.

Our eyes caught, and my chest grew warm and tingly.

As we stared at one another, I tried to tell him without telling him that he looked *perfect*.

I knew I'd done just that when he smirked at me and muttered, "Channing? I don't know how long it took you to do your hair, but if you don't stop looking at me like that, we'll be late—'cause you'll have to do it all over again."

I pulled my bottom lip between my teeth as I fought a smile.

His eyes dropped to catch a glimpse, then he shook his head at me. "Not kidding, babe."

I hummed a laugh, continued down the hallway and murmured, "I need to put my shoes on and then I'll be ready."

Ange, Penny, and I were in his truck ten minutes later.

I'd convinced Blake to let Penny tag along. Sylvie and Camille were going to *love* her.

The Wilsons lived in Westover Hills, twenty minutes outside of the city. We were pulling into their driveway a couple minutes after six-thirty. My nieces, who had obviously been anticipating us, were out the front door and bouncing around on the porch before I could even so much as reach for my door handle.

"Hi, Aunt Channing!" they cried in a chorus as I rounded the front of the truck.

"Hi, girlies," I called in response. "Hey, guess what?"

Cami twirled as she said, "Mommy says you have a boyfriend. Is that your boyfriend?"

A laugh bubbled out of me, and I skirted the question as I said, "That, in fact, is not the surprise."

No sooner had I said it than Ange had the back door of his Tundra open, allowing Penny to jump out. Sylvie gasped then dashed across the lawn in her bare feet. Penny met her halfway, excitedly sniffing her out.

She held open her hands for easy access and asked Ange, "Can I pet it?"

"Of course," he said. "Her name's Penny."

Sylvie buried both hands in Penny's fluff, and I swear I watched her fall in love.

Cami rushed to join her sister, stopping short the instant Penny caught sight of her. She took a step back, eyeing Penny cautiously. "Does she bite?"

"Nah. She's real gentle," Ange assured her.

"Look, her tail is wagging!" giggled Sylvie. "See, she likes it."

As if Penny was on a mission to win both girls' trust, she plopped down and rolled onto her back, offering them her belly. That did it. She had four little hands loving on her when Derek came through the front door.

He was tall dark and handsome in his own right.

What could I say? My sister and I knew how to pick 'em.

Even though he'd graduated almost two decades ago, he was tall enough people still asked if he played college ball. His classic response was, *You think I would have won Blake otherwise?*

He so totally would have won my sister over had he not been a college athlete.

But, safe to say, it didn't hurt.

"Chan, no pressure—but if this doesn't work out between you two, you're gonna have to steal his dog. You do realize that, don't you?" he asked, making his way toward us. "I mean..." He glanced at his daughters then raised an eyebrow at me. "You brought this on yourself."

I grinned at my brother-in-law even as I shook my head at him.

"*You* could always get a dog."

"Never gonna happen," he stated, draping an arm around my shoulders as he pulled me into his side. He stuck out his free hand toward Ange and greeted, "Hi. I'm Derek."

"Ange. Nice to meet you," he said, shaking hands.

Derek grinned. "When you walk into that house and smell what's comin' out of my wife's kitchen, on a Monday night of all nights, you'll know I mean it when I say—*the feeling's mutual.*"

I winced up at him. "Did she go overboard?"

He looked me right in the eye and asked, "You ever bring a man to this house to sit at my table before?"

I blew out a sigh, patted his chest, and extract myself from under his arm.

"She went overboard. We should probably get inside."

I took Ange by the hand. He called Penny to heel. Derek called the girls, and we all went inside.

Blake wasn't just in the kitchen.

She was in the kitchen *wearing an apron.*

This meant one thing.

She hadn't gone overboard.

She'd sunk the whole damn ship.

"Oh, hi," she said, turning away from the stove as she heard us approaching.

"Mommy, Aunt Channing is here!" announced Camille, racing toward the kitchen.

Sylvie, right on her heels, added, "Aunt Channing's boyfriend has a dog. Her name is Penny. She's *so* soft! Can we get a dog?"

"Hey," called Derek. "Did you actually say hi to your Aunt Channing and meet her friend? Or is it just the dog you've met?"

Both girls did an about-face and came charging toward me. Cami collided with my left leg, and Sylvie pressed up against my right hip as her little arms wound around my waist. I let go of Ange in order to return their affection.

"Don't worry. I get it," I assured them. "Penny is *way* cool."

Blake took off her apron as she made her way toward us, her hazel eyes bright as they darted between Ange and me. "Well, I would certainly like to meet Aunt Channing's friend."

This got her a smirk.

I knew she spotted it when her eyes didn't come back to me but stayed glued on Ange.

I smiled up at the handsome, bearded man at my side—whose presence in the Wilson household was starting to feel *surreal*—and began introductions.

"This is my older sister Blake, and my nieces Camille and Sylvie. Everyone, this is Ange."

"I can't tell you how excited we are that you're here. It's so very lovely to meet you," Blake practically gushed.

Ange's smirk morphed into a smile. It wasn't for me, but I felt the effects of it just the same.

"I appreciate the invite. It smells great in here."

Blake's expression turned into a guilty one. "I hope you're hungry. I may have gotten a little carried away with the food."

Sylvie peered around me as she said, "Mr. Ange, mommy made cannoli and monster cookies because she said she didn't know if you liked cannoli, but everybody likes monster cookies. But do you like cannoli?"

I bugged my eyes out at my sister as Ange replied on a chuckle, "I do like cannoli."

Uninterested in prolonging the pleasantries, Cami asked, "Is it time to eat soon? I'm hungry."

"Yup, sure is. Why don't you and your sister go wash up?"

Both girls released me as they did as their mother suggested, hurrying toward the powder room.

Derek played his part and asked, "Got a couple bottles of red on standby. Anyone interested in a glass?"

We all expressed our interest, and Derek headed toward the butler's pantry that doubled as their wet bar just off the kitchen. Ange pressed a kiss against my temple, where he told me on a mumble he was going to go lend a hand, then followed after my brother-in-law. As soon as they were both somewhat out of earshot, Blake was in my space.

She took hold of my arms, made sure she had my eyes, then whispered, "*Oh-my-god!*"

I couldn't help but giggle. She didn't have to say more. But it was Blake, so she kept going.

"You told me he was good looking, but, sweetie, *that man* should have his own calendar."

My giggle was on its way to a laugh, and she kept going.

"I adore my husband, you know this. He's the finest man I've ever met. But those eyes paired with that smile on *your* man..." Her own eyes got wide, and she shook her head, as if to express there were no words in the English language to capture the essence of Ange's smile.

I glanced toward the butler's pantry. Before I could look away, I caught green as Ange looked back at me from over his shoulder.

He winked. I grinned.

On a happy sigh, I tore my gaze away from his and said to Blake on a whisper, "I know what you mean."

It wasn't long before we were all seated for the *feast* my sister had prepared.

There was fresh salad. Focaccia she'd made from scratch. Homemade pasta with spaghetti and meatballs she'd been slow cooking all day. Plus, the cannoli.

I didn't even know my sister made cannoli.

It was too much.

There was no way I could skip the treadmill the next day.

But it was all delicious.

At eight o'clock, Derek took the girls to get ready for bed. They obeyed begrudgingly. By the time they were tucked in, Blake and I had her kitchen mostly in order. She then insisted Ange and I should stay for another glass of wine. We agreed. Derek poured another round. Then we all settled in their living room; Ange and I on one couch, Derek and Blake on another, Penny stretched out in front of the fireplace.

Ange did not shy away from tucking me under his arm, as if we'd gone long enough without physical contact. I felt the same, so he had no objections from me. Not to mention, my belly was full, the wine was smooth, and our company was great, which meant I was comfy and melting into his side only made all of that better.

The whole night, Ange seemed so at ease. For a variety of reasons, I shouldn't have been surprised. First, because he spent a lot of time talking with people on a regular basis. Second, because my sister and her husband were a couple of the warmest, most welcoming people I knew. They owned a *cookie* business, for crying out loud.

Nonetheless, as we sat for a while, allowing our food to digest, talking about nothing and everything, I felt a bit in awe of the man under whose arm I was nestled. This, in fact, may have mostly been because somehow, he'd steered us here. A month ago, I wouldn't have believed it.

No. More than that.

A month ago, I wouldn't have agreed to any of this at all.

But he'd convinced me to get in the boat. I knew that night, on my sister's couch, he'd steered us there. It hadn't been his idea, but he'd gotten me to a place where I felt like I could trust him with some of the most important pieces of me. My family at the top of that list. And *that*—that was downright unbelievable.

Moreover, it meant a whole lot.

I looked up at him, having lost track of the conversation, and made up my mind that when I had him alone, he was going to get one hell of a *thank you*—for being so great, and for sharing that greatness with the people I loved most in the world.

"Ange?"

My sister called his name, and I could tell by the tone of her voice she'd broken the stride of their conversation. This was confirmed when everyone looked her way.

She focused all her attention on Ange.

"I'm sure you are not ignorant of the fact that it's been *years* since my sister has let a man into her life. And I can't ever remember her looking at anyone the way she looks at you. And I know you're new, and I know we just met, but I've got to say—I sure hope you two go the distance. But even if you don't, I will be forever grateful that it was you who reminded that incredible woman next to you that she deserves the love of a good man. I needed you to know that. I needed you to hear it from me. Now, if I don't get up and go grab us a plate of cookies, I might start crying, and I know Channing would not take too kindly to that, so I'll be right back."

I watched her leave, then I looked to Derek. He was grinning, like he thought his wife was adorable and hilarious in equal measure. He set his glass down then excused himself to go help with the cookies not one of us had room in our stomachs to eat.

Then I looked at Ange.

He was already looking at me.

His green eyes caught mine and held on with a gaze somehow both tender and intense. Then he smiled, the skin at the corner of his eyes crinkled, my belly turned to mush, and I heard him promise me without telling me that when he got me alone, I was going to feel whatever he just felt.

That's when I knew.

What my sister said—and it was a whole lot—it didn't freak him out.

He liked it. A whole lot.

I also knew, we were going to need to leave.

Soon.

His front door closed, and I was in Ange's arms.

I didn't know if I'd jumped there or if he'd yanked me there—I just knew I was desperate for his mouth against mine, and I had it.

He kissed me hard.

I kissed him deep.

He reached down to palm my backside.

I reached up to bury my fingers in his hair.

He leaned into me. I leaned back, molding myself to the shape of him.

He gipped me tight around the waist, then muttered between kisses, "Up, babe."

I leapt. He hoisted.

I was around his hips, and we were on the move.

When we crossed the threshold of his room, he flicked on the lights, carried me to the bed, then gently laid me on top of it.

"Shoes."

He didn't need to say more. He sat on the edge of the bed and worked his way out of his boots. Sitting up next to him, I freed my feet of my wedge sandals.

I finished first, which meant I was ready to pounce at my first opportunity. I straddled his lap, immediately tugging the hem of his shirt from his jeans. He undid four buttons, then reached over the back of his head and yanked. He'd barely rid his arms of the garment and I was pressing in on him, pushing him on his back.

He let me have this.

I kissed his lips, his beard, his neck—my hands roaming over his chest and shoulders as I went. I had every intention of tasting my way down the length of his body, but he interrupted me.

Before I could descend any further, he curled up, taking me with him. Then it was my shirt that was getting tugged. It went up and over my head. My bra was discarded next. I didn't have a chance to get the upper hand again as he had me on my back on my next breath.

He kissed his way across my collar bone, then between my breasts. He teased me by swirling his tongue around each of my nipples. My ache for more was distracting. I was on the verge of surrender when he pulled away in order to peel off my jeans, and I rediscovered my focus.

Ange was on his feet as he dropped my denim to the floor, and I took advantage. I sat up and reached for his belt. I made quick work of the button and zipper of his jeans, then I shoved my hands into his boxer briefs, my palms flat against his backside as I pushed his clothing out of my way. He hadn't allowed me to get to my destination the way I wanted—but I took my chance as soon as I had it.

With one hand at the base of his hardening length, the other at his hip, I took him into my mouth. I'd yet to take him this way. After the night we'd had, I knew it was time.

He groaned as I maneuvered down onto my knees, and I had him right where I wanted him.

I felt a victory in my future.

I sucked. I licked. I stroked.

I worked him until he was so hard, I knew he'd come at any moment.

Then I lost him.

His hand slid over my hair before he took hold of my braid and gently but firmly pulled me away from him. My head jerked up so I could catch his eyes. His green irises were blazing, and it was unbearably sexy.

"I don't come in your mouth. *Ever*," he informed me, his voice gravely and low, his tone hinting at the little control he had left in his grasp.

I jolted in reaction to his declaration. He felt it and proceeded to explain.

"I don't come on my gut. I don't come on your tits. I don't come in your mouth. I come in one place, and that is between your legs after I've made you come or while you're strangling my dick so tight I can't hold back. Prefer the latter, but those are the rules, babe. So, as much as I enjoyed what you were doing—*you're done*."

There was a lot there, all of it hot.

I quickly thought back over the last several weeks. We'd had our fair share of sex. Okay, maybe more than our fair share, but that was beside the point. The point was, he never came first. Not ever. And if he had his way, I came at least twice.

I was so busy considering the merits of his rules, he caught me off guard when I suddenly felt his hands underneath my arms, hoisting me up and back onto the bed. I didn't have a chance to respond to anything he'd said before my panties were gone and *he* was on *his* knees.

He hesitated at my center, so close I could feel his breaths against my slick skin. I knew he was waiting for me to give him my eyes when I looked down at him and he told me, "You don't come in my mouth, either."

I had just enough time to realize he was right before his mouth was on me, and I lost track of anything that wasn't the feel of his tongue.

Now it was *him* who had *me* right where he wanted me.

I was powerless against him, and my surrender was bliss.

This time, when he brought me to the brink and pulled away, I didn't gasp my disappointment. Instead, I held out my hand, reaching for him as I breathlessly called, "Honey…"

Then he was there, hovering over me.

Except, rather than immediately uniting our bodies, he traced his nose down the length of mine before he pressed the softest kiss against my lips. When I felt him position himself at my entrance, he held my eyes for a long moment before he buried himself slowly—*so slowly*—until I had all of him.

That's when I felt it.

For one excruciatingly beautiful moment, I felt what Ange felt in my sister's living room.

My chest ached as I tried to keep my emotions in check.

I reached up to take hold of either side of his face. I hooked my legs around the backs of his, wanting to feel him *everywhere*. I felt desperate with a desire so pure and unadulterated, I thought it might split me wide open.

Then Ange pulled out of me, almost as slowly as he'd entered, his eyes still locked with mine. When he came back, he jerked his hips hard, paused, then did it all over again.

That's when I understood.

Oh, god, I understood.

I moaned on his next thrust, wrapping my arms around his shoulders, needing something substantial to hold onto.

Out slow.

In hard.

Out slow.

In hard.

Over and over.

He didn't hurry.

He didn't break rhythm.

I had his eyes until he brought his mouth to mine, kissing me deep and wet.

My god, he was ruining me.

The warmth he stoked inside of me grew gradually. After a while, it got so intense, I knew when I came, it was going to be ecstasy.

And if I was going to experience ecstasy, I wanted Ange to experience it with me.

"Ange, honey," I murmured against his lips, my hands traveling up the back of his neck.

"You there?"

"Yeah," I whimpered.

"Let go, baby," he breathed, jerking his hips.

I shook my head and whispered, "*Together*."

He touched his forehead to mine, then reached behind his head for one of my hands. I let him have it, and he held it against the bed beside my head, lacing his fingers with mine. He repeated the act with my opposite hand, then propped himself up, allowing him the leverage he needed.

Ange rolled his hips, his thrusts picking up speed.

My knees fell open as my grip around his hands got tighter.

I moaned, my orgasm coming closer to the surface.

He bucked his hips harder, and it felt *incredible.*

"Ange," I breathed, my back arching off the bed.

"Hold on, baby."

I tightened my grip, sealing my eyes closed as I held on the best I could.

He took me harder. Faster.

I wanted us to come together, but I was on the verge of losing it.

"Oh, god—*honey,*" I cried, my body tensing in preparation for a release of which I didn't know if I could ever be truly prepared.

"Channing, look at me."

"I—I can't."

My body was trembling. If I looked at him, I'd be a goner.

"Look at me, baby—look at me, and let go."

Yes. I wanted—no, *needed* that.

I opened my eyes and let go.

I came so hard I couldn't stop the sob that spilled past my lips.

Ange rode me through my orgasm, his rhythm totally lost.

Wave after wave of pleasure washed over me while I watched him unravel above me.

I'd assumed wrong.

This wasn't ecstasy.

It was *heaven.*

Ange stilled inside of me, but we both felt it as my core continued to clench and release around him, my orgasm tapering off as slowly as it grew. I was so focused on trying to catch my breath, I didn't even notice my tears until Ange let go of one of my hands in order to dry under my eyes.

He then held the side of my face and stared down at me.

I stared back.

Part of me understood what we'd shared should have scared the crap out of me—but I was already feeling too much. I didn't have the capacity to feel scared.

Besides, I wasn't done feeling *him*.

As if he'd read my mind, he thrust his hips one last time, and a sigh escaped from my mouth.

He traced a thumb across my cheek.

"Yeah," he murmured.

Somehow, I knew exactly what he meant.

This was why, on my next breath, I cupped my hand around the back of his head, lifted mine, and kissed him long and hard.

Later, after I cleaned myself up and Ange let Penny out one last time, we crawled between his sheets and snuggled close. It was getting late. We both had work the next day, and I knew we should get some sleep—but I wasn't ready to leave the day behind. I wanted to squeeze everything I could out of it.

I suspected, by the way Ange traced his fingertips back and forth across the thigh I had hitched over his, he felt the same way.

"I like Blake," he told me, breaking our comfortable silence. "Derek and the girls, they're great, too—but Blake, she loves you. A lot."

"Yeah, she does. She's known me my entire life. She's been looking out for me just as long."

He hummed his acknowledgement, and I wondered where his head was. I wondered if seeing Blake and I together made him think of Nico and their estranged relationship. I knew it wasn't any of my business, but I was too curious not to ask.

"Have you—have you tried reaching out to Nico since your falling out?"

His fingers stopped their journey across my leg for a moment. They started up again after he answered, "No."

I hesitated, then decided to press.

"Why not?"

"Guess I don't know what I'd say."

Ange had turned the lights out, so I couldn't really see him when I moved to prop my chin on his chest. I peered up at him anyway and replied, "You could tell him you miss him."

I felt him shrug. "Last we spoke, I was a total dick, babe. He might not give a shit."

"Maybe he won't. Maybe you call him, and he doesn't want to talk to you. Honestly, that's the worst that could happen, in which case nothing changes. Or—maybe he misses you, too. Maybe he needs his big brother to lay the first plank in order to mend the bridge that was burned in a stupid argument."

Ange said nothing in reply, but I didn't let that discourage me. I pressed a kiss to his chest, then returned my cheek to its resting spot.

"I don't know Nico, honey—but I do know what it's like to grow up with an older sibling. I think there's very little Blake could do that I wouldn't forgive, if anything. I'd be surprised if Nico felt differently. But you'll never know if you never ask."

I didn't say more. Neither did Ange.

I wasn't bothered. He was still tracing patterns on my thigh.

We lay silently for a while longer.

Then out of nowhere, Ange said, "I like her, but she's a nut. What am I going to do with all those cookies?"

I laughed, thinking of what couldn't be less than a five-pound bag of monster cookies Blake had shoved into his hands on our way out the door.

"Take 'em to the pub and share. Everyone likes monster cookies."

"Yeah, I guess," he chuckled.

When our amusement subsided and my eyelids grew heavy, I knew I wouldn't be able to hold onto the day much longer. Before I faded to sleep, I whispered, "Ange?"

"Right here, babe."

"Thank you for today. For all of it."

I felt his lips in my hair as he kissed me and replied, "For you? Anytime."

ANGE

He waited until he knew she was asleep, then carefully shifted out from underneath her and rolled out of bed. He grabbed his phone from his nightstand on his way out of the room. It was late—after midnight—but he needed to do it right away. He needed to do it while her words were fresh in his mind.

Earlier, the two of them out on his boat, he'd accepted the reality in which the woman in his bed was the same woman who'd carved out a chunk of his heart. She was in there, and she was in there deep.

That night, in her sister's living room, he'd seen it in Channing's eyes that he'd managed to do the same. Then he brought her home, made love to her, and he had no doubt.

He was in there, and he was in there deep.

This was why he found himself standing in the middle of his kitchen, Nico's contact information pulled up on his phone.

Channing was a good woman with a generous heart. She suggested reconciliation with Nico like nothing else made sense. She didn't cast blame or judgement, she merely looked at the situation through the lens of love.

She was right. At worst, nothing would change.

Ange admitted to himself that if his brother blew him off, it would hurt. But the alternative made it worth the risk.

Lately—the risks he took seemed to be paying off.

Nico and Ange had grown so far apart, he didn't know what was left to save. Except, they were brothers, and nothing would ever change that. It had been too long. It was time for Ange to swallow his pride, get over his shame and regret, and apologize.

That was the only version of himself Channing deserved.

It was the only version of himself he wanted to be.

He initiated the call.

It went straight to voicemail.

Ange left a message, then went back to bed.

CHAPTER *Seventeen*

Channing

Two Weeks Later

S OMEHOW, WE WERE A week into April, and Libby and Patrick's wedding was in a month.

Fortunately—or luckily, depending on the scenario—things were coming together.

We had Libby's mother to thank for finding a Catholic church with a Saturday available in May on such short notice. It had also been Libby's mother who convinced the priest who would perform the wedding mass that two and a half months was plenty of time for Libby and Patrick, who were both cradle Catholics, to undergo the required pre-marital counseling. I didn't know what kind of connections she had, but seeing as Libby was both dead set on having a Catholic wedding *and* in the timing she saw fit, we were all grateful Mrs. Chavez was supportive of her daughter and her choice in Patrick.

Phoebe had no trouble lining up the perfect caterer for the reception. Even though we were planning the post-ceremony celebration at

The Four Horsemen, the pub's kitchen would not be responsible for the food. Patrick didn't have a firm stance on much when it came to the finer details, trusting Libby with most of the decisions, but on this he was unwavering—his staff would be guests at their wedding.

I thought that was sweet. It was also, as I had come to know, classic Patrick.

As far as the guest list was concerned, Libby had handled that like the professional she was. She'd kept it tight with clear boundaries. Family and close friends *only*.

Coincidentally, for both Libby and Patrick, that included work colleagues.

And the only plus ones allowed were couples that were already married or engaged.

Fortunately for me, my date had his own invite to the wedding.

We didn't have time to design, print, and mail out official invites, so we'd gone the electronic route. That had been a tough compromise for Libby, but she understood it was for good reason.

She and Patrick still had a couple more days to chase down their final RSVPs, but they were really close.

Libby had booked a photographer. She and Patrick had a cake tasting the following week. Jorge had successfully sourced peonies and succulents. I was *this* close to finalizing the overall design, which meant I could start sourcing rentals. And while it was still undecided what I would be wearing to the wedding, that very afternoon, Libby, her Rusty Barn family, and her mom took a few hours to do a bit of wedding dress shopping.

I was very relieved that she hadn't taken long to say yes to a dress.

We may have still had a month to go, but alterations took time—regardless of our connections—and we had less of that than we liked.

Now, it was Saturday night. Libby, Jorge, and I were at The Four Horsemen, sitting at the bar, finishing dinner. Patrick and Ange were working. The band that was playing the night Ange and I first got together was back. Just then, they were covering "I Want to Rock" by Twisted Sister.

Needless to say, they were definitely rocking.

The only thing that could have made the night better was Russ—but it was still early.

I had a good feeling he'd turn up.

"Are you gonna finish those fries?" asked Libby, eyeing my plate.

I fought a smile, looking over at the remnants of her salad. I was not the least bit surprised her dinner had left her unfulfilled. It wasn't that the salad wasn't a completely adequate meal, it just wasn't really Libby's style. Even Patrick had given her a strange look when that was what she'd ordered.

"Nope. They're yours if you want them," I told her, pushing my plate toward her.

"Just one."

Jorge rolled his eyes. "You're joking, right?"

"What?" asked Libby with a shrug.

"This is about the dress, isn't it?"

"Of course, this is about the dress. My next fitting is in two weeks and—"

"I'm sorry..." He frowned, leaned forward in an exaggerated attempt to look at me, and asked, "Were we at the same bridal boutique?"

I chuckled and batted a hand, as if brushing away his concern. "This'll last two days, tops. She's not eating salad for the next month. I guarantee it."

Libby gasped. "You don't think I can do it?"

"Sweetie, I've seen you try to give up carbs. It's not pretty. Besides, you're going to look gorgeous in that dress no matter what you eat. Want to know how I know? Because you looked gorgeous in it today."

She looked at me, down at my leftover fries, then behind the bar at Patrick. He was busy shaking a cocktail; but, like he did about a million times every night Libby was at the bar, he glanced her way as he did it. When he saw her watching him, he smiled, then blew her a kiss.

She then pulled my plate in front of her and went in on my fries.

I grinned at Jorge. He grinned back at me. Libby changed the subject.

"So, you said you had an idea about how you wanted to transform this place for the reception. What did you have in mind?"

"Ah, yes," I stated, spinning my chair around so I faced the room. Jorge followed suit.

Libby grabbed a couple more fries, then did the same.

"It helps a lot that you and Patrick agreed on a DJ rather than a live band. I know they always put the band over there, but I think we'll really need that space for seating. While the DJ needs to be accessible, he doesn't need to be a focal point, so we'll put him towards the back on the opposite side of the room."

"Good idea," said Libby with a nod.

"Great. As for the bar, I want it to be a functioning bar. We'll dress it up a little, but it is what it is, you know? Why waste it? Except, I was thinking we'd ditch the chairs and butt the dance floor right up to it. If we use most of the booths, we should be able to clear the space for a twelve-by-fifteen floor with tables on either side. And we can put the bride and groom table—"

I was on a roll, talking with my hands, picturing the room transformed, when the door to the pub opened and I saw him.

He was laughing with someone as they entered, and all I could do was stare. It was like the sight of him immobilized me. Even with him across the room, we hadn't been this close to each other in nearly a decade.

I didn't understand how this could be happening.

It wasn't like I hadn't *seen* Dylan since our wedding day.

I had. Three times.

Twice, he'd been with Ava.

Once, he'd been with their oldest son.

Each time, I managed to get as far away as fast as I possibly could before he could see me.

Whenever I accidentally saw Ava, it was usually on a random weekday. It made sense that I wouldn't see Dylan with her, as he'd likely be at work, whatever that looked like for him. Until recently, I spent most weekends either at someone else's wedding or at home.

Now, it wasn't that I'd turned into some social butterfly. Ange and I went out occasionally, and I frequented his pub, but there was no way that slight change to my routine should have increased the odds of running into either of the Butlers. Not to mention, Austin wasn't a small city. The chances of me running into them ought to have been small. Miniscule, even.

And yet—it kept happening.

And this time, I had no place to hide.

What did the universe have against me?

A lot, as I would soon find out.

"Channing!" called Libby whilst snapping her fingers in front of my face.

I blinked and turned to look at her. I barely registered her confusion.

"Hey, are you okay? Chica, you look like you've seen a ghost."

She couldn't have been more right. Only, *this* ghost was still alive and breathing.

Worse, even—*this* ghost was staring right at me when I looked away from Libby to see if he was, in fact, actually there.

Yup. Definitely there.

He muttered something to his friend, his eyes still pinned on me, and then he was walking toward me.

Yeah. This was happening.

Unfortunately, the band chose that exact moment to take their first break. The sound system kicked on with overhead music, but it wasn't nearly as loud.

Dylan smiled hesitantly at me, waving at me unnecessarily as he drew closer.

All I could do was watch as he ate up the distance between us.

After he'd jilted me at the altar, that was it. We didn't talk. I had been so devastated and heartbroken, not just by the *timing* of his abandonment, but the whole *manner* of it, there was no explanation he could have given that would have made any of it better. Blake, Derek, and my parents had been my mediators after the fact. Not that there was a ton to mediate. It wasn't a divorce. We hadn't gotten that far. But I had no contact the weeks following the incident.

For better or for worse, neither Dylan nor Ava had ever tried to contact me in the months that followed. And neither had I.

This was why I found it a little difficult to breathe when he stopped two feet away from me and said, "Hi, Channing."

He looked good. Irritatingly good.

He wasn't nearly as handsome as Ange—but time had been kind to him.

His chestnut brown hair was grown out long enough you could make out its wavy texture. He wore it combed back, the ends just barely touching the collar of his shirt. Also, unlike the last time I saw him—a couple years ago now—he was sporting a bit of facial hair. His goatee was full, as was his jaw line, his cheeks less so, like he couldn't grow hair there. Still, he pulled it off.

He was wearing a polo shirt and khakis, both of which he wore well. He'd never been a particularly broad guy, but he took care of himself. He was all lean muscle and confidence. Always had been.

It took me a second, but I finally managed to say, "Hi."

I wasn't sure what the right thing to say would have been, but this was apparently the wrong thing; this evidenced by the fact that his smile grew, as if I'd given him an opening, and he kept engaging.

"How are you? It's been a really long time. You look great."

He thought I looked great.

I knew I looked great.

Not-summer was almost over.

It was early April and we already had ninety-degree days sprinkled about in our forecast.

This meant, when I got dressed that morning, there was only one logical outfit choice.

I was wearing a soft-pink, sleeveless dress with a lace pattern across the chest, the hem of which stopped just above my knees. I'd paired it with my kick-ass, tan cowgirl boots. Knowing I'd be seeing Ange that day, I took the time to curl my hair. And to top it all off, I wore my wide-brim tan felt hat.

So, yeah, I looked great.

But it certainly wasn't for him, and it bugged me that he'd said it.

"Thanks," I replied lamely.

I wanted our exchange to end.

Apparently my monosyllabic responses were not expressing that accurately.

He shifted his brown eyes to my right, clearly interested in the two people who—I had no doubt—were staring at him with a mix of curiosity and confusion. He then looked back at me, as if he thought I'd introduce him.

As if.

Unfortunately, my friends didn't feel the same.

"Hi, I'm Jorge," he said, reaching out a hand. "I work for Channing."

I could tell by the sound of his voice, Jorge found Dylan attractive, which was what fueled his intrigue.

"Hi," Dylan replied, his smile charming as he accepted Jorge's gesture.

"I'm Libby," she cut in.

I could tell by *her* voice that she was feeling suspicious and territorial.

She confirmed this when she continued, "I work for Channing, too. I'm also her best friend. And you are?"

"I'm Dylan."

Libby's spine straightened, and the electric current that shot through her with her new awareness was palpable. He wasn't sitting next to me, but something told me Jorge was adding his own charge to the atmosphere, knowing he'd just met the man married to Ava.

Even Dylan did a double take before he tried again to get me talking.

"I heard you're planning the wedding of the season. Dani's been following your work for a while. She says you're pretty in demand, and none of us should be surprised the congressman's daughter chose you," he said, speaking of his closest sister, Danielle.

I nodded. Not in response to what he said so much as what it implied.

I didn't start Rusty Barn until four years after Dylan left me. This meant Danielle had been interested enough to find out what had become of me, even though the end of my relationship with her brother really was the end of my relationship with *any* of the Butlers.

Which, point of fact, was not entirely my choice, thus making the breakup that much more painful at the time.

"It was great of you to include Ava and her shop. She drums up a lot of business on her own, but a feature in a magazine will be huge. She's really awesome at what she does. But, I don't need to tell you, that."

Jorge cleared his throat. *Loudly.*

I kept my mouth shut.

Dylan took a deep breath, then reached up to rub the back of his neck.

He felt awkward.

I was starting to get through to him.

Good. I wanted him to go away.

Still, he kept talking.

"Ava mentioned she saw you around town a few weeks ago."

This time, it was my spine that straightened.

"What? Where?" The words fell out of my mouth before I could stop them.

"She said she was at the library, and she saw you walking. I guess you were with someone." I saw it as his eyes traveled down to my hands and then back up again. "Are you seeing anyone?"

It was then I understood he'd been looking for a ring.

I couldn't breathe; therefore, I couldn't speak.

Fortunately, Libby had held her tongue for as long as her Latina spirit could manage, and that was over now.

"That, sir, is none of your business."

She slid off of her chair and took a step toward him. Even in her platform heels, she was a good six inches shorter than Dylan. She'd been taller in her chair. Yet, somehow, she was more formidable on her feet.

"As a matter of fact, *nothing* about Channing is any of your business. Given that she's said *four* words since you came over here, I think you should take that as a hint she has no interest in talking to you. And I, for one, don't blame her.

"It's obvious to me you're still feeling guilty about the horrendous way you treated her. Why else would you be asking about her love life? You, of all people? It's actually quite remarkable you could be so deplorable. Unfortunately for you, you're not gonna leave here feeling better about yourself. Any life Channing has managed to make for herself is *in spite* of you. The guilt you carry as a result of that? Sorry," she paused for a shrug. "Only God can absolve you of that. We're pretty fucking awesome, but we're not God, so we can't help you.

"Also, this is my fiancé's pub, and we were here first. In other words, you can leave now."

When she was finished, Dylan looked over her head at me.

I continued to say nothing.

Still—*unbelievably*—he kept talking.

"I meant what I said. You look great. Truly. I hope you've found happiness. Good luck with that wedding."

Finally, *finally*, he turned and walked away.

I didn't watch him leave the Pub.

I spun around in my chair in order to brace myself against the bar.

My eyes caught a green spark and locked in.

That just happened.

"He's gone," said Libby before she took her seat. She rubbed a hand across my back and repeated, "He's gone.

That just happened.

Those green eyes stayed trained on me, warm and intense.

I reminded myself to breathe.

"Babe? You okay?"

The tension in Ange's shoulders was not lost on me.

He was braced and ready for anything.

I knew, whatever I needed, he would do it for me.

Even if that meant I wanted him to go after Dylan and slug him hard across the face.

"Babe?" he called gently when I didn't answer.

I drew in a deep breath, and I felt it.

The pinch in my chest.

It sucked to admit it, but I knew what I needed.

"Channing, babe—" Ange reached for my hand, covering it with his. "Are you okay?"

I shook my head and whispered, "I don't know." I then flipped my palm up, so it was kissing his. I gave his fingers a squeeze, then pulled away as I began to dismount my chair. "I think I need to go home."

"Are you sure?" asked Libby.

The band's lead singer announced they were back, and they immediately started playing their next song.

I needed a moment alone—a moment to think.

I needed to process the fact that my ex-fiancé, who hadn't spoken to me since he'd humiliated me on our wedding day—that cowardly asshole—had seen me and decided the best course of action was to come over, tell me I was still hot, and then check out my *ring finger*.

Yeah. I needed more than a moment.

I wasn't going to get any in the pub.

"I'm sure. I, um..." I glanced back at Ange, and I knew.

Whatever I needed, he would do it for me.

Even if he didn't like it.

"I'll call you later."

I grabbed my purse, shot my friends an apologetic look, then got out of there.

I didn't even notice it was Russ who held the door open as I left.

I'd replayed my exchange with Dylan at the pub a dozen times.

After the wedding incident, for a good three or four years, I used to imagine what I'd say if we ever saw each other again. In some of these scenarios, there would be tears; in some, there would be shouting; in others, I'd say what I wanted to say calmly before I kneed him in the balls and walked away forever.

Somewhere, in the back of my mind, I knew it was all bullshit. I knew it would never happen, but not because we'd never see each other again. Within a span of four years, I'd spotted Ava a handful of times, so I knew seeing Dylan wasn't an impossibility.

No—I knew I'd never speak my mind because within a span of four years, I'd spotted Ava a handful of times, and I'd gone out of my way to make sure she hadn't seen me.

Conversations with Dylan weren't the only ones I'd imagined.

Ava had her own catalogue in my mind.

But I'd never said a word.

They weren't the only cowards.

Now, I sat on my couch, hugging a throw pillow to my chest as I stared out over my view of downtown Austin. I stared, but I didn't see—my brain too preoccupied.

I couldn't deny it anymore.

I'd been running scared for *years*.

It was easier to hide from Dylan and Ava than to confront them. It was easier to hide from the *why* behind the lies and the betrayal. Since we never sat down and discussed how it was possible that my best friend and my fiancé ended up falling in love with each other behind my back, my imagination dreamed up the extent of their deceit, and it was neither innocent nor pretty.

Though, I didn't think their version would be any better.

It was preferrable to shove it all in a box and bury it under mountains of work for *years*.

Rather than play the jilted victim, I decided what being in control looked like.

I defined *empowerment* as never dating anyone, ever; never trusting a man with my heart, ever.

For nine years.

Nine *fucking* years!

The pinch in my chest burned, and I hugged my pillow closer as my first tear fell.

It wasn't long before two tears turned into three turned into an ugly cry.

Dylan had looked down at my hand and saw my ring finger was empty.

It could not be denied, that was partially his fault. He'd been the one to put an engagement ring there. He'd been the one to break the promise which came with that ring. He lied and cheated and humiliated me, shattering my heart into so many pieces it took me years to put it back together.

But my empty ring finger wasn't entirely his fault. It was mine, too.

I had to admit that. I had to stop running from it.

I'd convinced myself I was better alone and all I needed was my life's work. Except, that wasn't true. I'd simply been too scared to hope for anything more. My hiding from Ava and Dylan wasn't just about me wanting to prevent them from getting so much as a glimpse of me or my life.

That was true. They didn't deserve any part of me.

Though, as I'd learned, my attempts at hiding weren't as fool proof as I'd thought.

But it was more than that.

It was me hiding from myself—hiding from the girl who was broken and angry.

I was hiding from the shadow of my cowardice.

I was never brave enough to stand up for myself and tell them how what they did was beyond awful. Not because I lacked a backbone but because I was afraid they might reveal something about me that justified what they'd done.

It didn't matter what Blake said, or what my parents said, or what *everyone who loved me* said. It seemed impossible that two people could do something so hurtful merely out of selfishness. There had to have been something I'd done. Or so I thought. For a really long time. So long, in fact, I didn't dare test the theory. Instead, I became the best daughter, sister, aunt, friend, wedding planner I could be, and I left it there.

It was safer to leave It there.

Except, Dylan had looked down at my hand and saw a ring finger that was empty.

Something about that implied he thought I'd be married by now. And it wasn't so much that I cared what he thought. I didn't. Certainly not after what he'd done and the years which had transpired. But that one glimpse had been painfully eye opening.

As I sat alone on my couch, I realized the only person I'd been punishing this whole time was *me*—and I wasn't going to do that anymore.

I let myself cry it out.

When I was done, the pinch in my chest was gone, and I knew it was gone in a way that it would never come back.

Then all I could do was think of Ange.

"If I'm a risk, a big one...we're in the same boat."

Ange thought I was a risk, too.

Weeks ago, he'd looked at me and saw someone he liked.

He looked at me and saw beyond all my red tape.

He looked at me—and I mean *at* me—and decided I was worth the risk.

Suddenly, I didn't want to be alone anymore.

I'd watched the sun set hours ago, but it was still only midnight, which was early for a man who tended bar until last call. I didn't care. I'd wait for him all night, if I had to.

I uncurled myself from the couch and went to the bathroom to freshen up a little. I didn't bother reapplying makeup after washing my face, too impatient to get gone. When I was done, I set about packing a light weekend bag. This didn't take me long. I had no intention of dawdling. There was someplace I wanted to be.

Twenty minutes later, I was in front of Ange's house. I got out of my car, made my way to his front porch, and got comfortable in his two-seater rocking chair. The night was slightly chilly with the breeze, and I tugged my denim jacket tighter around me. Ange wouldn't be home for a couple of hours, but I didn't care.

I'd wait for him all night, if I had to.

Fortunately, I only had to wait a couple of hours.

As he was pulling his truck into the driveway, I got up and went to stand at the top of his porch steps. I watched him as he got out of the driver's seat, letting Penny out after him. She barked her hello before cutting across the lawn to get to me. I bent to give her a quick rubdown, but I didn't take my eyes off Ange.

It was too dark to make out the green of his gaze, but I felt it on me as he approached.

At the pub, he'd let me go without argument, respecting what I told him I needed.

Now, I just needed *him*.

Admitting that should have felt monumental, but it didn't. It just felt true.

The porch light illuminated the green of his irises as he reached the bottom step. He hadn't said anything, so I didn't either. I simply held out my hands, reaching for him. I was up on my tiptoes, engulfed in his arms and pressed against his broad, hard, warm chest a second later. I held tightly to his shoulders, my face tucked into his neck, and I was certain there was nowhere better.

We stood like this for a solid sixty seconds before Ange asked, "You okay?"

I was about to be.

Lifting my head until my lips grazed the shell of his ear, I whispered, "I need you."

He didn't hesitate.

He reached down with one hand and tapped the side of my thigh.

He didn't have to explain.

I hopped up, circling my legs around his hips.

He unlocked the door, carried me inside, and locked up behind us.

He brought me to his bed.

He took off all my clothes.

I took off his.

Then he made love to me.

Slow. Hard. Bliss.

We came together.

And it. Was. Perfect.

"You want to talk about it?"

It was after three in the morning. We were in Ange's bed, shrouded in darkness, snuggled up together between his sheets. I should have been passed out—drained from crying or tired and sated after sex—but I wasn't. Attuned to me, neither was Ange.

I contemplated his question then decided there was something that was still bothering me.

"Remember when I told you Ava was in the industry? Events and weddings and such?"

"Vaguely."

I nodded. That was a fair answer. We tended not to talk about my ex-best friend on account of there were so many far more interesting things to talk about.

"Well, she's a florist. She owns Blossoms & Balloons Floral Design. She opened the shop just six months after I started Rusty Barn. The timing was interestingly coincidental, but I guess I wasn't all that dumbfounded. Flowers and those really elaborate balloon designs have kind of always been her thing.

"I can't say she's bad at it. It would be a lie," I said honestly. "But she's done the flowers for three of my weddings, and each time, she has managed to mess something up. Part of me thinks she does it on purpose, because it's me. I can't say for certain, because it doesn't make sense. She got the guy she wanted so, why try to screw me over even more?"

"How?" Ange interjected. "How does she mess things up?"

"The first time, it was the ribbon around all the bouquets. It was the wrong color. I know it might not sound like that big of a deal, but it was an error that shouldn't have happened. An error we had to go out of our way to try and fix. It's why I avoid hiring her as a vendor. Honestly, I probably would anyway—but it's her work that makes me steer clear whenever possible.

"Now, I say all that for context," I continued. "My big client I told you about?"

"The congressman's daughter," he stated knowingly.

"Yes, exactly. Well, they insisted on hiring Ava as their florist. I had nothing to do with it. But tonight, Dylan said it was great of me to include Ava and her shop. It was like he thought we were on speaking terms—which we certainly are not. Libby and Jorge have always handled that vendor relationship. But, I don't know, maybe Ava led him to believe otherwise and that's why he thought it was okay to come over and talk to me.

"I should have told him the truth. I should have said his wife is awful to work with and she's already made this high profile, super important, stressful wedding even more stressful than it needs to be. She's cost me time and money, and if I never worked with her again, it would be too soon." I paused for a moment, my frustration subsiding before I admitted on a whisper, "I should have said a lot of things tonight. I didn't say any of them."

Ange pressed a kiss into my hair and then mumbled, "Not telling you how you should think, but Channing? Pretty sure neither of them deserves the headspace you give them."

"No," I replied, still whispering. "You're right."

"That said, if she fucks with your business, you should sue."

"The thought has crossed my mind."

His arm around me squeezed reflexively before he muttered, "But?"

A half-smile tugged at my lips at his one-word inquiry. I kind of loved the straight-forward way he looked at any situation involving Dylan or Ava. In his eyes, if I was ready and willing to stand up for myself, I couldn't lose.

"*But*...I don't know. It feels like more trouble than it's worth. I just want them to be out of my life for good." I drew in a deep breath and blew it out in a sigh, ready to put our conversation to bed. I indicated as much when I turned my head, pressed a kiss to Ange's chest, and said, "I don't want to talk about it anymore. Sorry for running out of the pub the way I did."

"Babe, where are you right now?"

This brought a full smile to my face as I snuggled tighter against him. "In bed with you."

"Seems to me no apology is necessary. Though, I will say, I'm pretty beat. That mind of yours clear enough for sleep yet?"

"Yeah. Sleep sounds good," I said, my smile now a tired grin. "Goodnight, honey."

"Night, babe."

CHAPTER
Eighteen

I T HAD BEEN AN overwhelmingly busy week. Friday couldn't have come soon enough. Now that it was here—or, rather, now that it was here, and I was done with work for the day—I was in a celebratory mood.

I was going to the pub. I hadn't been to the pub since the night I ran into Dylan, but I wasn't going to let the memory of that keep me away.

I had plans to sit at the bar, have a couple drinks, flirt with the rugged man serving me those drinks, listen to some live music, and revel in the fact that it was Friday, and I didn't have to think about work again until Sunday.

Most importantly, I was going to look good doing it.

I'd purchased the denim jumpsuit that hugged my every curve on a shopping trip with Blake months ago. Until that night, I hadn't worn it anywhere other than the dressing room at the store. It had short sleeves and a wide collar, the first of only three buttons located in the middle of my torso. The leg had an elongated flared hem, which left enough room at the bottom for me to wear my gray, suede, ankle booties underneath. It was super cute, moderately sexy, and tonight felt as good as any night to debut it.

It was also the exact right thing to wear with my dove gray, tri-tip, felt hat. Still enjoying the last days of not-summer, I didn't think twice about putting it on over my now-dead curls.

The clock told me it was already after seven. I gave myself one last glance, grabbed my overnight bag, and headed for the parking garage.

I didn't usually spend Friday night with Ange. It didn't always make the most sense. One or both of us had work on Saturdays; and if I wasn't working, I was doing all I needed to do in order to be free to spend the day with him on Monday. But after an overwhelmingly busy week, we'd hardly seen each other, and I missed him.

I didn't fight the feeling.

I was done punishing myself.

I tossed my overnight bag in the backseat, and I headed for the pub.

The Four Horsemen was decently busy when I arrived. The bar was full, both Patrick and Ange obviously working through a rush of customers. I saw three servers out on the floor, taking care of those seated at tables. Willow breezed by me, flashing a wave and a smile on what I assumed was her trip to the kitchen. I waved back, then took a second look at the bar. Upon spotting Russ, I headed straight for him

.

He saw me when I was halfway there and was off his chair by the time I'd reached him.

"Hey, darlin'," he greeted with a dip of his chin.

"Hi, Russ. How are you?"

"Got a cold beer and a pretty woman to keep me company. Doesn't get much better than that." He nodded to his chair. "Take a seat. I'll buy you a drink."

There was no point in arguing with Russ.

I took his seat, and I waited for Ange to notice me so I could order a drink.

When he saw me, I got the eye crinkles, and my chest grew warm and tingly.

"Hey," he said when I was in earshot.

I lifted out of my chair enough that I could lean across the bar for a kiss. I stayed close so he heard me when I murmured, "Hi, honey."

There was a spark in those gorgeous eyes as he said, "Like what you've got on."

I grinned, leaned a little closer and replied, "Maybe I'll let you take it off later."

I knew I'd read the undertone of his comment accurately when that spark in his eye turned into a flame. "No *maybe* about it, babe," he declared.

I hummed a laugh, kissed him once more, than put my seat back on my chair.

"What are you drinking?"

I glanced beside me at Russ. He was leaning against his elbow, propped on the bar, his focus on the live band. He was cool and relaxed. Granted, I'd never seen Russ be anything *but* cool and relaxed, but I was feeling his vibe, and I wanted to join him.

Turning back to my man, I said, "I'll have what he's having."

He nodded, then went to pour me a draft.

Soon, I was facing away from the bar, like Russ, feeling cool and relaxed as I enjoyed the live music. The group that night was a country blues band. They were really talented and played both covers and a few originals. I hadn't heard them before and was glad I could be there to check them out.

The crowd at the bar had thinned enough that Russ had a seat next to me when Ange gave me my second beer. I was contemplating an order of fish-n-chips when something caught my eye.

It was the stuffed rucksack slung over his shoulder.

I did a doubletake as he stood a few feet away from the door. The man was in roughed up work boots, jeans that were faded from use but hung just right on his tapered hips. The tee he had on was well loved—threadbare but not ratty—and it clung to his hard-to-miss body. He had on a backwards baseball cap, his overgrown dark hair spilling from underneath the brim. It stopped short of his shoulders.

I could tell from where I sat his eyes weren't green—but I had a strange feeling I was staring at a younger version of Ange without a beard.

He peered around the room, not like he was looking for someone, but like he was taking in the pub's details. I was getting ready to turn away from him in order to catch Ange's attention when I noticed the man's gaze lock in on the band. His head tilted slightly, as if he found their choice of song intriguing. I recognized the cover of "Change on the Rise" by Avi Kaplan.

Apparently, so did he.

He lifted a fist and started pounding it to the beat on his chest as the female lead singer sang the first round of the chorus. I found this slightly odd.

Then the chorus was over, and the man with the rucksack tipped his head back and opened his mouth.

My eyebrows shot up my forehead as he *belted* the lyrics of the second verse, his voice astoundingly deep, resonate and beautiful, his tone rivaling that of the one over which he sang.

I certainly wasn't the only one to notice.

Even the lead singer of the band yielded the floor as the stranger continued to sing through the chorus.

And the lyrics? They were eerily appropriate.

When he was finished, he settled his eyes decisively behind the bar.

I swear, there was a crackle of electric energy that shot through the entire room.

My strange feeling was now certainty.

The man with the rucksack was Nicodemus Castellanos.

By the time I turned around to look for Ange, he was already on the move. He disappeared behind the bar, and I watched and waited for him to come through the hallway that would grant him access to the main room. He walked right up to Nico and clasped a hand around the back of his neck, then stared at his brother like he wasn't sure whether or not to believe he was really there.

Nico stared back, saying nothing.

They did this for a solid forty-five seconds.

Then Nico dropped his bag and crashed into Ange.

Ange heartily returned his brother's embrace.

"Well, I'll be damned."

I glanced over my shoulder at Patrick. He looked as amazed as I felt.

Ange had told me he'd left a voicemail on his brother's phone a couple weeks ago, but he hadn't heard anything in response.

This was way better than a callback.

Russ leaned toward me and muttered, "Family reunion?"

"Yeah," I replied with a smile and a nod.

He watched Ange and Nico then said, "Beautiful."

I wholeheartedly agreed.

The Castellanos brothers held onto each other a couple minutes, patting each other on the back sporadically. When they finally pulled apart, they still kept looking at one another like they found the other familiar but couldn't quiet recognize him.

From what I understood, it had been years. I supposed, after enough time, familiar yet unrecognizable would fit the bill.

Ange picked up Nico's bag and slung it over his shoulder, then the two of them headed toward the corner of the bar where Russ, Patrick and I were still watching.

"I can't believe you're fucking here," I heard Ange say as they drew closer.

"I was out of town workin' a job when you called. Just finished up a couple days ago. Stopped at home long enough to do a load of laundry then pack another bag and got my ass out here. Didn't have your address, but mom told me the name of this place. Figured if I got this far, you'd put me up for a few days."

"Hell, yeah. I've got room for you."

Ange set Nico's bag down next to my chair, aiming his smile at me.

I was already smiling at him, thrilled to see him so happy.

Before he could introduce me, Patrick called out, "Look what the fuckin' wind blew in."

I wasn't quite sure how well they knew each other, or how the status of Ange's evolving relationships with the two men over the years were intertwined, but I didn't give it much thought.

Not because I wasn't curious, but because it wasn't possible.

That was because Nico was smiling, and Nico's smile wasn't merely distracting...

It could break hearts.

He was aiming it at Patrick as he said, "'Sup, loser? Knew there was hope for him yet when he hooked up with you."

Patrick chuckled, then hitched his thumb over his shoulder and asked, "What are you drinking? First one's on the house."

"Whiskey neat. Best you got."

Patrick rapped his knuckles against the bar twice in acknowledgement before he turned to climb the ladder to grab the *best they had*.

"Nico, there's someone I want you to meet," said Ange, clasping a hand around his brother's shoulder. "This is Channing. Babe—meet my brother."

I extended my hand to shake his. "It's so great to meet you," I told him sincerely.

His heartbreaker smile slipped when he looked at me, and he didn't even try to hide it. Neither did he hide his open perusal of me, his hazel-brown eyes not so much appreciative as they were judgmental. He took my hand in his, accepting my gesture, but I didn't get more than a jerk of his chin in response to my greeting.

That told me a lot.

I was a woman, and I was involved with his brother. Given their history, those were two reasons for him not to trust me. Never mind that he didn't know me, or that it was his brother whom he needed to trust, Ange having chosen me.

Then again, as warm as their hello might have been, a single hug didn't solve the issues between them.

I needed to let this play out.

I forced my smile to stay intact as I let go of his hand and said, "I was just thinking of ordering dinner. Have you eaten?"

No sooner had the words left my mouth than Ange's fingers were in my hair, his hand at the back of my neck. I glanced at him, and he gave my nape a gentle squeeze. I knew he'd read his brother's reaction to me.

Then again, Ange didn't miss much.

"You should definitely sit," said Ange, speaking to Nico. "Order some food. I'm here for a while." He let me go, then reached for Nico's bag. "I'll toss this in the office."

"Sure," Nico replied.

Patrick set two fingers of whiskey in the empty spot opposite Russ. He nodded toward the chair, silently inviting Nico to sit as he said, "For the first timer—the best we got."

Over the next couple of hours, we ordered food, listened to the band, and chitchatted when Patrick and Ange weren't busy serving customers. Nico talked about work as a welder out in the oil field. Russ, who apparently had some knowledge of work in an oil field, engaged in the topic for a while. When Nico asked after the pub, he got the backstory from Patrick before Ange layered on about his involvement, how they managed to turn things around, and how much he loved it.

It did not go unnoticed how the brothers stuck to neutral topics, keeping things light and friendly. It made sense. They had a lot to discuss, most of it fit for a different setting—like out on Ange's back porch with a couple of beers. As I watched them interact, I changed my mind about where I'd be sleeping that night. Ange needed time alone with his brother, and I was happy to give it to him.

One o'clock hit, and the band started packing up for the night. As always, that was Russ' cue to close his tab. Patrick was off running his card when Russ looked between Ange and Nico and asked, "How long's it been since y'all last saw each other?"

Both brothers looked at one another, regret playing in some manner on each of their faces. Ange was the one who answered, "Seven years."

Russ nodded in that way I knew he was thinking something heavy, like life had taught him a few things, and he understood the pain that came along with *seven years*.

He confirmed what I thought when he next spoke.

"Two things a man needs money can't buy—the love of a good woman and his family. Nothin' more important than family." He then looked at me and added, "As for a woman, measure of a good one is seen in the way she takes care of her man. When you've found one, you don't let her go." Finally, he looked at Ange, dropped his cash tip on the bar and concluded, "When you've got both, you can't lose."

Patrick returned with his card, and I stared at Russ as he put it back in his wallet.

Russ only saw Ange and me at the bar. Most of the time, there was an entire counter between us. Yet, I shouldn't have been astonished by what he'd observed when he looked at Ange and me. He had vision only experience could earn him.

It warmed my heart knowing what Russ saw in us.

He said goodnight, shot a wink my way, then headed for the door.

"You should get out of here, too," insisted Patrick, jerking his chin at Ange.

"Are you sure?"

"Yeah. Go spend time with your brother. And while you're at it, don't bother coming in tomorrow."

Ange clapped a hand against Patrick's back in a manly show of affection, then said, "Thanks, Pat. I owe you one."

"No, you don't. Just get out of here."

Ange looked to Nico. "You ready to jet?"

"Gotta piss, then let's roll." He threw back the last of his drink, then hit the restroom.

I took advantage of his absence and told Ange, "I think I'll just head home."

This earned me a frown.

"You're at my place tonight."

"I know that was the plan, but now that Nico is here, I think I should give you two time to catch up."

"Babe." He paused, telling me with his eyes before he told me with his words, "He'll warm up to you."

"Oh, honey, I'm not worried about that. I—"

"Good. You're in my bed tonight. So, are you riding with us or meeting us at the house?"

His tone coupled with the fact that I'd been looking forward to being in his bed all day made me hesitate.

"I'm good to drive," I conceded.

Twenty minutes later, we were all walking through Ange's front door, Penny leading the way. I headed to the bedroom with my bag while the guys journeyed into the kitchen, Nico having dropped his bag unceremoniously on the floor. As soon as I hit Ange's room, I slowed down. I took my hat off and ruffled my hair, in an attempt to soften the effect of the weight of it on my head all night. I took my shoes off then hovered by the door, listening.

I heard them open the fridge and grab a couple beers. Nico cracked a joke and Ange laughed. It wasn't his big laugh, but it warmed my insides just the same.

I was glad he had that—a reason to laugh with his brother again.

Then I heard the back door slide open before they made their way out onto his screened-in porch. This was exactly what I thought they needed, and I'd already made up my mind I was going to let them have it.

I gave it a couple more minutes while I brushed my teeth. When I thought I'd procrastinated long enough, I made my way outside. Even though it couldn't have been cooler than seventy degrees out, Ange had turned on the firepit. He was sitting on the couch, sprawled in the corner like always. Nico was in one of the chairs across from him. They both looked at me as I stepped through the open doorway.

"Hey. Come sit with us," invited Ange.

"I'm actually going to head to bed. The week caught up with me, and I'm feeling pretty tired. I just wanted to come out and say goodnight."

"Okay."

I could tell by the way he looked at me he wasn't sure if he believed me.

It wasn't entirely false. It had been quite the week.

In any case, I was committed.

He tilted his head back upon my approach, granting me what I wanted as I went to give him a kiss. When I lifted my mouth from his, it was only so I could catch a glimpse of green. The moment I had it, I whispered, "Wake me if you want to." I watched his eyes glisten with a mix of desire and appreciation, then I kissed him one last time.

Before I headed inside, I turned to Nico and said, "Really glad you're here."

I didn't wait for him to respond before I left them to talk.

Sometime later, I woke with Ange's mouth between my legs.

A little after that, I came with his fingers inside of me.

Then a while later, I got a simultaneous orgasm.

I'd made the right move.

They'd talked it out.

He was saying *thank you*.

It was *so* worth the interrupted sleep.

Since Ange now had a free Saturday, he didn't bother setting an alarm. We'd both crashed after middle-of-the-night thank-you sex and, as I'd gotten a head start on sleep, it didn't surprise me when I woke to find him still dead to the world. Not wishing to wake him, I carefully got myself out of bed in order to make a quick trip to the bathroom. After I'd handled my business, I felt too awake to lay down again, but not awake enough to be considered fully functional.

I needed coffee.

I never packed a nightgown or a robe when I stayed the night at Ange's place. It was basically an unspoken rule that if I wasn't sleeping naked, he wanted me in one of his shirts. Since I liked the way his shirts tended to swallow me, and the fact that they always smelled like citrus and sandalwood—like *him*—I had no objections.

Except, usually his brother wasn't staying down the hall.

That morning, it seemed my options were to shower and get dressed or make do with what I could find. Certain a shower would wake Ange, something I was trying to avoid, I decided to make do whilst hoping Nico was prone to sleeping in. After a little quiet rummaging, I found a pair of jogger sweatpants with a drawstring in the waistband.

Score.

I pulled them on, secured them around my hips, then tossed on the henley he'd left in the middle of the floor on his way to bed that morning. I finger combed my hair, then situated it so it draped down either side of my chest. I still hoped Nico was asleep, but I'd be somewhat prepared if he wasn't.

Turns out, *he wasn't.*

I stopped short at the sight of him. He was in the kitchen, his chest and feet bare, his legs covered by the same faded jeans he had on the night before. He had a tattoo on the left side of his chest.

I didn't want to stare, so I didn't catch what it was.

His hair was wild from sleep, and he'd woken with a bit of stubble on his face. I wasn't sure how long he'd been awake, but it was long enough to figure out his brother's coffee machine and brew a pot. He was sipping his steaming nectar, his backside leaned up against the sink, his ankles crossed, when he saw me.

"Yo," he muttered over the rim of his mug.

"Morning," I murmured as I came unstuck. I went about preparing my own dose of coffee as I asked, "Did you sleep okay?"

"Fine, yeah."

I nodded, more to myself than at him.

What I'd said to Ange was true. I wasn't worried about Nico warming to me. I imagined it would happen in time. Given the way he'd greeted his brother at the pub, I knew he had it in him—he just needed to learn to trust me first.

That said, I suddenly wished I'd woken Ange. A buffer would have been nice.

"You around today?" Nico asked, catching me off guard.

I turned to face him and caught his hazel-brown eyes. They were unreadable. I took a chance and replied with a bold question of my own.

"Do you want me to be?"

This got me a smirk.

No doubt, he'd learned that from his big brother.

He set his coffee down and folded his arms across his chest. "Look, I don't know you and you don't know me. The last one didn't know me either, but I knew enough about her to know she wasn't worth the trouble. She was beautiful and far from dumb. I'll give her that much. Wasn't smart enough to do right by my brother, but that's neither here nor there.

"I walk in to reconnect with Ange after seven years of no contact—not even a birthday call or a Christmas drive-by on account of my job or his ex—I'm not with him five minutes, and already he's introducing me to a gorgeous blonde knockout, with eyes the color of the fuckin' sky, and all I can think is: he sure does know how to land the prettiest bitches."

I pulled in a deep breath and let it out slowly.

There was a lot there.

Some nice. Some not.

He was being honest.

I was trying not to bristle.

I kept my mouth shut.

Fortunately, he kept talking.

"Then I find out the voicemail he left was on account of you. That tells me, you're a different breed of woman. So, yeah, I want you around today. I don't know you and you don't know me, and somethin' tells me I shouldn't leave it that way."

Okay, so, it was touch and go there for a while, but I had to admit, that was a solid landing. I told him as much when I asked, "Do you brunch? Cause there's this place that's not too far from here I've been wanting to try with Ange, and today feels like the perfect day."

This got me his heartbreaker smile.

It didn't make me tingly, but warmth spread across my chest, and I knew then Nico and I would get on just fine.

CHAPTER *Nineteen*

"H EY, CHICA, READY TO get out of here?" Libby asked, poking her head into my office.

I hit *send* on the email I'd been writing then closed my laptop.

"Could not be more ready if I tried."

She smiled, exposing her dimples, and I finished packing up for the day before we both headed for the elevator.

It was Thursday night. While I'd gotten into the habit of reserving my Thursdays for Ange, Libby and Patrick's wedding was in nine days. It was crunch time, so I was taking my girl to dinner. Since I'd made plans, Ange picked up a shift, giving one of the other bartenders a night off. This meant after Libby and I nailed down any and all last-minute pre-wedding details, we'd head over to The Four Horsemen to have a drink and see our men.

We had reservations at Swift's Attic, and my stomach was already growling in anticipation of our meal. We made our way down to the parking garage, hopped in my car, then drove the short trip downtown.

When we arrived at the restaurant, checking in at the hostess stand, I couldn't help but notice a group of women who were already seated at a table. They looked to be about my age, maybe a little older, and it was obvious they were celebrating something and having a great time. It brought a smile to my face, the sight reminding me of Libby's bachelorette party just a few days ago.

Somehow, over the weekend, we managed to pull off a three-hundred-guest wedding in Boerne then have Libby's bachelorette party *and* live to tell the tale.

The wedding, at a historic ranch, had been beautiful.

Seeing as we were already traveling two hours out of town for the event, I decided it made sense to go a little further to Texas wine country for Libby's celebration. Fredericksburg was a classic choice for a girl's weekend, so we did it right. We met up with a few of Libby's cousins, her aunt, and her mom late Saturday night and partied it up—renting an *adorable* Airbnb—until Monday afternoon.

It was debatable whether or not I'd recovered from all of that yet, but it had been worth it.

Ange kept Patrick closer to home, but he took advantage of their Monday off and spoiled the groom. He rented a yacht, and they spent the day out at Lake Travis. Jack, Hector, and a couple of Patrick's buddies tagged along. When they got back to shore, they went for steaks, and stayed out drinking until the wee hours.

Needless to say, Libby had come around to my idea of separate parties.

She'd also thanked me about a half-dozen times for her last-hoorah girl's weekend.

I didn't tell her *I told you so*—but I knew I was well within my rights.

We were seated right away, and Libby and I decided to wait until we'd ordered food and drinks before we dove into work. By the time our dinner arrived, we'd gone through most of my checklist.

"Seriously, I cannot thank you enough," said Libby, not for the first time. "I know you've put in a ton of work to make this happen for me, on top of everything else you have going on."

"Sweetie, you know I wouldn't have it any other way, right? Besides, you're no slouch. We're doing it together. And we don't have any weddings scheduled between now and yours. We're so close to the finish line." I spread my napkin across my lap, the reality of what I just said hitting me in a whole new way. "How do you feel? Not about the wedding—about the fact that you're going to be a married woman in nine days."

She shook her head in disbelief. "Honestly? I have no idea. It seems so surreal, and it's all coming together so quickly. There's so much to think about, I don't know that my brain has fully wrapped itself around the idea. I mean—I'm excited. I love him and I cannot wait to call myself his wife, but I'm giving up my apartment in two weeks. I remember when I moved in there and how much I loved it. These days, I'm at his house more than I'm at my place, but it'll be different when we're married."

"Better, I hope."

"Definitely better." Libby picked up her fork, looked down at her plate, then nonchalantly asked, "So, what about you and Ange?"

"What about me and Ange?"

She peeked over at me, a mischievous smile playing at her lips.

"You're still going strong. Seems pretty serious between you two."

It was my turn to look down at my plate. I did it smiling.

Ange had that affect.

I pushed around my food as I said, "We're good. We're enjoying the ride."

"And where, exactly, do you think this ride will take you?" she probed.

My smile stretched into a grin, and I looked up to meet her curious stare. "I don't know—I just know we're going to keep on going for as long as it feels good."

Her face got soft before she said, "You seem happy. Happier than I've ever seen you."

I thought about what she said for a long moment. Not because I doubted it, but because it took me that long to think of all the reasons why she was right. I remembered dinner at Blake's house; hitting breweries one afternoon while Nico was in town; long mornings out on the lake catching bass, and cozy evenings sipping wine on Ange's back porch by the fire.

Of course, I couldn't forget all the times I found myself in Ange's arms. Clothed or naked, it would have been a lie to say it wasn't my favorite place to be.

"I am," I stated matter-of-factly.

Satisfied with my answer, Libby didn't ask for more.

We dug into our dinner, and it was everything I wanted it to be. When we'd finished, too full to even consider dessert, we asked for the check. We were only about a block from the pub, and we agreed the walk there would be nice. Before we left, I excused myself to use the restroom.

When I was finished in the stall and at the sink washing up, one of the women from the group I'd noticed earlier walked in. We glanced at each other in the mirror, both of us smiling politely before look-ing away. Except, rather than head into an empty stall, the woman changed her mind to address me.

"I'm sorry, I just wanted to tell you that I love your dress."

"Oh, thank you."

Reactively, I looked down at what I was wearing. It was a sleeveless wrap dress that tied in a simple knot at my waist. It had a stiff, layered collar that added a little dramatic flare. It was periwinkle, and paired great with my ankle wrap, wedge sandals.

"Did you get it locally, or do you remember?"

I met her eyes in our reflection, and I noticed they were dark blue and beautiful—especially with her pale skin and deep brunette hair.

I grabbed a couple paper towels and turned to address her directly. "You know, now that I think about it, I'm not sure I remember where I bought it. It might have been in Dallas."

"Ah. My friends and I are from out of town. We're trying to figure out the best places to shop."

"Oh, well, if you came to shop, you have plenty of options. Austin has a little bit of everything, so it depends on what you're looking for. I'm sure you've researched it already, but definitely hit Second Street. There's a boutique called Hemline, and they have some pretty good stuff."

"Thanks for the tip."

"Sure. Enjoy your trip."

The woman disappeared into a stall, and I discarded my paper towels on my way out to meet Libby. Ten minutes later, we were at the pub, sitting at the bar, and I'd all but forgotten the woman from the bathroom at Swift's Attic.

At least I had—until I saw her again an hour and a half later.

Ange was in the back, restocking a keg, when the group of women from the restaurant entered the pub. They were laughing as they came through the door, drawing Libby's and my attention. It appeared they may have had a couple drinks since we last saw them, and they were still having a wonderful time. They picked a long, high-top table near the side hallway and settled in.

For a second, I found it interesting how they'd managed to find their way to The Four Horsemen, of all places. It was a great pub, and competed well with all the other downtown bars, but it wasn't exactly a tourist destination.

"Huh. That's funny. They were at the restaurant, weren't they?" commented Libby.

"Yeah," I said with a shrug. "Strange coincidence."

"I would have guessed The Roosevelt Room was more their speed."

"Some might say the same about you, hot stuff," teased Patrick.

Libby and I smiled at each other, both of us still dressed up in our work attire.

He wasn't wrong.

We hardly had a chance to change the subject before the woman from the bathroom bellied up to the bar. Patrick had gone to the other end, which meant she had to wait. While she did, she recognized me.

"Small world. I swear, we aren't following you."

I smiled and told her, "Never a bad thing when you visit a place and end up where the locals like to go."

"Good point. Though, I have to admit, this wasn't exactly on my friends' itinerary. They're here to indulge me."

I didn't have time to consider what that might mean before I heard Patrick mutter, "Oh, fuck."

My eyes snapped in his direction only to find him staring at the woman from the bathroom.

I frowned, now wondering what *that* was about—and then Ange came back, and it all became very clear.

I saw it, the moment he recognized her. He jolted to a stop, and his eyes devoured her, like he'd seen her a million times, but she was still a sight to behold.

Suddenly, my dinner wasn't sitting so well.

"What are you doing here?" he asked, sounding as astounded as he looked.

"Hi, Ange," she murmured.

As if his brain was rebooting itself, it took him a second to register that she hadn't answered his question. When it clicked, he semi-repeated, "Stephanie, what are you doing here?"

For reasons I couldn't in that moment understand, hearing her name on his lips like that caused a pinch deep in my chest.

I felt Libby lean toward me before I heard her whisper, "Stephanie, like, *ex-wife* Stephanie?"

All I could do was nod.

"Officially, we're in town for Bekah's birthday. She's turning forty, and we wanted to get away and make a long weekend of it. I convinced them we should come to Austin. Unofficially? Well...I wanted to see you."

"Why?" he asked, matter-of-factly.

Stephanie hesitated then said, "It's been a long time. So much has changed. I've been thinking a lot about you, about the way things ended between us. It was—well, you were there. You know. Anyway, I just wanted to reconnect. I wanted to come see how you were doing."

I watched as Ange shook his head in what appeared to be disbelief more than anything else.

When he didn't respond, Stephanie pressed on, not ready to claim defeat. "We're staying at the JW. If you have any time, I'd love to meet for coffee and catch up. Maybe tomorrow? We likely won't get up to anything until late morning."

Ange scowled, and I held my breath.

What was happening?

"Okay," he said.

All the air whooshed out of me.

"Great. I look forward to it. My number—my number hasn't changed."

"Sure," muttered Ange, still scowling.

He looked as confused as I felt.

What was happening?

"Anyway—officially, I'm over here to order a round of shots. Could I get six? Tequila, please."

I looked away from her and focused my gaze on what was left of my old fashioned. It was basically gone, only the cherry left to consume, but I didn't want it. Not anymore.

Ange was going to meet his ex-wife for coffee.

His ex-wife who didn't seem like the heartless woman he'd described.

His ex-wife who complimented me on my dress. Me, a random stranger in a bathroom.

His ex-wife who was beautiful, just like Nico told me she was.

So beautiful, in fact, that when Ange looked at her, it was like he'd seen her a million times, but she was still a sight to behold.

Ange was going to meet his ex-wife for coffee.

What was happening?

The pinch in my chest began to burn.

"Hey, chica, you okay?" asked Libby.

I looked at her, unsure if she'd asked me once or three times.

"Sure, yeah," I lied.

"Channing, I'll admit that was weird, but whatever that woman wants, you and Ange are solid. You know that, right? I've seen the way he looks at you."

"Mmhmm," I hummed.

I didn't bother asking if she happened to notice the way he looked at *her*.

"Babe?"

Startled, I looked at Ange and caught green. My eyes lingered for only a second, then I glanced at the spot where Stephanie had been. She was gone.

"Channing," Ange called a second time.

I met his gaze.

"We're still in our boat, yeah?"

I wanted to stay in the boat.

I wanted so desperately to get lost in pools of gorgeous green.

I wanted Ange—but I couldn't forget the way he'd looked at her.

"It's just coffee. I'm not trying to be a dick. You hear me? I'm still in the boat."

He was still in the boat.

I nodded.

He was still in the boat.

"Okay," I murmured.

He stared at me.

I stared right back.

"You're in my bed tonight."

Before I knew what I was saying, I told him, "No, honey—I'm fine. You're going to be here late, and I have to be to work early." I didn't mention his coffee date, but I could feel my unspoken thought as it drifted between us. "I'm fine. In fact, we should probably get going. We have to walk back to my car."

"Babe…"

"It's okay," Libby piped in, coming to my rescue. "I've got her."

She reached into her purse for her wallet. Ange looked between the two of us, then silently relented. When she held out her credit card, he took it and closed out our tab. While his back was turned, I peered over my shoulder, curiosity getting the best of me. Stephanie was listening to whatever conversation was happening at her table.

But just as I was getting ready to look away, she cut her eyes behind the bar.

I didn't understand how any woman in her right mind could have Ange and then let him go.

A single glance from across the pub let me know *she couldn't*.

Libby and I said our goodbyes. When she didn't reach for a kiss from Patrick, I was relieved, because it meant I didn't have to reach for one from Ange, either. I didn't know why, but I didn't want Stephanie to see that.

We didn't say much as we walked to my car. Libby knew me well. I needed to sort through my thoughts, and she let me have that. It wasn't until I pulled into the garage at our office and parked next to her vehicle that she turned to me and laid it out.

"I know you're kind of freaking out. You say you're not, but you are. And I get it, I do. He was married to her. But you just have to remember they took their shot, and it didn't work out for better or for worse. Now he's here, and she's there. Texas and New York are literally separate worlds. So, he's going to meet her for coffee. He's being a nice guy. That's who he is. It's part of why you like him. But you also need to trust him. He's not Dylan."

I almost flinched when she spoke his name.

I didn't want to go there. Not even a little bit.

Instead, I told her what I knew she wanted to hear.

"You're right. You're right," I repeated, lightening my tone the second time. "It's going to be fine."

"Yes, it is." She reached over and gave my forearm a squeeze. "Go home and get some sleep, okay?"

"I will. You, too."

We said goodnight.

I watched as she got into her car and started the engine.

I backed out first and headed home.

Once inside, I locked myself in.

I got ready for bed.

I slid between the sheets, pulling my covers close.

I shut my eyes, but all I saw were his.

They were devouring her.

Like he'd seen her a million times, but she was still a sight to behold.

Ange

H ER HAIR WAS DIFFERENT. Shorter.

But that was the least of what he'd noticed.

She was different.

As he drove toward the JW, Ange thought back over his marriage. Stephanie had never been one to put on an act. She wasn't manipulative or cunning. She'd always been honest and upfront about who she was and what she wanted. It had been something that attracted him to her in the beginning.

In the end, it had been what made it so clear they were over.

That was why he'd said yes to coffee. Because the woman bellied up to his bar wasn't the woman he remembered. The woman he remembered wouldn't have even stepped foot into The Four Horsemen. Even her desire to reconnect, to see how he was doing—like she was curious about whether or not he'd found happiness—it seemed genuine. It took him by surprise. More than that. It damn near shocked him. Now, it was his own curiosity he wanted to satisfy.

He valeted his truck but didn't immediately head into the lobby. He took out his phone and initiated a call to Channing. He'd recognized the spooked look on her face after he'd agreed to meet Stephanie. She was so quick to leave, he hadn't had the chance to explain himself. They needed to talk, and he'd see that they did—but for now, he just wanted to hear her voice.

The call rang through to voicemail.

He left a message, promising he'd call again, then pocketed his phone and went inside. As he stepped into the lobby, he saw Stephanie right away. She'd been waiting for him. She smiled as she stood from where she'd been sitting and helped close the distance between them. She was in a pair of tight jeans and a top that was cut to drape off one of her shoulders. With her hair and makeup done she looked as put together as she always did.

He wondered how early she got up to do all that and how long she'd been waiting.

He also couldn't help but notice—she was still beautiful.

"Hi. Thanks for meeting me."

"Sure." He tucked his fingertips into the front pockets of his jeans, her proximity a reminder there wasn't a bar between them anymore.

"Um, we can grab coffee just over there and then sit."

"Okay," he agreed with a nod.

Stephanie hesitated a second, her dark blue eyes roaming over his face before she turned toward the Starbucks kiosk. There were a couple people ahead of them in line, and she was quick to fill the silence of their wait.

"You grew a beard. I like it."

He unconsciously reached for his face, smoothing his hand over the hair at his chin. Not knowing what to say, he commented, "You cut your hair."

"I chopped it a couple years ago. It's actually a bit longer now."

Ange nodded but said nothing more as they moved up in line.

"The pub is great. It looks like you guys are doing well. It's impressive, given what the pandemic did to the restaurant industry."

"I'm still surprised you came," he admitted.

"I know. It's not exactly my scene, but I'm really glad I did. And you know what? I'd go again."

Neither of them had a chance to say more before it was their turn to order. Stephanie insisted it be charged to her room, and Ange conceded. His black coffee and her Americano were ready shortly, and he followed her to a place where they could sit.

"So, besides the pub, how are you? How's life in Austin? Is it everything you wanted it to be?"

He didn't even have to think about it.

"Yeah. It is. It's a different pace of life down here."

"You wanted something simpler, and you got it," she observed with a nod.

"I did."

Smiling, she asked, "Do you still go fishing?"

"As often as I can."

She laughed softly. Knowingly. "Good for you. I mean that. So often people talk about what they want their lives to be, but they don't make the hard decisions or put in the extra work to make it a reality. I look at you and I see you got exactly what you wanted. I admire that."

Ange studied her for a long moment. It had been nearly four years since they'd last seen each other, but that wasn't long enough for him to forget the things she'd said. The life he'd wanted, it wasn't one she supported—and his decision to go after it wasn't one she'd admired.

He didn't know why she was there, in Austin. He didn't understand what she wanted, and he was growing impatient waiting for her to make it clear.

"You're different," he stated, hoping to shift the direction of their conversation.

She set her coffee on the table beside them then rested her forearms atop her knees and leaned toward him "I am. Or, I'm working on it. I got myself a therapist. She's brilliant."

"Is she the one who put it in your head to come down here?"

"No. But it would be a lie to say we didn't talk about you a lot. You, our marriage, our relationship—how it ended."

Ange merely nodded in reply. He wasn't sure he wanted to get into all that. If that was why she came, she'd be disappointed.

Stephanie wasn't deterred. She continued, "After our split, I was single for about a year. Then I decided to put myself out there again. It took longer than I'd like to admit, but I realized I was attracting a certain kind of man and every relationship felt hollow, somehow. I wasn't happy, and a friend of mine referred me to Dr. Ghirelli. It didn't take long for us to uncover that letting you go was one of the greatest regrets of my life.

"Anyway, I admitted it and I moved on. Or, at least, I tried. Then this year rolled around, and we started planning Bekah's fortieth. It hit me that I am closer to forty than I am to thirty, and I feel like my life is still missing something. It made me think about you, and I wondered how you were doing. I thought about the fulfillment you were seeking and the happiness you were chasing, and I really started to understand it; that is, your longing for change. I wanted to see you and see how your life was turning out, so I talked my friends into making this our destination, and now here we are."

She paused and took a breath.

Ange didn't know what to say, so he didn't.

Stephanie nodded, as if to express she understood.

She sat up, reached for her coffee, then said, "I notice you don't have on a wedding ring."

Fuck.

There it was.

"I'm seeing someone," he told her.

"I'm not surprised," she said, lifting her bare shoulder in a shrug. "A man like you with a face like yours?"

"Steph—"

"Is it serious?"

He knit his eyebrows together in confusion. None of this made sense.

His ex in Austin. The two of them sitting down to coffee.

It suddenly felt very strange.

"Yeah, it is," he answered.

"Lucky girl."

Ange frowned. "You can't have come down here thinking—"

"No, I know. Trust me. It was a long shot."

"A long shot?" He shook his head in disbelief. "You were born and bred on the Upper East Side. This life, my life, you said no to it for a reason. And maybe you regret it, and maybe you've changed—but I think we both know you like the idea of me and my life more than the reality of it."

"I don't know. Maybe."

"If it was me you really wanted, you wouldn't have come down for a long weekend with your friends and a reservation at the JW. You would have followed me here a long time ago, but you didn't. We took our shot. We wanted different things."

She smiled, but it didn't reach her eyes. What he said was the truth. Nevertheless, he could tell it stung. He couldn't say it brought him any sort of solace, learning of her regret. He did feel a measure of respect knowing she was trying to find her own version of happiness—even if that meant a detour to Austin.

Ange felt his phone vibrate with an alert in his pocket. He was getting ready to reach for it when Stephanie asked, "Will you at least stay long enough to finish your coffee? I'd like to talk a little while longer. How's Penny?"

He didn't reach for his phone.

He stayed for another fifteen minutes.

When his coffee was gone, he told Stephanie he needed to get to the pub.

They said their goodbyes, and he felt sure he'd never see her again.

While he was waiting for the valet to pull around with his truck, he remembered his unread text and pulled his phone out to read it. He wasn't taken aback to see it was from Channing—but what she'd sent hit like a sucker punch.

Hey. I think I need a little space right now. I think we both do.

He didn't hesitate.

He pushed a call through and immediately brought the phone to his ear.

She answered on the second ring.

He didn't even give her a chance to say hello.

"Babe—"

She was just as quick to cut him off.

"I saw the way you looked at her last night. I can't stop thinking about it."

"Channing—"

"The crazy thing is, she had dinner at the same restaurant where Libby and I had dinner. I ran into her in the bathroom. I mean, I didn't know it was Stephanie, but she came in and saw me and complimented my dress. She seemed nice. Maybe even fun."

"Channing, babe—"

"She's different than I thought she'd be. She's different than you described her."

Ange closed his eyes and let out a breath. "You're not wrong. She's different than I remember."

"Exactly."

He opened his eyes and shook his head, not even noticing his truck as he replied, "Babe, what are you trying to say?"

"Tell me something," she challenged instead. "If she hadn't chosen money over you, would you two still be together?"

A frown tugged at Ange's brow. "What?"

"Would you?" she pressed.

"I—I have no idea."

"But you met her for coffee."

"Babe...it was just coffee. Nothing more, nothing less."

"Right," she whispered.

"Channing—"

"I can't. I can't do this—I can't do this right now. I need some space. I need some time. I'm sorry."

"Babe—"

"I'm sorry. I have to go."

She ended the call, and he pulled his phone away from his ear to stare at the screen.

Fuck.

She was freaked.

No. She was one step *beyond* freaked.

Fuck.

It had been two months since she'd walked into his pub, and he first laid eyes on her. Two months, two years, it was inconsequential. She was his, and he knew his woman.

Channing took one look at Stephanie and saw a threat that didn't exist. He and Steph had a history, but they didn't have a future.

Except, he wasn't at risk of losing his woman because of *his* history—it was *her* history that was still wreaking havoc.

Fuck.

He thought they were past all that. He remembered the first night he made love to her. It was so damned beautiful she cried. *Fucking cried*. She felt it as much as he did. And when their roles had been reversed, it was his porch she ran to; it was his bed she'd wanted to fall into; it was him she needed.

Ange knew he started as a risk. A big one. But she was his, and he was hers, and there was no going back. Not anymore.

He was in there. He was in there deep. Deep enough to be familiar with his woman's scars.

Ange wasn't Dylan, and Stephanie wasn't Ava—but Channing jumped out of their boat, on account of his ex, like it was haunted.

They'd been coasting on the water for a while now.

They were nowhere near a shore.

She'd drown trying to find her way back—or *he* would, trying to catch her.

Cause there was no way in hell he wasn't diving off that boat and going in after her.

CHAPTER
Twenty-one

Channing

Three Days Later

AFTER HAVING ANGE FOR one night—just *one*—I'd needed five miles on the treadmill and a few hundred meters on the rowing machine. It didn't do much to help me forget him, but it wore me out. It was a distraction. At the time, it did the trick.

After having Ange for two *months*—I was doing two-a-days. It was the only way I could find sleep. If I didn't completely exhaust myself, all I could manage was to toss and turn and ache for him. I'd done that Thursday night, then again on Friday night. I hit the gym Saturday morning before I busied myself with chores and errands, both of which I neglected the previous weekend being that I was out of town. Still, I slept restlessly.

On Sunday, I figured it out. I did an hour at the gym in the morning. I sorted through my inbox and took care of a bunch of admin work throughout the day. Then after dinner, I hit the gym for another hour. By the time I'd showered and gotten ready for bed, I was exhausted.

I slept all night.

The only trouble with trying to distract myself all weekend—a weekend without a wedding on the books—was that I had efficiently taken care of everything on my to-do list. Now it was Monday, and I didn't know how I was going to distract myself all day, but I did know it was going to start with a trip to the gym.

After wearing myself out for an hour, I slowly trudged my way back to my building. On my way there, I got a call from Blake.

I let it ring through to voicemail.

Chances were good she was calling to demand an hour. We'd met for lunch three weeks ago, but since she found out about Ange, she was checking in more frequently. She wanted updates on my relationship. I didn't have it in me to tell her the latest. I certainly didn't feel like reliving any exchange involving Stephanie. So, I didn't answer when my sister called. I'd figure out what to say to her later.

When I arrived back at my building, my phone rang a second time.

It was Libby.

I'd call her back.

I needed a shower and coffee first.

I couldn't put Libby off like I could my sister. She was getting married in five days. I was the wedding planner *and* the maid of honor. This meant I had to put on a happy face. I still wasn't sure how I was going to manage that while being in the same room as Ange, but I'd figure that out, too.

It was imperative.

I would not ruin my best friend's wedding.

Fortunately, I had a couple more days to get myself sorted. In the meantime, I just needed to perk myself up enough to handle a conversation with my best friend and bride-to-be.

I boarded the elevator and rode to the eleventh floor.

I was contemplating whether or not binge-watching *Emily in Paris* on Netflix for the rest of the day would make me feel better or worse about my love life when I caught a glimpse of her down the hall. I stopped in order to draw in a deep breath.

I had about thirty seconds to perk up.

Libby was sitting in front of my door. She had a drink carrier with two coffees sitting next to her. Her attention was focused on the phone in her hand until she sensed my presence. When she looked over at me, I put one foot in front of the other and continued toward my unit.

She stood, bringing the coffees with her as she announced, "These babies are definitely going to need a few seconds in the microwave. You were gone forever."

"Sorry. I had no idea you were coming over."

"Oh, I know. It's no problem." She smiled at me then nodded toward the door. "I am dying for this latte though, so, let me in."

I obeyed, and she was quick to make her way inside. Except, rather than head to the microwave, she set our coffees on my kitchen island, planted her hands on her hips, and pinned her eyes on me.

I closed the door, then proceeded with caution.

"Libby, what's up?"

"What's up is on Friday morning, you told me you were good. You told me you spoke to Ange. Therefore, I thought you were good. At least, on your way to good. On your way back to happy. Then yesterday when I texted, because I thought I ought to double check, you told me you were good. Busy but good. Then I find out from Paddy, my girl is *not* good. My girl is not taking her man's calls which means she is *not* on her way back to happy. Then, the icing on the cake, *I* call you—five minutes ago—and you duck my call. So—*what's up* is you've been lying to me and that's not okay."

I exhaled slowly, hoping a few deep breaths would help stave off my tears.

I cried a decent amount on Friday night. Ange called five times after I'd hung up on him. Not all at once, but sporadically throughout the day. When he stopped calling, I felt it. I knew he was done and giving me the space I demanded.

It was what I wanted, but that didn't mean I didn't cry when he gave it to me.

I'd been trying not to cry since then.

"Channing, what the hell?"

"I know he's Patrick's best man and I'll be seeing a lot of him next weekend. I swear, I'll be fine, and I won't make it awkward."

Libby scowled at me as if I'd lost my mind.

"Are you serious? I'm not worried about my wedding. I'm worried about my friend! I'm worried about *you*, chica! It was just a couple days ago, and you confirmed you were happier than I'd ever seen you. You're falling in love with this great guy one day, and then the next day you're not returning his calls. And I'm sorry, but his ex, showing up out of the blue? I know you want that to be a good excuse—but it's because I love you that I'm telling you it's not."

The humorless laugh that forced its way out of my mouth would not be silenced.

She had laid it all out there, and I had three days of pent-up emotions I couldn't hold back anymore, so I gave her all I had.

"His ex is not a good excuse? That's what you think? Okay, well—let me tell you what I *know*. I know what it's like to think you have the love of a man only to find out that you don't. I know what it's like being the one he settled for before he realized he could have the one he really wanted all along.

"Dylan leaving me at the altar *destroyed* me. It took me *years* to get over it. Somehow, I managed to find happiness on my own after that. It might not have been the dream, but I was okay with that. I was at peace with it. Then, along comes Ange. He's handsome and sexy and thoughtful and smart—he's wonderful, in every way. And just when I think I may have found the great love of my life, the universe just swoops on in with a warning of what it will cost me if I let myself fall for him completely.

"I can't be the one discarded again. My heart can't take it. And I know that Ange is not Dylan—but *I saw* the way he looked at Stephanie, and I know he loved her once. She loved him, too. And a woman who has Ange and lets him go is insane; but a woman who goes out of her way to reconnect with him while in the middle of a girls' trip is obviously a woman who has come to her senses. Even Ange confirmed she's different than he remembers. And just the thought that he could love her again hurts so badly, I know if I wait to let life play out, if I wait and he chooses her again, there will be no pieces of my heart to pick up and paste back together. I can't let that happen. I need my heart to survive, so I'm going to protect it while I still have it."

I was out of breath when I finished, but I'd said all I needed to say.

Libby didn't respond right away. She stared at me for a solid minute, and I let her—hoping what I'd said would sink in.

"Damn," she finally murmured. "It's messy in that head of yours."

"Yeah. I'm well aware," I muttered.

I really wanted that coffee, now.

"Listen, that was a lot," she began carefully. "Unfortunately, we're not going to be able to unpack that standing here. I'm going to need you to shower and get dressed. We're getting out of here and grabbing some food."

I shook my head. I didn't want to unpack my feelings. I didn't want to think about Ange. I needed to figure out how to let him go.

"Libby, I appreciate what you're trying to do, but—"

"*Channing*, we can talk about it or not talk about it, but we're not staying here. What I mean to say is, I'm not leaving you here. You cannot be left alone with that monster of a brain. As your best friend, I can't allow it. Go get in the shower. Please."

I took a second to think about it.

Honestly, I needed the distraction.

She'd promised we didn't have to talk about Ange, and I'd make sure we didn't.

She was getting married in five days, which meant I was sure we could fill a couple hours with wedding talk, and that was going to be better than a Netflix binge.

"Okay," I agreed. "Give me twenty minutes?"

She nodded, and I headed for the shower, grabbing my cold latte as I went.

We went for a late breakfast before we hit the mall.

Libby knew how to shop on a normal day—but on her last day off before her wedding, she was a force to be reckoned with.

It was a distraction.

It was exactly what I needed.

God, I loved her.

We ate an early dinner and then she dropped me at home.

Before she let me out of her car, she made me promise to call if I needed help battling my brain. I said the words, but I broke the promise.

The moment I closed myself into my condo, it was just me and my brain.

I didn't call Libby, I suited up for the gym.

My body was going to hate me, but at least I'd sleep that night.

I wore a pantsuit to work the next day.

It was beige, the pants cropped at my ankle with a wide belt that accentuated my waist. The blazar had a notch collar rather than a regular lapel. Underneath it, I wore a strapless white top, to keep the whole thing from looking stuffy.

It wasn't often I pulled out the pantsuit. Especially not when it was going to be over eighty degrees outside—but I needed the armor. I was going into the office. My best friend's wedding was in four days. The Jackson-Ford wedding was in two and a half weeks. My interview with *Southern Bride Magazine* was the following Wednesday.

In other words, I had things to do, and I didn't have time to wallow.

Libby dropped by my office before our staff meeting to assess how I was doing. I convinced her I was fine and that I didn't want to talk about Ange. I understood there would come a time—in the very near future—when we *would* need to talk about Ange and how I was going to make sure things weren't awkward in three days, when Ange and I would be forced in the same room at the rehearsal dinner, but that day was not today.

Not to mention, I hadn't quite figured that part out yet.

Obviously, he and I needed to talk. We'd been going hot and heavy for weeks now. I couldn't just end things over the phone.

I knew that.

I also knew any woman who had Ange and let him go was insane.

Seeing as I wasn't insane, I was having a really hard time letting him go—but I needed to.

Before we talked, I needed to.

I didn't tell Libby all of that. I told her only as much as was required for her to let me leave my office so we could get on with our staff meeting.

Jorge and Phoebe were already in the conference room when we arrived.

Phoebe looked like she was ready to go into over-protective mom mode.

Jorge looked like he was pissed right the hell off, his face stony and his jaw locked.

I braced and proceeded with caution.

"Okay. Something is obviously going on. Let's hear it."

"It's Ava," said Jorge.

I closed my eyes and tried to keep it together.

I did not need this.

Not today.

Aware I wasn't going to be able to feign patience, I opened my eyes and asked, "What now?"

"Came in this morning to an email. She's now double booked the day of the wedding. We have her scheduled to arrive at the venue at eleven o'clock. She's telling us the soonest our order can be delivered is one o'clock."

I curled my bottom lip between my teeth and bit down *hard*.

Ava was *not* an idiot. Neither was she a novice.

The Jackson-Ford wedding was less than *three weeks away*. She knew we already had every moment of the day plotted out to a T.

On the day of any wedding, I was the conductor, and my vendors were the orchestra. Every note had a time and a place to create a beautiful symphony of sound.

She *knew* that, and she had a mind to fuck it all up.

I shook my head and turned to make my way back to my office.

"We will have this meeting later. I'm over this shit. I'm calling my lawyer."

"Wait, what?" asked Libby, trailing after me.

"Thank *god*," muttered Jorge, sounding genuinely relieved.

"That a girl," added Phoebe.

I didn't know why Ava played the games she played, and I no longer cared.

She'd pushed me too far. I was done.

Five minutes later, I was on the phone with my lawyer's receptionist.

Two minutes after that, I had a meeting on the books.

He had a slot open up just that morning.

I'd see him at three o'clock.

Maybe the universe didn't hate me after all.

CHAPTER
Twenty-Two

Three Days Later

L IBBY AND PATRICK WEREN'T having a formal rehearsal. Given the wedding party consisted of Ange and me, the plan had been that we would sit down with the priest at Saint Austin with Libby, Patrick, and their parents, we would discuss the ceremony, and then we would go to dinner.

The rehearsal dinner was also a bit of an exclusive meet and greet. It would be Libby's immediate family, Patrick's immediate family, plus Ange and me. Since all of Patrick's family was coming from out of town, that night was going to be the first time even Libby got to meet a couple of her soon-to-be in-laws.

I hoped, given the circumstances, Ange and I would be mostly ignored.

It had been a week since he met Stephanie for coffee.

Since that same day, after his fifth failed attempt to reach me by phone, he hadn't called. He hadn't texted. He hadn't dropped by my office. Nothing.

I asked him for space, and, boy, did he give it to me.

For my part, I hadn't reached out at all. It would have been easy to blame it on work, but after the life I'd lived for the last two and a half months, that excuse was as flimsy as they came.

Did I bury myself in work? Yes.

Was it an act of avoidance? Also, yes.

But the time had come when I would have to deal.

That night, whether I was ready or not, we needed to talk. I figured we could step away for a few minutes at the rehearsal dinner, get on the same page about how we were going to handle the next day, and then get on with it.

When I showed up at the church and Ange wasn't there, I started to feel out of sorts.

"It's all good," Patrick assured me. "He just needed to see to some things at the pub. His job tomorrow is easy. Walk a pretty woman down the aisle then back me up."

I forced a smile and nodded. He wasn't altogether wrong. Though, I had hoped for a warmup before dinner; a chance to remind myself what it felt like to stand in a room with Ange and then get over it so I could say what I needed to say.

Though, admittedly, I still wasn't entirely sure what I was going to say.

There were two things of which I was certain.

First, if Ange wanted Stephanie—even a tiny little part of him—we needed to quit while we were ahead.

But the second thing was, in order to quit while we were ahead, I couldn't already be in love with him.

I'd spent the better part of the last week trying to convince myself I wasn't.

I needed that warmup, but I wasn't going to get it. And I couldn't help but wonder—did he really need to *see to some things at the pub*, or was he avoiding me?

If he was, I couldn't blame him. I'd been doing it to him all week.

The rehearsal dinner was being hosted at the pub. Ange and Patrick had agreed to close The Four Horsemen to the public all day Friday and Saturday. They would take a hit, but Patrick and Libby had saved a ton by not having to rent a venue, so Patrick insisted he'd work it out.

They'd arranged to have a deep clean earlier that morning. Hector and Jack would be cooking The Four Horsemen's noteworthy fish-n-chips for both families that evening. Harper would be manning the bar while Willow worked the floor.

The next morning, a crew would show up to transform the space to suit a wedding reception. It was all arranged. Phoebe was going to meet the caterer at the pub to make sure they got in and situated. Jorge would oversee floral installation at the church then at the pub. They were going to work together to make sure everything was running smoothly so I could spend the day as maid of honor first and wedding planner second.

Everything was sorted, except for Ange and me.

We were finished at the church after forty-five minutes.

As we all headed to our vehicles to make the short trip downtown, I ignored the nervous tension in my belly.

It was time.

Since it was nearly seven o'clock on a Friday night, the closest parking I could find was almost a block away. I didn't mind. In fact, I took my time walking to my destination. I needed the chance to deep breathe for a couple more minutes.

When I was finally standing in front of the double red doors, I rolled my shoulders back, raised my head high, and yanked on the handle to grant myself entrance.

I stepped inside and barely had time to survey the place for Ange's whereabouts before his big, warm, calloused hand wrapped around mine and *tugged*. I just about got whiplash as my feet got a delayed start before moving to prevent myself from falling.

"Ange," I called, not entirely sure what was happening.

Obviously, he was dragging me somewhere.

Clearly, he hadn't taken a second to notice my three-inch stilettos, which were, coincidentally, *not* meant for hurrying *anywhere*.

He also wasn't listening to me.

"Ange!" I tried again.

He ignored me.

Actually, his grip around my hand tightened and then he started walking even faster, escorting me past the restrooms and down the side hallway.

He didn't bother to look back at me, so he was oblivious to the fact that my three-inch stilettos weren't the only part of my attire that made this sprint a challenging one.

My one-shoulder, tea length dress, with the cute, ruffled cap sleeve, fit me like a glove. The short slit up the back was there to make walking possible. *Walking.* But when Ange's speed was combined with the length of his stride, that same slit might as well have been non-existent.

I didn't bother calling his name again, I was too busy trying to keep up with my short, quick steps.

When we reached his office, he pulled me through the open door, made the door not open, then pinned me to the back of it, his hand no longer wrapped around mine but gripping me at the waist as he got close—real close—*too* close.

I dropped my purse at our feet.

He smelled like citrus and sandalwood.

His green eyes met mine and my breath caught.

Damn, but he was handsome.

I didn't get my warmup.

Instead, his proximity coupled with the way he was looking at me—and I mean, *at* me—it made me so warm and tingly I couldn't think of a single word to say.

Not that it mattered.

Ange had enough words for the both of us.

"You said you needed space, and you seemed hell bent on taking it, so I gave it to you. Now I'm done."

"Ange," I managed on a whisper.

He kept talking, like I hadn't spoken at all.

"*In another life*—pretty sure that's how you described it. *In another life*, you loved that bastard who let you get all the way down the aisle before he decided he was done with you."

I tensed, but my attempt to brace was too late.

Ange wasn't done.

"That first night, you and me at ATX Cocina, you told me that shit, you showed me that scar, and I knew two things." He raised his free hand, and I watched him in my periphery count with his fingers the two things he knew. "He was a dumb fuck, and if I wanted you, I was gonna have to play the long game. So, I settled in to play the long game."

He dropped his hand and pressed in closer, so close I could feel the heat radiating off his chest.

"Not three days later, I was in your bed. Two days after that, we got in our boat, and we set sail. A month ago, when that bastard walked into my pub and sent you running, after you sorted your shit, you were in my bed. I thought that meant I was in there," he said, pressing two fingers to the center of my sternum, "and I was in there deep—deep enough to chase away your doubts about us, about who we could be.

"I had no idea it was going to be *my* past that would have you jumping out of our boat, but that's exactly what happened. You took one look at Steph, my ex *from another life*, and you jumped, babe. You jumped.

"I let you swim a little while, but that's over now. I can't let you go any further because you carved a hole in my heart where only you can fit, which means it's hollow without you. And even though you jumped, I'm pretty sure there's a hole in your heart where only I can fit, too, which puts us back at the same damn boat, Channing. And I'm alright with that, because I've been enjoying the ride; so much so, I plan on staying in the boat and loving you until we reach the end of the world. Seeing as how I don't think that place exists, I'm feeling pretty sure I'll be loving you in our boat for a good long while.

"So, you've got a choice babe. You either admit I'm bad company and a horrible lay after all, or you admit I'm worth the risk I know you are, and you get back in the damned boat so we can see where it goes."

I'd started crying somewhere between him telling me I'd carved a hole in his heart only I could fit in and him wanting to stay in our boat until it reached the end of the world.

There was no denying it now.

I was head-over-heels.

I wanted to say so much. Where I was at a loss for words when I was trying to figure out how to let him go, the floodgates had been opened after all he'd just said. But the giant knot in my throat, preventing me from bursting into a sob, made it difficult to speak.

I could manage four little words, though.

"I—I love you, too."

Apparently, that said it all.

Before I could take my next breath, Ange's mouth came crashing down on mine.

He licked my lips open as he brought his hand up, buried his fingers in my hair, and took hold of the nape of my neck. I whimpered when I got the first taste of him I'd had in over a week. He pressed his body closer, pinning me completely to the door, and I slid my arms around his waist and across his back as I let him own my mouth.

It was his, after all.

God, but he could kiss.

We kept at each other like neither one of us would ever get enough.

I gave him my fear, my pain, and my regret.

He swallowed it all, then gave me nothing but love.

It was inexplicably delicious.

When he started pulling up the hem of my dress, I moaned my approval.

There was no stopping this—*us*.

I didn't care where we were.

I wanted him, too.

No. *Needed* him. All of him.

I made this clear when I reached down to free the button of his khakis. As soon as I had his zipper open, I dove in to take hold of his length and found he was already hard.

I had him in my grasp only for a moment, then he was out of reach, yanking my thong down to my ankles. I stepped out with no instruction, then I was up—my dress bunched at my waist, my back against the door, my legs around his hips, and my hands holding tight to his shoulders.

When he drove into me, I saw nothing but green.

Bliss.

He paused, all of him filling me full, then brought a hand up to wipe away the tears I'd forgotten. "Beautiful. Every time, baby," he whispered.

"Ange..."

It was all I could say before he readjusted his hold and started moving in and out of me. He felt so good, I could hardly stand it. I'd missed this, missed him. I was kidding myself thinking I could ever let him go.

He set a steady rhythm, and our bodies coming together against the door made a low, pounding sound that I was sure no one could mistake if they walked by. I didn't care. I wanted more.

"Harder, honey," I begged unabashedly.

His grip on my thighs got tighter, and he gave me what I needed. He rode me hard, stoking the warmth within me, beckoning it closer to the surface.

I slid one of my hands across the back of his shoulders, up his neck, and into his hair as I dropped my forehead down to kiss his. Him as my anchor, and the door as my leverage, I moved with him. I knew he liked this when he picked up the cadence of his hips, and I was suddenly on the verge.

"Yes, don't stop," I gasped. "Honey, don't stop."

The pressure of his fingertips digging into my thighs let me know my rugged man was one step removed from out of control, and this—miraculously—turned me on even more. I expressed as much with a moan.

"You there, baby?" he asked, his lips barely grazing mine.

"Yes, yes," I panted.

He pounded harder. Faster.

My orgasm got closer. Bigger.

"Let go, Channing. Come for me," he demanded.

He thrust, and I felt the promise of something sensational. He thrust again, and my breath hitched. He jerked his hips, slamming into me with a grunt, the sound implying he was barely hanging on, and I let go.

I held on tight—my arms and legs locked around him as my sex constricted with immense pleasure, sending wave upon glorious wave of delight right through me.

Even my scalp tingled.

Ange lost his rhythm, and I saw his face change, his handsome features distorted as he surrendered control for the sake of release. He groaned softly as he came undone right along with me. It wasn't merely beautiful. It was *everything*.

Neither of us moved when we were both spent, panting for breath.

I could hardly remember where we were or why.

But I did know I was back in the boat—and that's where I was going to stay.

Ange thrust his hips one last time, eliciting a whimper.

I felt his forehead relax before I saw the creases at the corner of his eyes as he gave me a smile that made my chest warm and tingly.

Then he said, "Love you, baby," and my belly turned to mush.

"I love you, too, honey," I whispered.

He kissed me long and sweet in response.

It was another fifteen minutes before we were both straightened out and presentable. Ange having gone to get what I needed to clean myself up, I didn't have a mirror to see what I looked like—but I didn't need a mirror to see how obvious it was I had just had sex.

No. Not just sex. Hot-against-the-door-of-Ange's-office-make-up sex.

Ange hadn't messed up my hair, my dress wasn't overly wrinkled, and I'd put my thong back on, but I knew my cheeks were flushed and my eyes were happy and bright, because that was exactly how I felt.

That said, I didn't care who knew I'd just had hot-against-the-door-of-Ange's-office-make-up sex, because he was mine and I was his and that was all that mattered now.

"You ready?" he asked, his hand extended toward me.

I took it, lacing my fingers between his as I murmured, "Ready."

He opened the door, and we took our leave to join the others.

When we reached the main room, everyone was seated, and dinner had already been served. As I'd hoped, nobody paid us any mind as they went on conversing.

Everyone except Libby.

She took one look at me and knew.

I was certain of this because before I could even blink, she was all dimples.

CHAPTER
Twenty-Three

Four Days Later

ANGE COULD DANCE.

Out on the dance floor at Libby and Patrick's wedding, I'd learned my handsome, rugged, bearded man was also *suave*. He wasn't over the top or goofy. He had the necessary rhythm and the perfect amount of sway that he just looked cool out there.

We danced all night.

Much like we'd done after the rehearsal dinner, after the send-off of the bride and groom, he took me back to his place and made love to me until neither of us could keep our eyes open.

Mr. and Mrs. Moore weren't going on their honeymoon for a few months yet, but they'd taken the short flight to Dallas for an extended, romantic weekend away. This meant on Sunday morning, Ange had to work. He left me naked in his bed with one simple request—that I still be there when he got home.

I didn't spend *all* day in bed, but I did my fair share of lazing with Penny around the house. At sunset, we went for a long walk. I'd put in more than enough hours at work the previous week to have a real weekend, so I took it and didn't feel bad about it.

I was showered and naked, tucked between Ange's sheets when he got home.

He liked that a whole lot.

I knew because he showed me—enthusiastically.

I came four times before we both passed out.

It wasn't until Monday that we talked about Stephanie.

We were out on his back porch, each of us with a mug of coffee, enjoying the coolest part of the day—me in one of his undershirts, him in a pair of boxer briefs. He told me about the forty-five minutes he gave her at the JW. I apologized for not giving him a chance to tell me sooner. Then we put it, and her, behind us.

After we finished our coffees, we spent the rest of the day in bed.

Needless to say, I hadn't been to the gym since Friday.

But every night since, I'd slept like a baby.

Except, just because I slept *well* didn't mean I slept *enough*.

Tuesday morning came way too soon.

I was at my desk, sorting through emails, and mid-yawn when Libby floated into my office.

"Hello, hello. *Buenos días*. Good morning, good morning!" she practically sang.

I laughed and replied, "Good morning, Mrs. Moore."

She sighed joyfully. "Feel free to call me that as often as you'd like."

"I will," I promised. "How was Dallas?"

She plopped down in one of the chairs opposite my desk. "Short but sweet."

"You really could have—" I paused, interrupted by another yawn, then finished, "—sorry, excuse me. You really could have stayed a couple more days. You didn't have to rush back."

Libby gave me a suspicious smile. "No, I needed to come back. We have to make sure you're good to go for tomorrow's *Southern Bride* interview."

"Mm, yeah."

Still smiling at me, she tilted her head and asked, "You know, I'm beginning to wonder—which one of us had the most sex this weekend? The newlyweds, or the newly-reunited?"

I grinned, totally unable to lie.

She mirrored my expression, flashing those dimples.

As if she'd conjured him with her question, Ange filled my doorway not two seconds later.

"Knock, knock."

We both looked his way, and I almost whimpered at the sight of what I knew would be a large vanilla latte with my name written all over it.

Libby turned back to face me and hummed, "Mmm-hmm," like she had her answer.

She waggled her eyebrows at me before she stood and made her way to the door.

"Morning, Ange."

"Morning, Mrs. Moore."

His greeting elicited another lyrical sigh. "That's me," she sang before she disappeared down the hallway.

I stood to make my way toward Ange as I commented, "This is unexpected."

He lifted the coffee in his hand and said, "It's not a vat, but it does have an extra shot of espresso."

When he was close enough, I didn't bother reaching for the coffee, more interested in reaching for him. I circled my arms around his waist, surrendering some of my weight as I leaned into his chest and asked, "Have I told you I love you today?"

"Think you just did, babe," he said with a quarter-smile, his fingers finding their way into my hair and around the back of my neck.

God, I loved it when he did that.

"Well, you should also know, that extra shot of espresso makes you my hero, too. Remind me to order you a cape."

He chuckled, and I felt the sound as it reverberated subtly through his chest.

That was nice.

Then he lowered his mouth until his lips grazed mine and muttered, "Cute as fuck," before he kissed me.

That was even better.

"You're *suing* me? *Seriously?*"

My whole body jolted, startled as I was at the sound of her voice.

Ange's hand still at my neck, my jolt only resulted in the end of a great kiss before I snapped my gaze toward the door.

Ava, decidedly more pregnant than the last time I'd seen her, had stormed into my office with the papers I knew she'd been served the day before.

I'd asked my lawyer to make sure they weren't delivered until after Libby's wedding.

I wasn't altogether stunned by her visit first thing in the morning.

It was Dylan, taking her back, that caught me off guard.

"Well, shit," Ange muttered under his breath.

It was barely audible, but I heard it.

He was impressed.

I looked up at him and whispered, "I'm done hiding."

He grinned, and my belly turned to mush.

I fought a smile as I let him go.

He gave my neck a parting squeeze, then took my back.

That felt good. Better than good.

Finally, calmly addressing my visitors, I said, "Yes, Ava, as evidenced by the papers you've got in your hand, I am, indeed, suing you. I'm also firing you. Your services are no longer needed for the Jackson-Ford wedding in two weeks."

Her jaw dropped and her face grew pale.

Checkmate.

"You can't—you can't *do* that," she gasped. "The Jacksons—"

"Oh, the Jackson's and I had a nice long chat last week," I interrupted. "They now understand why Blossoms & Balloons Floral Design has never, and will never, be a vendor of choice here at Rusty Barn Wedding Co. They also gave me the green light to do what I had to do—and what I had to do was get you and your shoddy-ass work as far away from this wedding as possible."

She huffed, her face turning red in agitation.

Dylan stepped up and said, "Channing, come on, be reasonable. Ava's been planning for this wedding for months. It's two weeks out. You can't possibly find another florist capable of fulfilling this order in two weeks."

I smiled and folded my arms across my chest.

It took a lot of work, more than a few phone calls, the cashing in of a couple favors, and the promise of a few owed, but Jorge and I had got it done. It was going to be a team effort. In our industry, it usually was, and the three florists we'd managed to get on board to put their necks out there for me understood that. We were a community—we were in this together.

"It's amazing the things I can do when someone pushes me too far."

"You're making this personal," muttered Dylan.

My arms fell to my sides as my eyes widened in exasperation. "You're damn *right* I'm making this personal. That's because it *is* personal, Dylan." I looked at Ava. "I'm not a luddite. I know how to use the internet. I've looked you up and read your reviews. There are too many to consider them bullshit. You're good at what you do. I'll give you that, but that's all I'll give.

"Every time we partner on a wedding, you fuck something up, and it comes with a cost. Every time, Ava. Not to mention, you've been jacking us around on this wedding, even though you know it's a huge freaking deal. I'd say that's pretty personal. Pretty unprofessional, pretty petty, and pretty immature—but, first and foremost, pretty damn personal."

Ava narrowed her eyes at me. "Did you ever stop to ask yourself *why* I might have done those things?"

"Yeah. I did. Now I just don't care."

"Channing—"

Dylan started to speak, but Ava held up a hand to silence him as she confessed, "I was trying to get you to *talk* to me. Instead, you always sent one of your staff to deal with me."

I lifted my brow and spread my arms open wide. "You wanted to *talk* to me? Well, congratulations. You got your wish. We're *talking*."

"Oh, don't be such a bitch, Channing! You're suing me, for god's sake."

At this, my spine straightened, my face became an expressionless mask, and any modicum of patience I might have had was gone.

"I'm going to need you to leave. We're done talking. Anything else you have to say, you can tell it to my lawyer."

"Channing, please, don't do this," said Dylan, trying one more time. "The amount you're suing for—"

"The amount I'm suing for is justified."

"It's outrageous."

"You want to know what's outrageous?" I snapped. "The two of you, coming into my office, completely uninvited. Your *wife*, purposefully screwing up and putting my brand at risk just so I'll *talk to her*. Why on earth would I want to talk to either of you about anything, ever? You broke my heart," I stated, pointing at Dylan. I then pointed at Ava and continued, "but you ripped it out and sent the pieces scattering. Then you just ran off into the flipping sunset, got married, and started making babies. Not once did either of you even so much as *apologize*, as if I wasn't even owed that much.

"So, no, I don't want to talk to you. Not to either of you. After nearly a decade, what you two did to me might be water under the bridge, but that doesn't make us friends. It barely makes us acquaintances. Now, having cleared that up, please leave."

They didn't leave.

Waving the papers around, Ava cried, "You'll get me blacklisted."

"Can't we just discuss this like adults?" Dylan began. "Can't we come to an agreement amongst ourselves, without getting the courts involved?"

It was like talking to a brick wall.

"I'd rather not call security to escort you out, but I will."

Ava's eyes glanced behind me and locked on Ange.

My half-smile couldn't be helped.

"Oh, he's not security. He's the love of my life. Though, he is bigger than most on our building security crew, and I'm sure he would have no issue making sure the both of you got out of my sight immediately. All I'd have to do is ask nicely."

"Babe—snap of the fingers would do it," he corrected.

I grinned as I tried not to laugh.

God, I loved him.

Ava's eyes shifted to meet mine for a second before they were back on Ange.

I lifted my right hand and positioned my fingers to snap as I told her, "I know. He's *real* easy on the eyes. But he's mine," I cut my eyes at Dylan. "Got an upgrade." It was low, but it felt good. Looking back at Ava, I concluded, "You can't have him. For real, this time. Now I'll ask you once more to leave."

I started a mental countdown from five.

With two seconds to spare, Dylan took Ava by the hand. "You'll be hearing from our lawyer," he said before finally, *finally* leaving.

I drew in a deep breath, filling my lungs completely, then let it all out in a satisfied sigh.

"Channing?"

I turned, my gaze instantly colliding with his.

Green and gorgeous.

Warm and intense.

"Hmm?"

"That was fucking awesome."

I smiled, but he wasn't done.

Wrapping an arm around my back, he pulled me against his chest and told me, "Proud of you."

My belly turned to mush, but I still managed to say, "Thanks, honey."

"Blake'll get a kick out of that."

I chuckled just thinking about it. "She'll wish she could have been a fly on the wall."

"Lucky for her, she'll get that wish. Recorded the whole thing."

"What? No, you didn't," I said, gaping up at him.

He nodded as he told me, "Just the audio. Hit record then dropped my phone back in my pocket. You're suing her, babe. She shouldn't have shown up here like that. Doubt you'll need it, but in case you do, your lawyer can have it."

I stared at him.

He stared right back.

This lasted for a good twenty seconds.

Then I asked, "Have I told you I love you today?"

His eyes got bright with his smile.

My chest grew warm and tingly.

He didn't even have to say it.

I saw it. I *felt* it in his gaze.

He said it anyway.

"'Til we reach the end of the world, babe."

Epilogue

Rusty Barn Wedding Co. had a good reputation that drew in plenty of business *before* the Jackson-Ford wedding feature in *Southern Bride Magazine*. After the article hit the shelves, we had more inquires coming in than we could handle. In the month that followed, I'd turned away enough couples, the crew and I decided we needed to hire one or two more people to help increase our bandwidth.

Turned out, when you got a glowing review in a major bridal magazine, brides weren't the only ones to take notice. Erin and Jamie didn't come with just experience; they also hit the ground running as soon as they started, proving their value in a matter of *days*.

This was good. Better than good.

This was what I needed.

Not simply because it killed me to turn away so many couples when I wanted to be able to help curate as many dream weddings as I possibly could—but also because, one of those dream weddings I desperately wanted to plan was my own.

Three days before the Jackson-Ford wedding, which happened to be three months after our first date—which Ange insisted was dinner at ATX Cocina, even though I knew it was breakfast at 24Diner, while one could argue it was dinner at Péché—Ange proposed.

I wasn't crazy or pregnant, but I was happy and in love—so, of course, I said yes.

I probably would have given us a bit more lead time before the wedding, but Ange told me he didn't care when we got married just as long as it was within the year. With no desire to compete with the holidays, I picked the latest date I could before we hit Halloween.

I had to admit, I did love a good October wedding.

While four and a half months was a little longer than two and a half months—because, you know, math—it still felt like it came and went just as fast.

In that time, I'd moved in with Ange and started renting my condo.

We would find a place of our own in the new year.

We would definitely need more space. But for now, it was home.

We'd also done the meet-the-parents routine.

My parents met Ange at my sister's Fourth of July bash. He took the day off, knowing it was my favorite, and we spent hours in the pool with Sylvie and Camille. Ange made the mistake of tossing the girls up in the air, launching them toward the deep end one time.

Let's just say, he got an unexpected arm workout that afternoon.

When the sun went down, we snuggled up and watched fireworks.

Mom thought he was dreamy.

Dad was content to see me so happy.

I didn't need their blessing, but I had it just the same.

With Libby taking on a larger role at Rusty Barn, this allowed Ange to whisk me away from the blazing heat of Texas in August for a long weekend in the cooler temps of Michigan. We'd timed it when we knew Nico would be home, which also made it a bit of a family reunion.

It was awesome.

Then suddenly, it was October.

And now, it was time.

We were getting married in Austin Hill Country.

I was standing out of view in my backless, lace, boho wedding dress. It had long-sleeves and a short train. It was my dream dress. Nothing *glam* about it. When I'd originally tried it on, it reminded me of the lacey, wine-red dress I'd worn the night I first kissed Ange.

That did it. I was sold.

My hair was down and styled in big, loose curls—the way Ange liked it best—and I had on enough makeup to befit a bride at her sunset wedding.

My bouquet was filled with the colors of autumn in Texas. Orange dahlias. Burgundy English roses. Cream peonies. Dusty rose ranunculus. An assortment of green foliage that brought the whole thing together.

It was a beautiful gift I'd been given from one of the florists who came through for me after that whole debacle with Ava.

In fact, *all* of my flowers—the huge arrangement that served as the focal point on the wooden arch I knew was at the end of the aisle, the bouquets for my matrons, the centerpieces for my reception—*all* of them had come complimentary from the teams that helped me pull off the Jackson-Ford wedding last minute.

Needless to say, they'd gotten one hell of an honorable mention from me in the article.

The flowers were a sign of their appreciation.

It made me a little teary every time I thought about it.

"You ready, kiddo?" asked dad, offering me his elbow.

My belly tensed in nervous excitement, and I looked out in front of me.

Blake and Nico had already started to make their journey toward the altar.

Libby and Patrick would be next.

Sylvie and Camille would make the trip last—Cami in charge of tossing rose pedals; Sylvie in charge of Penny's leash; Penny in charge of carrying the rings.

It was a little unconventional, but I thought it was adorable.

Besides, we didn't have any little boys in our family.

At least, not yet, we didn't.

I looked at my dad, slipping my hand into the curve of his arm as I murmured, "More than ready."

It felt like it took forever before it was our turn.

Finally, Jorge winked at me, and I knew that was my cue.

We made it to the back of the aisle, the breeze causing my hair to brush softly against my bare back, and all I could do was smile.

That was because my groom was grinning.

His green eyes locked on me, and my chest got all warm and tingly.

Beautiful as it was, *this* moment wasn't the one I was dying to witness.

It wasn't *this* look I couldn't wait to see.

I didn't need to catch a glimpse of his face the second he first laid eyes on his bride because I was his bride, and I already knew we were going to make it.

We were in our boat, sailing to the end of the world.

What I was really looking forward to, was the look on his face when I told him we were going to need a bigger boat.

We were expecting an additional passenger.

I was going to tell him just as soon as he walked me down the aisle as Mrs. Michelangelo Castellanos.

THORNHILL *Road*

Tess McBride is on a bad boy hiatus. After trusting her heart to one too many men with that devil-may-care attitude, she's decided it's time to consider other options. She's on the lookout for someone less rough around the edges. A safe man. A reliable man. Though, given her challenging work hours as a hospice nurse, finding that man is a bit of a struggle—especially considering her most sacred rule to never get involved with a grieving family member.

A rule she's tempted to break after a single visit with a new patient has her walking into a biker bar.

Mustang has been a member of the Wild Stallion Motorcycle Club for half his life. He knows no other family, except his little girl, whom he loves with all his heart. When he's not busy being a dad, he's with his brothers. He spends his working hours at his bar, on the Stallion compound in Gillette, and whatever time he has left riding wild and roaming free.

She walks into his bar in pink scrubs and white sneakers asking for him, and he knows one look will never be enough.

Trouble is, the only way to get her is to travel down a road he hasn't been on in years. It doesn't take much for Mustang to concede, the woman he intends to make his is worth a trip down Thornhill Road.

Turn the page and meet Tess in the first chapter of the next Love Me Tender novel – Thornhill Road.

CHAPTER *One*

I PULLED INTO THE driveway on Ramshorn Avenue and checked the time.

A sigh of relief passed between my lips when I saw I was ten minutes early.

"Hey, Siri—set timer, ten minutes."

My phone talked back to me, alerting me to my ten-minute timer, then I leaned my head against the seat and closed my eyes. I was four hours away from the end of my double shift. That meant two more stops. Two more patients.

Ten minutes.

Ten minutes of sleep was going to carry me through.

It was all I needed.

Just ten minutes.

A knock sounded at my window.

I pulled in a deep breath and opened my eyes.

Seven minutes. I'd gotten seven minutes.

It would have to do.

Glancing out the driver's side window, I saw Mitchell Jones offer me an apologetic smile and a timid wave. I smiled back at him. Not timid. Not apologetic.

Real.

Genuine.

Tired, but genuine.

He was a major reason why I was there. His mother was dying. Stage four lung cancer. Inoperable. Never smoked a day in her fifty-nine years. Her life expectancy when I met her had been three months. Now she had weeks left. Six, maybe less. She wanted to spend what time she had remaining on this earth in the comfort of her own home, surrounded by family, and it was my job to make sure she got her dying wish.

I also considered it my responsibility to make sure both of her sons were well supported and looked after during such a difficult time.

I canceled my timer, grabbed my purse and my bottle of water—water I wished was coffee, even though I'd already had my fill—then moved to get out of my car.

"Hi, Mitch. How you doin'?"

"I'm so sorry to wake you. I'm sure you're burning it at both ends. I saw you pull up, and I wanted a chance to talk before you came inside."

Mitchell was average height with dark blond hair I was sure he got cut every four weeks, like clockwork. He had brown eyes, a strong, masculine jaw, and a subtle cleft chin that wasn't unattractive.

"No need to apologize," I said.

I meant it. Mitchell was the eldest of the two brothers. He was always so kind and gracious. It was obvious he loved his mother and felt quite helpless. He couldn't fix her, but wherever he could step in or show up, he would. He was a good son. A good man. The kind of man I thought I should consider for myself.

Not *him* of course. Aside from the fact that he was already married—and I made it a point not to date married men—he was related to one of my dying patients. Family members were strictly out of bounds. For ethical reasons, first and foremost, but also because I had unwavering boundaries when it came to mixing my work and my emotions.

It was critical in the field of hospice care.

All that aside, someone *like* Mitchell was who I thought I should keep an eye out for. Someone stable with a good head on his shoulders. A man with a corporate job. Maybe even a job that required him to wear a tie.

As boring as it sounded, it also seemed quite safe.

My dating history was littered with men who were far from safe. Mitchell wasn't exactly my type—but for the last couple months, I'd thought it was time for me to reconsider my options.

However, at present, my pathetic dating life was not a priority.

I was at the house on Ramshorn Avenue, which meant I was there for Sharon.

"What's on your mind?" I asked Mitchell as we slowly made our way toward the front door.

We chatted for a few minutes on Sharon's porch. Mitchell's youngest daughter, Emilia, had come down with a cold. She'd been in the house the day before, and he was worried. I reminded him that sick toddlers were inevitable, he couldn't possibly blame himself, and I'd monitor Sharon carefully for any sign of a cold—then we both headed inside.

I could barely remember a time when I didn't want to be a nurse. Since I was twelve years old, it had been my plan. I had no alternate routes for my future. Hospice care, in particular, was my end goal. For the last six years, that's exactly what I had the privilege of doing.

And it truly was a privilege.

It was exhausting in every way—mentally, emotionally, physically. It was hard work. The schedule was shit, and I didn't know the meaning of *work-life-balance*, but it was worth it. Not once had I regretted my career choice, because it was more than a career.

It was a vocation.

It was my calling.

It was medicine, sure. I was a registered nurse. But a hospice nurse was so much more than that. I addressed my patient's spiritual and emotional needs, too, as they journeyed toward death. I was there to make dying dignified, peaceful, and comfortable—or as comfortable as possible. It's what made the job such a challenge. It was also what made the job so rewarding.

Hard as it was, I loved it.

I went through my usual routine with Sharon, checking her from top to toe. Once I was done with her physical exam, we discussed how she was feeling, and I got an assessment of how alert and oriented she was. Then, like I did with most of my patients, I sat with her for a few minutes and visited while I charted. I was wrapping up, checking to see if she needed any of her prescriptions filled, when the sounds of an argument drifted into the room. I looked toward the doorway and frowned.

Lance had arrived.

"My boys...they're having a rough go of it lately," murmured Sharon.

It had become clear to me where Mitchell had gotten his personality. She was busy dying, and Sharon hardly spent any time worrying about herself, too concerned with the family she would leave behind. It was why I liked to spend a few extra moments with her each visit, so we could focus on *her* for a little while each week.

I offered her a small smile, then reached for her hand and gave it a gentle squeeze. "I'll talk to them. You get some rest, okay? Call me if you need anything."

I stowed my tablet in my purse, then double checked to make sure I had all my supplies. I bid Sharon farewell and ventured out toward the living room.

I didn't need Sharon to tell me her sons were having a *rough go of it* lately. This wasn't the first argument to draw me away from my patient. They were two men who were losing their mother. Rather than bond over it, they were hurtling their grief at each other like grenades.

"Guys—guys," I interjected as I went to stand between them. "We agreed. No arguments without a mediator. As I understand it, Renee is home with a sick toddler, which leaves me. So—are we good here, or do I need to get a chair?"

"No. Sorry, you're right," said Mitchell.

"Yeah. All good here," agreed Lance.

Lance, though younger, was the taller of the two brothers. His hair was lighter. His nose was sharper. His jawline squarer. One might have said he was the more attractive brother—until he opened his mouth.

I hadn't met their father. He and Sharon were divorced. When I considered Lance, I wondered if his personality was his own, or if the apple hadn't fallen far from the tree. He was certainly the more selfish of Sharon's offspring. Most of the arguments were instigated by him; and most of the time it was about money, or whose turn it was to help with laundry or house chores.

In the two months I'd been coming around, I hadn't seen Lance even so much as fold a single piece of laundry.

There was also something slimy about him that made me feel uncomfortable.

Nevertheless, people experienced pain in a variety of different ways, so I did my very best to offer him as much patience and grace as I could muster.

"I'm going to go check on mom," Mitchell told us before he left.

I blew out a breath and looked up at Lance. "You sure you two are okay?"

"We'll be fine. Thanks for stepping in." He reached for my shoulder and gave it a squeeze. "I don't know what we'd do without you."

As he began to let me go, he trailed his fingertips a short way down my back before dropping his hand to his side.

I gave him no response to his touch but did a mental shiver.

He made me feel so *ick*. Like he was incapable of platonic affection.

"I should get going. I've got another patient to see."

"Of course. It was good to see you, Tess."

I nodded, waved, and said, "I'll be back in a couple days."

Once on the other side of Sharon's front door, I closed my eyes, stretched my neck, then rolled my shoulders back.

One more patient. Two more hours.

I was on the home stretch.

On my way to my car, I pulled up Edmond Thomas' address. He was my newest patient. This was going to be my first trip to his house on Thornhill Road. My GPS told me I'd be there in about twenty minutes, and I didn't waste any time before I began the short trek north.

When I pulled into the driveway, the first thing I noticed was the unkempt yard. It was the middle of June, and we hadn't had snow in several weeks, which meant it was lawn mowing season. Only, Edmond Thomas had a yard full of weeds, not grass.

The house looked old and almost as neglected as the lawn, and I wondered what I'd find on the inside. Since it was my first visit, I took some extra time to go over his chart before I got out of my car. He was dying from pancreatic cancer. According to his list of medications, he also had cirrhosis of the liver and a few other long-standing conditions he'd been dealing with, as well. Aware I wouldn't know the full extent of what I'd be dealing with until I met him, I grabbed my things and was at his front door in under thirty seconds. After a quick knock, I waited for someone to answer.

Edmond filled the doorway a minute later.

He was a tall man with hunched shoulders. One look at him, and it was obvious he'd once been formidable. Now, at only sixty-one years old, he was on the verge of appearing frail. His clothes hung on him like they belonged to someone else, and his eyes—while a pretty hazel-blue—were sad.

"Mr. Thomas?"

He jerked his head in a nod. "You my nurse?"

"Yes. Theresa McBride," I said, extending my hand as I offered the name the care center would have provided. "But, please, call me Tess."

He accepted my hand with a stronger grip than I anticipated, and this made me smile.

"Call me Ed. Come on in," he muttered.

He turned and left the door open as he made his slow return trip deeper into the house. I followed after him, closing us inside. We didn't go far. It was a split-level home, but he'd obviously dispensed with dealing with the stairs. In what I assumed was once a living room, there was an unmade bed, a well-used recliner, a television that sat on top of a wooden dresser, and a bunch of clutter on every flat surface there was. On the opposite side of his living area, partitioned by a wall, was the kitchen. I assumed the bathroom wasn't far, either.

Ed made his way to the edge of his bed and took a seat.

"So, how does this work?"

I set my purse at my feet, took out my tablet, and proceeded to explain what a typical visit would look like. I then asked him a list of questions and proceeded with my exam. When I was finished, I grabbed a chair from his kitchen table so I could take a seat next to him while I charted.

"Ed, other than me, who is going to be helping with your care?"

"Got someone who drops by to take care of the laundry and cleaning 'bout once a week."

I nodded, hugged my tablet to my chest, and clarified, "What about any family or loved ones?"

He shook his head. "My wife died a lifetime ago, and I haven't seen my son in years."

When he said *son*, I saw the slight nod he gave to the frame that sat beside him on his nightstand. It was the only picture frame I'd seen on the main level of the house.

"May I?"

He nodded and I laid my tablet in my lap in order to pick up the frame. I was surprised to find not a picture but a clipping out of the *Gillette News Record*, our local paper. There was no date, so I wasn't sure how old the clipping was, but I recognized the establishment in the photo and knew it couldn't have been more than a few years old.

The article was about Steel Mustang, a popular biker bar located on the edge of town on the Wild Stallion Motorcycle Club compound. Even though bikers were the typical patrons, the bar wasn't exclusively for those in the club, and it drew quite the crowd. They were known for their live music and the great bands they hosted.

I didn't know this via hearsay.

I'd been a couple of times.

I could attest, it was awesome.

However, I didn't recognize the man in the photograph.

Not that it was a great quality photo. It was black and white. He was leaning against his motorcycle with his arms folded across his chest and a pair of sunglasses covering his eyes. I knew enough to be sure the leather vest he wore was a *kutte*, and I was certain the patch on the back matched the tattoo he was sure to angle toward the camera on his right bicep. It was difficult to see the details in the clipping, but everyone in town recognized the Wild Stallion logo. It was a skeletal stallion head, only it was designed to appear made out of metal. And the mane wasn't hair, but fire.

It was badass.

I'd never officially met anyone who rode with the Wild Stallions—but the members who made up the *heartbreaker club,* known informally as my *exes,* were men who could have been cut from the same cloth.

Or, if not the same cloth, they'd at least be found in the same fabric section at the store.

All that to say, I didn't need to actually read the article to know what it was about—but I did glance at the caption beneath the photo.

Sullivan Thomas, long time member of the Wild Stallion MC and majority owner of Steel Mustang, poses in front of the up-and-coming biker bar.

"Sullivan, that's your son?"

"Sully," Ed corrected. "Turned out alright, no thanks to me."

I studied the dying man in front of me for a second, curious about the details behind the sad look in those hazel-blue eyes. He was all alone, and I didn't like it.

"Says here he's the owner of this bar. That means he's local," I pressed gently.

"We don't talk, Tess. He doesn't even know I'm sick. It's just me. Move slow on account of the pain, but I can still manage to get around most of the time. If you're gonna be comin' by for night visits, I got a spare key I can give you."

"Okay, Ed," I murmured, setting aside the photo frame. "Let's try that for a while and see how we get on."

I stayed for a few more minutes, then collected my things and the spare key to the house on Thornhill Road. I bid Ed farewell, assuring him I'd be back in a couple of days and insisting he call me should he need me before then. It was a few minutes after four when I got behind the wheel of my car. I was done for the day. I could go home and sleep, which was exactly what I wanted to do.

Except, I couldn't.

Ed Thomas was all alone in the house I'd just left, and that didn't sit right with me.

I understood families were complicated. People had falling outs and relationships fell apart. But I also knew what it was like to lose a parent to an illness they couldn't beat. Sully didn't even know his dad was sick. I didn't understand what that was all about, but death had a way of changing people's perspectives. Maybe whatever was broken between father and son could be reconciled with the threat of losing their chance on the horizon.

I figured it was worth a shot.

I didn't know Ed, but I knew it was my job to make sure he died in peace and comfort.

It was obvious he was lonely, and it felt like my duty to reach out to Sully, just in case all they needed was a little intervention.

So, I didn't go home.

I put my car in reverse, I backed out of the driveway, and I pointed my car toward that bar.

Follow me on Instagram (@annie.winston_author) and stay up to date on what I've got coming next!

xoxo — Annie

ALSO BY

Love Me Tender

Thornhill Road
Tattered Edges

Wild Stallions Motorcycle Club

Ridin' Wild

Follow me on Amazon and never miss a release!

www.ingramcontent.com/pod-product-compliance
Lightning Source LLC
Chambersburg PA
CBHW051812150726
47998CB00001B/122